War of Legends

Book 1

Ancient Gifts

Melanie Deer

This novel is entirely a work of fiction. The names, characters and incidents portrayed in it are the work of the author's imagination. Any resemblance to actual persons, living or dead, events or localities is entirely coincidental.

Cover by: Etheric Designs

Map by: Rebecca Dunkleberger

First edition

ISBN: 979-8-9936253-0-0

I would like to dedicate Ancient Gifts to all those throughout the years that influenced it. Whether you were a classmate that I based a character on (sorry if your character got cut) or someone who read it for edits or just someone cheering me on. Thank you.

MAP OF EYLAOUR

PROLOGUE

The Divine Sisters were a gift to the plane; a gift that came with a promise of protection, but a warning of possible doom. Thousands of years ago, Jahola, the Ring of Protection, and Keelhola, the Dagger of Life, were given by the Ainjeal Jehepsu to defeat the Grand Fiends. For millennia, the bearers of the Divine Sisters were held in high regard and many held esteemed titles, but as the centuries passed, they faded into myth. People of the Eylaour began to wonder if the Divine Sisters were even real. The peace the Divine Sisters had promised remained, and no interplanar war took place. However, that promise was not to last.

Prophecies of strife and conflict began pouring out. The Divine Sisters would once again be needed. People had been warned: if one Sister became known, but the other remained hidden, all the Ainjeal had fought for would be lost. Darkness would overtake Eylaour. Realizing the plane once again depended on them, the bearers of the Divine Sisters began looking for each other before it was too late.

❧

The elf, Saelethil, made his way through the mountain. He heard a rumor that the bearer of Jahola might be in the Northern Lands. If he could just bring Keelhola to them, they could prepare for whatever was to come. Night was starting to fall, so he made camp.

The moon was mostly gone, and the stars seemed dim. He settled in his bed roll, next to the fire, and began to drift off to sleep.

About midway through the night, he was awoken with a start by the sounds of rocks crunching under foot and saw three figures standing over him. They were dressed in all black and had cloaks on so he could not see their faces.

"Hand it over and we'll let you live," one hissed.

"Hand what over?" Saelethil reached for his sword as the dread of knowing what they were looking for filled his blood.

Another one of them thrust their black blade against his throat. "I wouldn't if I were you."

He froze.

"Give us Keelhola." The first one leaned in.

"I...I don't have it." His heart raced. His fears were valid. They were after the Dagger of Life.

"Lies!"

The third one grabbed the collar of his shirt and picked him off the ground. "We know you have it. We've been watching for some time. The time has come for the Divine Sisters to be revealed to the world. In our hands!"

Sealethil felt the cold metal blade push against his throat and said a silent prayer to Etienne. He had failed.

CHAPTER I

The seven-year-old elf's heart pounded as she ran to find her mother in a panic. Watching her sister leave the city with a sack scared her. She knew her parents did not approve of what Kindy had been doing, but she didn't think it was enough to make her leave.

"Mom! Where is Kindy going?" The girl tugged on her mother's arm to get her attention.

"What do you mean?" her mother looked down from her stitching.

"She just left."

"She's been out of the house for a while now." The older elf said simply.

The young girl got frustrated; she didn't understand. "No! She left town! Where is she going?"

"She did what?" Her mother practically threw the cloth and needle to the side as she rushed out the door.

"She left," the child said softly as she watched her mother leave.

After tucking her into bed, the young girl's mother kissed her on the forehead and began to walk out of the room.

"Mom!" she called out.

Her mother stopped and turned around. "Yes?"

"When is Kindy coming back? It's almost her birthday."

She walked back over to her daughter's bed and sat down. "I don't know."

"I'm worried."

"So are we...so are we." She stroked the young girl's hair. "Just try to get some sleep."

The girl nodded and closed her eyes. She finally drifted to sleep. Shortly after midnight, the young girl was violently woken as someone grabbed her. A gloved hand covered her mouth. She pulled on the arm, trying to get the hand away from her as she continued to kick and scream. The person was clothed in all black, with a hood casting shadows over their face. She felt a warmth in her arm, where they held her, and all the muscles in her body began to weaken.

Right as her vision went dim, she heard her mother scream, "Catherine! Catherine!"

A small five-year-old boy stretched out his arms as his mother bent over to pick him up. "When are we going?" He bounced excitedly in his mother's arms.

She laughed with a bell-like chime as she answered, "Tomorrow. We set sail tomorrow."

"Are we visiting Daddy's brother?" The boy's eyes lit up with eagerness; he'd never met any of his father's relatives.

"I'm sorry. No. Maybe someday we can visit them."

"Promise?"

His mother sighed sadly. "If the opportunity ever comes up, we will take you to see them." She brushed some of the boy's blond hair out of the way of his soft brown eyes.

The boy grinned, satisfied by his mother's answer.

"There you two are!" his father exclaimed as he walked towards the two.

"Daddy! Mommy said we could visit your family!"

"Oh, did she?" he looked at his wife questioningly.

"If the opportunity ever presents itself." She raised her chin slightly.

The boy's father laughed. "I suppose that's fair enough. Alright, time to pack up." He took the boy into his arms. "We have a big day and a long journey ahead of us."

The five-year-old clung to his mother's skirt as he watched a strange ship sail closer. He heard his companions all shouting and pulling out weapons. The other ship came up on the starboard side. The young boy watched as hooks and boards started to attach to their ship.

His mother crouched down, cupped his face in her hands, panic in her eyes, and whispered, "Hide."

ॐ∙ॐ

The boy stumbled along the path. He was lost and confused. His head hurt. He felt blood running down the side of his face. The world around him was a blur. He didn't know where he was or where he was going. All he knew was that he had to get there. He had cried all the tears he had, so all he knew to do was walk, one foot in front of the other. Eventually, he tripped and fell to the ground. He wasn't even sure how to get back up.

He feared what would happen, but had no other choice, and so he cried out, "Help! Someone, please help!" His breath shook violently as if he were crying, letting out gasps, but no tears rolled down his cheeks. Consciousness was about to leave the young boy when he spotted a light casting the shadow of a woman as she came over.

"Oh my!" she knelt down next to him, placing her hand gently on his forehead.

He winced in pain.

"What happened?" She looked around desperately. "Where are your parents?" She turned her attention back to the boy. "Are you alone?"

He nodded slowly.

"Here, come with me." She went to help the boy to his feet, but, as his legs gave out from underneath him, she picked him up and carried him in her arms. "Don't worry. I'll get you to a healer...what's your name?"

The boy softly whispered, "Aaron."

☙❧

The twelve-year-old Catherine walked through the crowded marketplace. There were too many people there; even just one more person than necessary for her to trade there would be too many people for Catherine. She feared they would learn her true identity. A despised elf. She carefully weaved through the crowd, keeping her pointed ears hidden and taking precautions to avoid spilling the berries she gathered, the only thing she could use to trade. All she could remember was waking up in an abandoned shack with only the knowledge of her name and age. She never revealed where she lived to anyone, always afraid that they could be part of why she was there, an orphaned elf in a human city with no memories.

She paused as she passed the seamstress's shop. They always had the most beautiful fabrics. There was one bolt she had her eye on. If she could ever get enough coin, it would be the first thing she would buy. The bolt was a velvety green with golden embroidery. It always reminded her of the forest. How she longed for the forest, to be amongst elves again. Even though she had no memories of what it was like, she still felt the emotions of her past.

She finally reached the only stall that gave her more than her berries were worth. "Good morning, Sohar," she said with a smile.

"Ah! Young Lady Catherine!" He smiled as he spread his arms wide.

She couldn't help but blush at the title she didn't deserve. "I had to fight the birds for this batch." Catherine placed her poorly made basket on his table.

"That means they're the best ones." Sohar winked at her. "Unfortunately, I've been running low on grain."

Catherine's shoulders slumped. She knew she couldn't get enough wheat to last a week from anyone else.

"Oh, don't go worrying. My supply should be stopping by today." He leaned in as if to add a secret, "He has a tendency to be late."

She couldn't help but giggle even though she had no idea who he was talking about. "Well, should I come back later?"

"Hm...how 'bout you give me a hand? I still have some other items to set out, and I can give you a couple coins for your effort."

Catherine's eyes widened. She had never had any money other than the few coins that slipped through their owners' hands by the end of the day. "You   don't-"

"Yes, I do. Good work deserves payment."

"Thank you!" She placed her basket of berries underneath Sohar's table and began to help him organize and unpack things from his cart. She longingly looked at the apples, daydreaming of the day she could afford one. Sohar, despite being one of the smaller vendors, always had the best ingredients.

After several minutes, Sohar quickly turned and exclaimed, "Aaron!" He turned to Catherine and softly said, "Your wheat is here."

Catherine looked over and saw a young boy, about her own age, walking towards them, guiding a chestnut-brown horse loaded with heavy bags. The tips of his blond hair brushed against the tips of his ears, and he looked straight at Catherine. The closer he got, the larger the smile on his face got.

"Good morning, Sohar," he said kindly while placing the bag on the table. "Who might this be?"

Catherine felt a small shiver throughout her body when she made eye contact with Aaron. She couldn't help but smile in return, enjoying the sensation. "Catherine." She extended her hand before Sohar could answer the boy's question.

Aaron took her hand and kissed it. "It's a pleasure to meet you. My name is Aaron."

ᔰᦺ

He couldn't stop thinking about her. There was something about that girl. His adopted parents claimed he fancied her, but it wasn't that. He couldn't explain what he felt, but it intrigued him; besides, he was only thirteen, not yet a man, and had never planned on finding anyone. Aaron couldn't help but secretly hope she would be at Sohar's stall whenever he brought the wheat by, but every time, he was disappointed.

His intrigue was answered one day while riding his horse, Juniper. He decided to take a path he had passed hundreds of times but had never taken. The path led through the nearby forest, one of Aaron's favorite places. He slowly began to feel reinvigorated, as if he had never felt that way before. The sounds of the birds, the smell of the trees, everything felt amazing to him. As he started to head back to the farm, he saw a small path that he had missed before. After gauging that he had enough time, he turned Juniper down the path. It led out of the forest faster than he expected, but once he exited, he was greeted by a wide opening with nothing but a single shack sitting out in the open. It was clearly an old, abandoned structure, just stable enough to remain standing. He had never heard of this place.

Cautious but curious, Aaron got off Juniper, tied her loosely to a tree, and walked towards the structure. As he got closer, he saw a young girl with gorgeous, long, flowing brown hair sitting in the grass next to the shack. Aaron purposefully rustled some fallen leaves to make sure she was aware of his presence.

Catherine looked up at Aaron with wide blue eyes and stood up hastily. "What are you doing here?"

Aaron smiled at Catherine. "I just saw a path I'd never taken before and decided to take it." He saw fear in her eyes, and his smile faded. "I can leave if you want."

"I...I suppose you can stay for a while."

ॐ◦ई

"And where have you been?" Aaron's middle-aged, adopted father, Thomas, asked as he returned.

"I told you; I went for a ride."

"I suppose you found somewhere interesting again?"

Aaron shook his head as he dismounted. "I found *someone* interesting."

Thomas raised an eyebrow.

"The girl from the market I told you about. She lives alone," Aaron cast his gaze to the ground. "She was abandoned."

"Like you," his father said in a hushed voice.

The young boy nodded. He had been adopted only three years ago. He felt a little jealous that Catherine did not have to suffer in an orphanage but felt sympathy that she had not found a family yet.

Aaron looked back at his adopted father. "Can we help her?"

CHAPTER 2

I t had been ten years since that fateful day. Catherine's life had changed in immeasurable ways. But two things remained: no one knew she was an elf or where she came from. The small room was lit by a single candle. The quarter moon and stars seemed dim. Though the light was eerie, the owls and crickets created soothing music for the lonely elf. She gazed out the window, watching the chestnut-brown horse Thomas gifted her get settled for sleep. The young elf soon turned; her brown hair flew naturally and gracefully. Her kind, blue eyes looked at a book and a quill lying next to the candle on the desk. The twenty-two-year-old's left hand brushed her hair behind her ear. Catherine then sat down at her desk and began to write in her journal.

The 10th Day of the 1st Moon of the 35th Year of King Hargon
    The wind blew hard today. It was very difficult to keep my ears from showing. Sometimes I just wish that it didn't matter, but if I want a chance with Aaron, I know people can't know. If I want a chance to keep living, I can't let people

know. The persecution of elves is getting worse. Last week there was a traveling merchant with an elven necklace; the guards kicked him out of the city and told him to never come back if he were to continue bringing in those "vile artifacts."

I helped Aaron and Thomas today on their farm, which is where the wind caused the most difficulty. Aaron told me he found somewhere he wanted to take me, swearing I've never been there before. How he finds all these places I never know. We're going to meet at the marketplace and will head to wherever it is he wants to take me after we've sold their wheat for the day. I'm so curious...where is he going to take me?

Catherine put down her quill, blew out the candle, and laid down on her bed. The soft breeze whistled outside and gently fluttered around her bedroom. The air's calming movement eased her to sleep.

ॐ∽

"Kindy, what are you doing?" the little five-year-old Catherine asked curiously.

"Nothing of importance," Kindy snapped, forehead wrinkled, as she slammed close a large black book.

"I don't think you should be doing that," Catherine sang innocently.

"I can if I want to!" the older girl spat.

"What is going on?" Catherine's mother asked as she entered the room. "What are you holding? Is that...? Kindy go into my room right now!"

"Why?" Kindy got defensive.

"Now!"

❧❦

Catherine's eyes shot open. Her heart beat fast. She looked around her room. Not knowing what to expect. She took a deep breath; it was just another dream. But she couldn't shake the feeling that the dream was a memory. To clear her head, she went for a ride on Chestnut.

As her horse began to gallop down a short path, Catherine closed her eyes. The cool air of a fall morning hit her face and tossed her hair around. Catherine didn't have to guide Chestnut; the horse knew the path they always took. Catherine loved those morning rides; she got to escape, feel free, as if there was no one to hide from, and think. That morning, she needed to think.

Her dreams had to be memories. They felt too real not to be, and the names and faces were always the same. She had an older sister named Kindy. Her mother was the loveliest person she had ever seen, and her father's arms could hold her tight yet gently, protecting her from everything.

But those memories became just dreams. Catherine was no longer with her family, among fellow elves. She was somehow alone in a human kingdom that was on the verge of war with her kind. There was only one person she felt she could trust: Aaron, and yet, she still feared his feelings would change the moment she told him. Why would anyone love an elf, the race despised by humans for reasons she's never known? She couldn't keep it hidden forever; she just prayed that only the right people would be the ones to know.

After the short sprint, Catherine slowed her horse and they slowly trailed through the forest before headed back to get ready for the marketplace. Right as she reached her home, the sun's rays started to show from behind the trees, and the birds greeted it with their songs.

≈∞≈

Catherine approached the marketplace as the merchants placed their items on their tables for the first time that day. The rim of her forest green dress brushed against the ground. With only part of her hair tied back, she slowly pushed her white, long sleeves up above her elbows. The straps of her overdress stayed where they were, right below her shoulders. She glanced up at the sun. He would be there soon.

She leaned against a nearby fence, her arms crossed for warmth since the mornings were growing crisp, looking down at the dirt path that led toward Aaron's home. A figure slowly appeared, walking down the road towards the marketplace. After a few moments, Catherine could make out a large sack that had been flung over his shoulder, which was probably full of wheat based on the deep bounce in his stride despite the ease with which he appeared to be carrying it.

A small smile crossed Catherine's face as Aaron came into view. She felt the urge to run to him, but knew it would be foolish, so she just stood up straight and let her arms fall to her sides. The sun's rays reflected off Aaron's blond hair, casting an almost elven glow. Catherine felt her heart flutter for a moment with the desire for him to be kin, and then she felt her heart fall as she was forced to silently acknowledge that Aaron wasn't an elf. She had fallen in love with a human who might no longer love her if he were to ever learn the truth about her heritage.

Aaron tossed the sack of wheat to the ground as he approached Catherine. "Good morning," he said as he wrapped his arms around her.

"Hello," she whispered back, loving the strength and warmth of her beloved's embrace.

They stood there for a moment, just as they were, until Aaron ran his hand gently through her hair.

After they slowly let go of each other, Aaron flung the bag over his left shoulder, looked at Catherine, and asked, "Shall we?"

Catherine reached out, brushed a few strands of Aaron's hair from in front of his eyes, and let her hand stroke against his cheek as she removed it from his face. "Okay."

They made their way further into the marketplace, nodding hellos to familiar faces. When they finally reached his stall, Aaron placed the heavy bag on Sohar's table.

"Good morning, Aaron," the old man behind the table said, smiling through weariness.

"Good morning, Sohar," Aaron responded, with a similar expression on his face.

"And good morning to you too, Lady Catherine."

The corners of the elf's mouth curled upwards as she blushed and responded, "Good morning."

"Have you two met my new worker?" the man asked, while pulling out a small pouch of money.

"You have someone to help you now?" Aaron asked.

"I do...Jithu, come here!"

All friendly emotions fell from Aaron's face at the sound of the assistant's name. A man, about the same age as Aaron, walked over. He placed his hands on his hips, flexing his broad muscular arms.

"This is my new hand." Sohar leaned forward and whispered, "He came for cheap."

"I bet..." Aaron mumbled, inaudible to all but Catherine.

Jithu looked Aaron up and down, eyes narrowed. Aaron shifted uncomfortably.

The muscular man eventually saw the fair woman standing next to Aaron. A smile crept onto his face as an eyebrow rose, and he asked, "Who might you be?"

"Um..." Catherine shifted her weight from her right foot to her left, leaning closer to Aaron. "My name is Catherine."

Jithu's smile grew. "What might a lovely lady like you be doing out here? Especially with..." he paused, looked Aaron up and down again, "*him*?"

Aaron took the small pouch from Sohar, didn't bother to count the coins or even test for approximate weight, as usual, and then took Catherine's hand as he said, "She can do whatever she pleases. She doesn't need approval from the likes of *you*."

If it were naturally possible, Jithu's eyes would have had fire in them. But before he could say anything, Aaron guided Catherine off.

After they were halfway on the other side of the marketplace, Catherine questioned, "What was *that* about?!" as she slid her hand slowly out of Aaron's.

"It's a long story." Aaron waved his hand and tilted his head towards her slightly.

"I have time." She crossed her arms and lifted her head upwards.

"I knew him in the orphanage...okay?"

"Why don't you ever tell me what happened?" Catherine struggled to contain her frustration.

"Because I want to forget it."

"Why would you want to do that?" Catherine was horrified at the thought of wanting to forget one's past.

Aaron shook his head. "The memories are more painful than helpful."

"That's what makes you who you are!"

"You don't understand." He looked at her, pleading with his eyes.

"No. I do." Catherine placed her hands on her hips.

Aaron looked around and whispered, "Not here, please."

"Fine." She grabbed his hand and pulled him slightly outside the marketplace. "Even if it's painful to remember, aren't the good memories worth the pain?" Her mind flashed images from her dreams. Her mother's smile and tears danced through her thoughts, making her desire for them to be memories of events rather than dreams stronger than ever.

"That's the problem." Aaron looked at the silver ring he wore on his right ring finger and twisted it slowly. "I don't have any good memories."

Catherine paused for a moment, startled by what he said. "What do you mean?" she asked softly.

Aaron inhaled deeply. "I barely remember anything from before the orphanage; none of what I remember was good, and almost all memories from the orphanage are bad. I'd much prefer to have no memories and make up good ones than be constantly tortured by my past." He looked up and made eye contact with Catherine again.

"I...I never thought of it that way."

Aaron let out a small laugh. "You've thought about it?"

Catherine looked down at her own hands, unsure of what to do with them. "I live alone and have no idea why. I have dreams of a family, but no way to prove them." Catherine looked back at Aaron. "I don't even have a past I want to forget. I just don't have one."

They were both silent and still for a moment. The realization that Aaron might be more understanding of her other secret suddenly dawned on Catherine.

Aaron reached out and took Catherine's hand. "I will tell you what I remember, just not now." Before Catherine could object, he placed his finger against her lips. "I'm still trying to figure it out myself."

Catherine nodded. "I understand." She still didn't like his secrets, but she acknowledged she was keeping a large one from him as well. She took Aaron's hand and said, "Let's finish our errands so we can get out of here."

He responded with a half-smile, and they went back into the crowded marketplace.

After they had weaved through the marketplace for a while, Catherine spotted their friend's stall. "Thynan!"

The tall, brown-haired human laughed. "Hello, Catherine." Thynan reached out over his leather goods and kissed Catherine's hand. He then turned to face her suitor. "Aaron!" The tall human clasped one hand around Aaron's wrist and patted the back of Aaron's hand with the other. "It's been a while."

"I know...what?... Two days?" Aaron laughed.

Catherine laughed as well but did not join their conversation. She looked around, observing the many people filling the small circular clearing in the center of the town. She could name most of them, if not identify them as someone from Dovan at the very least. But soon, one man caught her eye. "Who's that?"

23

Thynan and Aaron halted their friendly conversation about various creatures that unexpectedly destroy crops and turned to look at her.

"Who?" Aaron questioned.

"Him." Catherine motioned with her head to a man who clearly stood out from the rest.

He was several inches taller than most other people there, with long, dark hair tied behind his head. He wore a blue robe with a red border, embroidered with silver, and carried a redwood staff carved in a twisted pattern.

"What is he buying?" Catherine questioned, since neither Aaron nor Thynan answered her first question.

"It looks like food...well preserved food..." Aaron stared at the man just as intently as Catherine.

"He's been here for a few days...Doesn't really talk to anyone," Thynan informed, leaning on his table.

While Aaron thought, Catherine asked, "Where's he staying?"

"The old tavern near the Jayid residence."

"He looks too rich to be staying there..." Aaron observed.

The mysterious man looked over his shoulder at the three staring at him. He simply raised an eyebrow, smiled, picked up the food he had purchased, turned, and walked away, somehow vanishing into the crowd.

"I don't like him," Aaron stated, folding his arms in front of his chest.

Catherine rolled her eyes. "You don't like anyone."

Thynan laughed.

"No...he doesn't make sense. Think about it. He's staying in one of the cheapest taverns in town, when there are several decently priced ones with relatively good service. He wears fine clothing and carries a rather expensive-looking staff, showing that he can afford better. *And* he didn't seem at all bothered by all three of us obviously staring at him...not even a tad bit annoyed."

"Huh..." Thynan leaned on the wall of a building behind his table. "You're right, at least on the last part. With how he behaves around everyone else, it would be no surprise for him to growl a curse on someone if they just accidentally look at him the wrong way."

Aaron looked over his shoulder at his friend. "What do you mean? How does he behave around everyone else?"

"Like I said, he doesn't talk to people. Also, I heard rumors from some of the 'regulars' at the tavern he's staying at that he actually threw one man across the room."

Catherine's eyes widened a good deal, but before she said anything, Aaron replied with, "You're trusting the information given to you by drunkards?"

"Who said they were drunkards?"

Aaron raised his eyebrows, arms still crossed in front of him.

"Who knows...He still doesn't seem all that friendly to me..." Thynan then began to set a couple more items on the table.

Aaron looked back at where the mysterious man had walked off to and whispered, "Me neither..."

Catherine reached out and took Aaron's hand, squeezing it to let him know she agreed. Thynan's mention of curses rang all too true with what she felt from the stranger, even at a distance.

☙◦❧

Aaron and Catherine both climbed over the fence next to Aaron's adopted family's house. He handed his father the pouch of money and the two bags of goods he had been sent to buy.

"Take Juniper out," Thomas instructed Aaron. "She hasn't been ridden in about a day."

Aaron nodded but didn't say anything. Catherine followed him to the stable. There were only two horses there. One was a typical brown horse, but the other was Juniper. Her coat was a silvery white. Her mane was pearly white, and her hooves were a shimmering black. There was no gate keeping her in. Aaron clicked his tongue twice, and Juniper came out of her stall. He touched her on her chin

26

and guided her out of the stable. Catherine had gathered the saddle and riding cloth, and then, with Aaron's assistance, placed and secured them on Juniper.

Catherine's beloved got on Juniper, reached down, and pulled the elf on in front of him. He wrapped his arms around her and took hold of Juniper's mane because he did not use reins with her. He kicked the horse just hard enough to get her moving. They left the farm and headed out towards the forest.

"Where are you taking me?" Catherine inquired as they headed deeper into the woods.

"You'll see." Aaron smiled but did not look at Catherine and just kept guiding Juniper along.

Eventually, they approached a small clearing. The sun shone down upon the velvety grass through the leaves of the trees, causing a greenish glow. Catherine noticed there were small lights of various colors floating around the area.

Noting Catherine's curiosity, Aaron said, "This area is believed to have some sort of magical power."

"Oh? What kind of power?" she looked over her left shoulder.

"Don't know."

Catherine laughed. "You don't know? Then how do you know it's magical?"

Aaron got off Juniper and answered, "The fairies."

She looked back over at the small lights. She still could not see them as well as she desired, so she got off Juniper and walked slowly towards the clearing. Once she could examine the orbs, she saw that they were the radiant glow of small girls flying around. Each had long hair and wings that resembled stained glass windows, glowing in the colors that matched their hue. "I've never seen a fairy before..." she said softly, mouth opened slightly.

"Really?"

"At least not that I can remember..."

Aaron wrapped his arms around her waist and kissed her softly on the cheek. Catherine giggled and turned around. They stared into each other's eyes for a moment. Aaron slowly leaned in and tilted his head to the side. Both closed their eyes, and their lips met. He lifted his left hand to her cheek and held the side of her face gently. Their kiss finally ended, and Aaron guided her to the edge of the clearing, and they sat down underneath a tree. Aaron's back was against the tree's base. Catherine leaned on Aaron. He embraced her, and she rested the back of her head on his chest, both just watching the fairies fly around playing with each other. Aaron began to run his fingers through her hair slowly.

After several minutes of silence, Catherine turned around and kissed Aaron. He brushed some of her hair out of her face, gently stroking the top of her finely pointed ears, and just stared into her eyes. At first, Catherine simply responded with a smile, but soon after, she realized what had happened. Panic took hold of her heart, and her eyes widened.

Aaron's eyebrows creased as he asked, "What's wrong?"

Her hand instantly went to her bare ear. "I'm sorry I didn't tell you! I was hoping I could...but...I..."

He laughed. "Don't worry about it. I already knew."

"But... how?" Catherine's eyes did not go down in size at all.

Aaron simply shrugged and responded, "I've seen your ears."

"*You've seen my ears!* When have you seen my ears?!"

Aaron chuckled slightly. "That's not the first time I've seen your hair behind your ear. You're not very good at hiding it."

"You haven't told anyone...have you?"

"Don't worry," Aaron's tone changed from playful to calm as he gently touched her arm. "I haven't told anyone. As far as I know, I'm the only person who knows." Aaron looked into her eyes with more intensity than she had ever seen. "And no human will ever know without your permission. I promise."

Catherine felt as though Aaron's eyes were burning through her. "What...what do you mean?" she stammered.

"I will not let any human harm you."

Catherine pulled her arm away from Aaron, fearing the anger in his eyes. "Why are you talking like this?"

The anger in Aaron's eyes melted into concern. "What do you mean?"

"You were saying 'humans' like...like you aren't one."

Aaron took a silent breath as his features froze.

Catherine stood up. "Aaron?"

"Oh, Catherine..." Aaron reached out towards her.

She took a step back. "*What* are you?"

"I'm like you...I'm..."

"What?" Catherine's heart stopped. "You're... an elf?" Confusion consumed her thoughts: his ears were rounded, like a human's.

"Not quite."

"Not quite?" She took a suspicious half-step backwards.

"Not like that! I might not be fully elf, but...at least half."

"How do you know? You have no memories." Catherine couldn't help but become accusatory. The likelihood of that many similarities was too low for it to happen.

"I can't explain exactly how I know, but this," Aaron slipped off his ring, "was my mother's." He handed it to Catherine.

She cautiously took the ring and examined it more than she ever had. It had three intertwining engraved lines that circled the ring in never-ending waves. "It's elven," she whispered.

Aaron nodded. "I always knew I was different. I can feel and sense things most others can't." He looked down at a fairy that landed next to him. "And fairies typically run from non-magical beings."

Catherine sat down next to Aaron, staring at the ring. It suddenly dawned on her: they were kin. He didn't care. Their eyes met, and she could feel every beat of her heart. Her secret doesn't matter for their future together. She had never dared to say it before, but the feelings she felt were too overwhelming for her not to say, "I love you."

Aaron took her hands in his, the ring trapped between them. "I love you, too."

The next day, Catherine met Aaron outside the marketplace again, this time it was later in the day. The crowd had grown to a steady and busy pace.

When she saw him walking towards her, Catherine couldn't help herself; she ran to meet him, threw her arms around him, and kissed him. They had never kissed in public before, but she couldn't help herself. They were descended from the same race; there was nothing to hide.

Aaron laughed after their kiss ended. "Hello."

Catherine smiled innocently. "Hello."

Aaron put his arm around her, and they began to walk down the dirt path that led to Thomas's farm. Instead of following it all the way to his home, Aaron guided Catherine off a side road that led towards the slums of Dovan.

"Why are we going here?" she questioned, shifting slightly away from him.

"Don't worry. There's something I want to show you." Aaron kept his arm firmly around her and moved his fingers so that they massaged her arm softly.

Catherine sighed. They continued walking until they reached an alleyway, then Aaron took Catherine's hand and guided her along one of the decaying walls.

Whispering, Catherine asked, "Where are you taking me?"

Aaron looked over his shoulder, smiled, and answered, "To that inn."

"You mean where that stranger is?" Catherine jolted to a halt, tugging Aaron's arm.

"It will be fine. I'll keep you safe." He waited a moment, then motioned for her to follow him as he left the alleyway and onto the street of broken stones.

The inn stood before them, dark and dreary. The windows were covered in soot and one of them was broken; the door looked as though it was about to fall off its hinges. Aaron opened the door, and it squeaked loudly. He led her in. There was a single bar, behind which the innkeeper stood, with stools lining one side, and about ten tables with five chairs around each. Everything was made from wood and looked as if it would crumble into dust with a single breeze.

The innkeeper only glanced at the two who had just walked in, and then back down at the glass mug he was cleaning. Aaron looked around, his right arm behind him, lightly touching Catherine in a slightly protective stance. There were only three other people and the innkeeper in the room: one at the bar, one at a table in the center of the room, and then another one in the far corner, cast in shadows.

"I think that's him," Aaron whispered to Catherine.

She looked over. The man was clearly tall, even when sitting down. The corner of his robes was in the light; it was blue with a red border embroidered with linked gold circles. Aaron began to guide her to an empty table, far away from the stranger. The two sat down, Catherine's back to the man while Aaron faced him.

Not too long after they sat down, the man in the corner stood up. He picked up his redwood staff in his right hand and walked towards them. He was tall, with long black hair and eyes a deep, fern-green. Aaron stood up and stepped to the side, making sure the stranger focused on him instead of Catherine. She turned around. They could see him clearly in the light now. He appeared to be in his early thirties and smiled at them with the same smile he had in the marketplace.

"I couldn't help but notice you two yesterday...and it appears you noticed me too..." He chuckled slightly. The man made direct eye contact with Aaron. "Since you are brave enough to stalk me," he paused for a moment, one eyebrow raised with what appeared to be mild displeasure, "I shall be blunt. I don't want to talk to you."

"That's unfortunate," Aaron retorted, "That's why we're here."

The man raised his free hand. "I don't want to talk to you *here*." He glanced at Catherine and then back at Aaron. "You might be able to help me."

Catherine knew she wouldn't like what was about to happen, but knew she couldn't stop Aaron.

Aaron stared at the man for a moment and then responded, "When and where?"

"Two days from now, just after sunrise, outside the marketplace to the north." He spoke bluntly.

The half-elf glanced at Catherine. She sighed and nodded.

"We'll be there."

CHAPTER 3

Aaron raised his axe and slammed it down on the log, causing a crack and thud that resulted in the one piece of wood becoming two. His adopted father had arranged with the local woodsman to obtain logs at a lower price if they weren't fully cut. Finishing the job became Aaron's as soon as he was old and strong enough to handle it on his own. When he was younger, Aaron resented being given the chore as much as an orphan in a loving home could resent a task, but he had begun to understand.

Things were not well in the kingdom, and it was having a profoundly negative impact on his family. Some nights, food was on the table simply because of tasks such as chopping wood. His father used to scoff at his mother teaching Aaron to sew soon after he was adopted at age ten, but recently his father became more grateful that there were two pairs of hands to handle the mending as they needed the expensive material to last longer, including the tough leather that required stronger hands than his mother ever had.

Aaron found himself thinking more and more about the future of their farm. He wasn't sure if he was worried about it failing, his parents' health failing, or him leaving. Ever since he met the stranger, two days ago, he had odd dreams including those that cloud one's mind during the day; one was of the orphanage; one was of a human man sword fighting with an elf, but Aaron had no fears knowing they were just practicing; one was of the day he found Catherine's house; and the strangest one was of him, Catherine, and the stranger eating around an open fire in woods he has never been in. The last dream had just been an image that interrupted his thoughts the other day. He feared that dream would come true, but he couldn't figure out why he would leave, at least if nothing catastrophic happened.

Once he finished chopping the wood, Aaron went into the house to change, rinsed his face off, and made himself presentable. As he pulled his shirt on, he glanced out the window at the sun; Catherine would be arriving soon. He walked down the hallway and into the reading room. Aaron placed his hand on his adopted mother's shoulder as she rehemmed their drapes.

"Done with the wood already?" she asked without looking up.

"I even made a batch of smaller ones for the stove, like you like."

She looked up at Aaron with a grateful smile. "Thank you."

Aaron leaned over and kissed her forehead. "Anything for you."

As Aaron turned to leave, she took his hand, causing him to turn back around. "What's bothering you?"

"What do you mean?" Somehow, she always knew when something was bothering Aaron, even though there were no blood ties.

"You've been...distant." She looked down at the cloth on her lap. "Not when you're around your father and I, but when you're alone." She looked back at Aaron. "I've seen your face. It's been a while since I've seen that face. Are you having those nightmares again?"

"No, mother." Aaron stared into her eyes, and he could feel her concern flood over him. "I just worry about the farm. Father is losing strength and the amount of work required of him is increasing."

His mother smiled. "Don't worry yourself with that. This isn't the first time we have had hard times. Besides, in a few years you'll have some help." She winked at Aaron, but as he opened his mouth to protest, she interjected. "Don't think we haven't seen the way you look at Catherine, and how she looks back at you." She raised a finger before Aaron could respond. "It's exactly how your father looked at me before we were betrothed and how he still looks at me. Since your father is not one for formalities, I'll just tell you now. You have our blessing for whenever you are ready."

"But...I..." Aaron stammered.

His mother just laughed. "Don't worry. Everything will be just fine. Etienne is smiling upon us all; don't you forget that."

Aaron smiled at his mother and shook his head before walking out the door. He knew she was right; he couldn't imagine his life without Catherine. But as he stood outside the house, looking out over their simple farm, he didn't know how he could provide for her, let alone a family. And if they did have children ...he twisted his ring.

"Aaron!" Catherine called out his name as she walked down the path to his house.

He met his beloved before she reached the house and embraced her. It was time to meet the stranger and figure out what brought him to their town.

୬୦୶

The stranger stood at the edge of the marketplace, precisely where they agreed to meet. His black hair was tied tight behind his head. His robes were a solid dark blue with a simple golden band on all edges, and he leaned slightly on his twisted redwood staff.

Aaron walked one pace in front of Catherine as they approached. Before they were within hearing range of the man, Aaron whispered, "I think he's from the Northern Lands."

"Why do you say that?" Catherine asked softly.

"His robes have both been primarily the dark blue that is typical of wizards from the Northern Lands."

"So, you think we can trust him?"

"I didn't say that."

They greeted the stranger with a simple nod, which he reciprocated.

"I am glad you actually came," the stranger said with a smile.

"We'll honor our word, as long as you do," Aaron responded bluntly.

"Understood."

"Who are you?" The half-elf started the grilling immediately.

"Now, why is that of your concern?" The stranger raised a single eyebrow.

"Because you will insist on the same information from us." Aaron stepped slightly in front of his beloved.

The man smiled, and his face relaxed. "How many outsiders have you interrogated?"

"That is none of your concern. Who are you and why are you here?"

"My name is Klew and I am simply passing through."

"I do not believe you. You are too far from your home to be 'passing through.'"

Klew raised his eyebrow again. "Give me your names and we'll discuss this disagreement further."

Aaron knew they would get no further if he refused, so he reluctantly said, "My name is Aaron, and this is Catherine." He barely motioned towards her, trying not to draw too much attention to her.

"Pleased to meet you," Klew said with a small, nodded bow.

Aaron could not determine whether Klew was being sincere or not. "Why are you so far from home?"

"And where precisely do you believe that is?"

"Based on the color of your robes and your staff, I'd say the Northern Lands."

"You are rather...observant," Klew said smoothly. "And you would be correct. However, I am simply passing through *your* town while on my way elsewhere."

"Then why have you been here for over a quarter of a moon's turn?" Aaron shifted uncomfortably.

"Because I have been looking for someone." A smirk crept across his face.

"So, you do have alternative reasons you are here." Aaron perked up. He enjoyed being right but also feared the motive behind Klew's actions.

"Why must you know all of this?" The smirk never left his mouth.

"Because strangers, such as yourself, typically only come to cause trouble, and I do not appreciate someone bringing trouble to my city. Who are you looking for and why?"

"I wasn't told his name, or why."

Aaron stared into Klew's eyes and had a sinking feeling that he was being told the truth. The half-elf's shoulders dropped; a sinking feeling filled his stomach. "Who sent you?"

"I am not at liberty to say."

"How will you know who you are looking for with so little information?" Aaron didn't hesitate; he wanted to know everything he could.

"I was told *he* would approach *me*," Klew glanced at Catherine, "protecting his beloved."

Aaron sharply stepped between Klew and Catherine, his left arm extended behind him as a guard for Catherine and placed his other hand on his hunting knife. What did this man want with them?

"Be calm," Klew spoke softly. "I am not here to harm anyone."

"And why should we trust you?" Aaron's heart raced.

"Because I have come to offer protection."

"From what?" Aaron spoke harshly as his trust faded fast.

Klew paused, glanced around, and then answered, "I was sent here to wait for a man who would risk his life for those he loves to approach me. I am to accompany him on his journey."

"How do I know you are speaking the truth? And why did you not say this when I first asked?"

"I wanted to be sure you were the one I was sent to find. She told me you would be a brave man, unafraid to oppose unknown power."

"She? You do not mean-"

"Annathalinda," Catherine whispered with a gasp.

Klew nodded.

"Why would Annathalinda care about us?" Aaron became very uncomfortable and fearful of deception. What kind of journey would the most powerful elven seer require him to go on?

"There is a journey I am to protect you during. That is all I have been told and so all I need to know." He shrugged shallowly.

"What journey?" Aaron snapped at Klew slightly.

"You tell me." Klew glanced from Catherine to Aaron.

Catherine reached out and took Aaron's hand.

Aaron's vision of the three of them sitting around a fire flashed through his mind.

"Can you help us find our families?" she asked.

"Your families?" Klew's features softened.

"We..." Catherine glanced at Aaron, then turned her attention back to Klew, "Our birth families are from far away. However, we don't know how we got here."

"Do you have any more information than that?"

Catherine looked at Aaron once more, took a deep breath, and whispered, "We are of elven heritage."

Klew shifted his gaze back and forth between the two of them, pausing momentarily on Aaron. "You are not safe here then."

Catherine squeezed Aaron's hand; he replied by doing the same, but he believed the squeezes were conveying different messages.

"I will help."

Her face lit up. The half-elf felt his chest tighten. He thought about the farm and his father, who was slowly aging.

"Do you know where your families are? How long have you been here?"

"We don't know where they are. I was kidnapped and Aaron..." she paused as she turned to her beloved.

Aaron stumbled over his words. "I...uh...I have a memory of a ship then here in Dovan."

"Hm..." Klew seemed to ponder the situation. "We may have to go directly to Annathalinda."

"Why would Annathalinda concern herself with us?" his cynicism came out.

"I do not question her," Klew made eye contact with Aaron. "She saw value in me helping you, and so I will do so, no matter if it makes sense or not. Now, knowing your heritage, it would be wise to get out of Bellmora as soon as possible. How long do you need to gather your belongings?"

"A quarter moon!" Catherine answered abruptly.

"Catherine," Aaron whispered.

She turned to him.

"I...I can't just leave."

"If you need some time, I understand," Klew added. "But with the current climate, I wouldn't suggest taking too long to decide. I will wait for half a moon. If I hear no more from you, I will move on."

And with that, their future was to be decided in less than a moon.

∂∾∾⋄

Catherine silently practiced what she was going to say as she approached Thomas's farm. She paused at the gate and watched her beloved tending to the horses. She took a deep breath and continued forward.

Aaron looked up as she approached. There was a slight smile on his face. She saw it fade as she drew closer. "What's wrong?" he asked.

She couldn't manage pleasantries. "I think we should go with Klew." Those were not the words she had rehearsed.

Her beloved remained silent for longer than she had anticipated. Finally, he said, "We can't."

The tension in her shoulders released as she leaned forward. "Don't you want to know your past? Don't you want to know where you came from? Don't you want to find your family?"

"My family is right here." Aaron extended his arm towards the house.

"But what about your past?" Catherine felt desperate.

"I have no past." He dropped his arm to his side.

"You don't know that." Catherine almost bounced with her frustration.

"Catherine," he furrowed his brow, and there was a hint of anger, "I can't abandon my family."

"Well, I don't have a family!" she snapped.

His voice softened, and his shoulders drooped. "What about us?"

"Aaron. I'm not you. I can't just walk in the open without a care in the world. I'm tired of hiding who I am. I'm tired of fearing what would happen if people found out. I'm tired of not feeling welcome in my own hometown. Which, by the way, isn't my actual hometown. It's where I've been stuck for most of my life!" She saw pain pierce Aaron's expression, and her heart stopped.

"I know." Catherine watched as his chest rose and fell. "I know it's not easy on you. But I just..." He turned his gaze to the ground. "I just thought I'd done enough to make up for it."

Catherine couldn't speak. She tried, but it got caught in her throat.

"If this is what will make you happy...go."

ᕱ৹ᕲ

As Aaron helped his mother clean up after dinner, someone knocked loudly on the door. He touched his mother's shoulder, indicating to her not to worry.

47

He met his father by the door. Aaron opened it and paused a moment before asking, "Can we help you?"

Three guards stood in front of him. "You haven't paid your taxes."

"You must be mistaken," Aaron doing his best to remain calm, "I brought them four days ago myself."

"Our records show it wasn't complete."

"I brought twenty sacks full of wheat." Aaron shifted uncomfortably.

"That is only half of what is required."

"You are asking for half our crop!" Thomas outburst.

Aaron placed his hand on his father's shoulder and gripped it.

The guards seemed unfazed. "You have until midday tomorrow to bring the remaining sacks." They then turned and left.

Aaron guided his father away from the door, closed it, and turned towards his mother. "I'll get started before dawn."

"They've doubled taxes?" his mother asked, wiping her hands with a towel as she stood in the doorway to the dining area.

"Apparently," Aaron said with a sigh.

"This is unacceptable!" Thomas clenched his hands into fists. "How *dare* King Hargon do this!"

"Father," Aaron placed his hands on Thomas's chest. "Breath. We'll be fine. We still have enough extra to afford it."

Thomas took deep breaths, only partially controlled, ran his hands through his hair, then finally gave in and sat down, exasperated.

"When did this happen?" Tammy asked.

"Since I turned the original sacks in. They confirmed it was all present at the time." Aaron's hand rested on his father's shoulder, appreciating his mother's calmness.

"Will you need help in the morning?"

"No. Most of the wheat is already bagged up; there is just a little bit more to make up a full twenty more bags."

"That's half our supply," Thomas muttered, his head in his hands.

Aaron patted him gently on the shoulder. "We'll get through." He just wished he believed it as much as he said he did.

That night, Aaron's mind did not remain calm. He woke long before he intended to but decided to get ready to work anyway.

The waning moon was low in the sky, and the air was icy. Aaron pulled a coat on and started filling sacks with the grain he had separated just the other day. It didn't look like there would be enough prepared to fill the twenty sacks.

After emptying the bin, Aaron headed to their pile of dried stalks. He glanced towards the sky and knew the sun would rise sooner than he would like.

Large armful by large armful, Aaron began threshing the wheat. With every swing, he did what he could to silence his mind. But his mind didn't quiet; the early morning stillness merely allowed his thoughts to spiral around the decline of the kingdom and whether he should join Catherine or not. No matter what he did, he would be abandoning someone.

Ever since Queen Idalga passed away, King Hargon kept changing things. The guards' behaviors began to change; the actual guards' assignments changed; the royal presence changed as palace servants disappeared from the marketplace. Aaron had also heard that foreign ambassadors had visited the palace three moons ago; he didn't know from where they hailed, but he had heard a rumor that they had left on unpleasant terms. King Hargon was not known for his skills in diplomacy, though, so no one was surprised by the rumor. However, the king was also not known for his military skills.

Things seemed to be going poorly fast after the Queen died. Rumors of King Hargon going insane spread. Aaron hadn't believed them before, but his mind was changing.

The King doubling taxes after they were due lacked support for sanity.

The sun had risen above the horizon, and the air warmed enough for Aaron to remove his coat. Once all the stored grain was threshed, Aaron switched to winnowing. He placed the winnowed grain directly in the sacks. Soon, he realized that there was not enough trade wheat, and he'd have to start collecting from their personal reserves.

As Aaron walked through the field to where the rest of the wheat was stored, he noticed someone approaching on horseback. At first, Aaron feared it was another guard coming to tell them they owed even more, but he was soon relieved to see it was Catherine on Chestnut.

"What are you doing?" she asked as she dismounted. "I thought you were set on wheat for a few days."

Aaron let out a huffing laugh as he leaned against the fence directly across from his beloved. "King Hargon had different plans."

"What do you mean?" She leaned so that only the fence was between them.

"Taxes have doubled."

"I thought you already paid them?"

"I did, but we still have to pay more."

"But-"

Aaron cut her off by raising his hand. "I don't know why; all I know is we can't afford not to pay it." Aaron reached out and took Catherine's hand. "I'd love to continue talking with you, but I still have one more sack to do by midday."

She held tight to his hand, not letting him walk away. "I have just one thing I have to tell you."

Aaron thought he caught a hint of urgency in her voice and on her face. "What is it?"

"I've changed my mind."

"What do you mean?" He turned his attention fully to her.

"I won't go with Klew without you."

"But what about your family?" Aaron wasn't sure whether to feel happy or guilty.

Catherine smiled. "I've gone this long without them."

"No, I can't let you." Guilt won the battle. "Don't do this for me."

"Aaron," Catherine shook her head, "I'm not. I'm doing it for me." She looked him directly in the eyes. "I don't want to leave you."

Relief flooded over Aaron, and he reached over the fence and pulled her close for a loving kiss. "I love you," he whispered.

"I love you, too," she whispered in reply, before kissing him once more.

বেজ্জ

Aaron and Catherine guided one of their horses pulling a cart full of twenty sacks of wheat. Since taxes were past due, the guards were no longer located right outside the marketplace. They had to travel to the guard house, at the edge of the nobles' area, separated only by an elaborate metal gate.

Aaron saw glances of disgust as some of the nobles walked past and looked at them. It was nothing new, but Aaron noticed it more often recently.

"What do you want?" a guard barked, leaning back in a chair outside the guardhouse.

"I was informed King Hargon requested more wheat in taxes last night," Aaron replied, more diplomatic than he would have preferred.

The guard grunted. "So, you're the farmer trying to refuse the King what's rightly his."

"Excuse me?"

"You've skimped on your taxes."

"It was raised after I had already turned it over. I was informed of this last night. So, here I am with the rest of what is due, before midday."

The guard laughed. "You're a bad liar. The notice went out a week ago and was due by sundown last night. You are late."

"No," Aaron blurted.

"Are you calling me a liar?" The guard stood up, his hand on the hilt of his sword, prepared to draw.

Aaron suddenly realized what he had just said. "No."

"Now, which is it? Are you lying, or am I?"

Aaron knew it was a trap, but he had no idea how to escape it. "Neither."

Before Aaron could continue his defense, the guard laughed and said, "Neither? I'm sure the King would love to hear how that works!"

"The – no!" So many thoughts and feelings flooded through Aaron that they became indistinguishable from one another: his parents, Catherine, their farm, anger, fear, and desperation. How had he let this happen?

"Good thing you came to me." The guard picked up a pair of shackles. "These are heavy."

Catherine touched Aaron on the shoulder, "What are we going to do?"

Aaron turned around, looked his beloved in her eyes, and gripped her shoulders. "Tell my parents what happened."

"I won't leave you!" She almost hung off his arms.

"There's nothing you can do. Go." He released her with a gentle push.

The guard took Aaron's right arm and pulled him away from Catherine. "Time to go to your new home." The guard locked the thick metal shackles around Aaron's wrists and led him away.

CHAPTER 4

❧

Catherine guided the horse and cart back to Aaron's parents' farm, unsure of what to do or how to tell them that Aaron was arrested. When she finally reached their fence, Thomas was in the field. He froze when he saw her and called out for his wife. Tammy came out and stood on their porch, just staring.

Thomas walked with Catherine to the house.

"Where's Aaron?" Tammy asked.

Catherine could no longer hold it in. She broke down crying.

❧

Thomas slammed his fists onto the table and shouted, "They have no right! We paid our taxes when they were due. We even brought more when they asked. King Hargon has lost his mind!"

"Keep your voice down, if you're going to say anything like that," Tammy said with a hushed voice. "We don't need anyone using that against us."

"What are we supposed to do? Just sit here as he robs us blind?"

"Yes. What can you do other than get yourself arrested or killed and leave me here alone?"

Thomas fell silent.

"We have to save Aaron," Catherine said softly.

"How?" Thomas asked just as quietly.

Catherine sighed.

Tammy reached out and took Catherine's hand. "Stay the night. I'd worry about you being by yourself, and, well, Aaron's..." her voice trailed off.

Catherine took her hand. "Thank you. I'll try to help however I can."

෧•෧

That was the longest night of Catherine's life. She could hear Thomas and Tammy discussing how they would handle their lives. When she finally tried to sleep, Aaron's bed smelled like him, and she could not bear all the memories that flooded her mind.

She sat up and moved to Aaron's small writing table. She lit the candle and pulled out her journal.

The 27th Day of the 1st Moon of the 35th Year of King Hargon

I don't know what to do. Aaron has been arrested for doing nothing wrong. Thomas and Tammy cannot afford it, and there is nothing I can do. The past three moons have brought nothing good.

I almost fear Thomas is right. Maybe King Hargon has lost his mind.

Catherine looked out the window, hoping an answer would suddenly dawn upon her. It didn't. She turned back to her journal.

I wish there were some way I could fix this. Some way to free Aaron. Summon an Ainjeal to change King Hargon's mind. A disgruntled guard set him free. I'd even settle for casting a spell!

Catherine's heart stopped. A spell was exactly what she needed.

෨ඁ෧

"Thank Etienne, you haven't left yet!" Catherine ran over to Klew as he strapped a saddle onto his horse.

He raised an eyebrow as he looked over his shoulder at her. "Changed your mind?"

"Aaron needs your help!" Her heavy breathing gave away how long she had been running.

The Northerner turned all the way around. "What happened?"

"Aaron's been arrested!" She placed her hands on her hips, trying to stabilize herself.

"Why was he arrested?"

"King Hargon raised taxes after they were due." She took a controlled deep breath. "His guard claimed Aaron hadn't paid in time."

"*After* they were due?"

Catherine just nodded.

"This is worse than I thought," he said, almost too soft for Catherine to hear. Louder, he said, "I'll help."

☙❧

"Catherine?" Tammy stepped into the doorway.

Catherine's hand stopped, midway between the bed and her backpack, briefly before she sped back up to try to appear normal. "Yes?"

"Why are you packing your things? You're welcome to stay as long as you need. You're no burden."

Catherine turned to face Tammy. "Oh, it's not that. I just..." she hadn't thought of what to tell Thomas and Tammy.

Tammy remained silent.

"I just can't bear it without him." Her hands shook with the truth of her words. "I have a friend who is willing to help me."

"Catherine?" Tammy stepped forward, concern flooding her voice and face.

"Oh, do not worry about me," Catherine turned, a forced smile on her face and a confession in the form of a tear on her cheek. "I'm going to trade beyond Dovan's limits. Travel with them. Maybe I can manage to get enough gold to set Aaron free and get things back to normal."

Aaron's mother embraced Catherine. "This isn't your burden to bear. But I know there is no stopping you. Please write us letters so we know you're safe."

"Of course."

❧

"This is a pleasant surprise," Aaron whispered as he reached his hand partway between two thick, cold, steel bars and brushed his fingers through a small cluster of Catherine's hair that hung from under her hood.

She turned her head so that his fingers touched her cheek. "Please forgive me."

"For what?" His thumb rubbed against her cheek.

Catherine looked into his eyes. "I'm getting you out of here," she whispered.

"What?" He stopped moving his fingers.

"Klew and I have a plan. You don't have to do a thing. Other than trust us." She wrapped her fingers around his still hand.

"I don't understand."

"No need to."

"I can't let you-"

Catherine placed her finger on his lips. "Please don't fight. We'll explain once we've reached the forest." Before Aaron could respond, she kissed him and turned and left, making sure to note every guard as she did.

∂∘⌒

Aaron was lying on his uncushioned cot, trying to convince himself to sleep and failing. It was cold in prison. He wondered what Catherine meant earlier that day. How were they going to free him? A guard was always stationed outside the cell. Why a "tax dodger" would need this much guarding, he had no idea.

Aaron sat up at attention when another guard came in.

"Time to go to trial," the guard half-grunted.

"Trial? It's the middle of the night." Aaron was confused; it had to be a codeword or something.

The guards just laughed. He opened the cell, went to Aaron, roughly grabbed his arms, and clasped shackles around his wrists. The guard yanked on Aaron as he guided

61

him out of the cell. Aaron stumbled as he tried to keep up with the guard, who was pulling him at an awkward and careless angle. As they walked down the hallway, another guard joined them and grabbed Aaron's other arm just as roughly.

"Where are you taking me?" Aaron demanded to know.

The first guard laughed gruffly. "Wouldn't ya like to know? Suppose you could just wait and see." He laughed. "Ah, don't you worry. You're getting to meet King Hargon's advisor. They wanted to meet you."

"What?"

The other guard laughed. "Seems he doesn't know his own fame."

The two guards laughed in unison.

The hallway had been fairly empty, but another guard approached them.

"Out of our way," the first guard scowled.

"King Hargon sent me to retrieve this prisoner," the new guard informed.

Aaron was thoroughly confused.

"Well, isn't that odd. So were we." The two guards pushed Aaron slightly behind them.

The new guard sighed and raised a hand. The two guards who had been escorting Aaron fell to the ground. Aaron jumped back and looked at the new guard in a panic.

"I'm Klew," the guard whispered. He placed a hand on Aaron's shoulder. "You now have a disguise as well." He looked down at Aaron's wrists. "This was not what we had in mind. Play along." He began to guide Aaron by one arm, much gentler than the previous guards had been.

"Did you..." Aaron glanced over his shoulder where the two guards lay as they walked away. "Did you kill them?"

"No, they are just in a heavy sleep."

They did not see another guard until they were about to exit the building.

"Act embarrassed," Klew whispered to Aaron as they left.

The guards on watch stood up and began to ask questions about the handcuffed guard.

"Damned fool went and lost the keys. Thought I'd teach him a lesson," Klew replied.

The guards began to laugh.

They walked down the street to a young woman standing with two horses.

"Well, hello there, m'lady," Klew said.

Catherine turned.

"It seems my partner here got himself into a bind. Mind giving us a ride to the nearest blacksmith?"

Aaron raised his hands enough for the light on a nearby lantern to reflect off the cuffs encompassing his wrists.

She smiled. "Of course."

As they walked toward the edge of town, Catherine whispered, "This was not part of the plan."

Klew whispered back, "We had to improvise."

Once they reached the forest, Klew waved his hand once in front of him. The disguise spell dropped, and a magical glowing globe appeared.

Catherine flung her arms around Aaron. "I was so worried about you."

Aaron kissed the side of her head. "You really shouldn't have done any of this."

She pulled back.

"But since you did. How do I get these things off?"

"Easy," Klew brought Aaron's cuffs into the light of the orb, ran a finger over the keyhole, and the cuffs unlocked. Aaron didn't have a chance to comment before Klew said, "We don't have much time, let's get moving."

⤙⤚

The road was heavy on Aaron's shoulders; not only was he unaccustomed to traveling, but he thought of home often. It was good to be free, and he appreciated what Catherine and Klew had done for him, but the state of what he left behind continuously came to mind during the monotony of the path.

That night, Aaron volunteered to be the first watch. Once Klew and Catherine had fallen asleep, Aaron gathered nearby eitine plants and tossed their white flowers one by one into the campfire. "Etienne, hear my request. Watch over Thomas and Tammy. Their hearts are broken and their bodies weak. Send one of Your spirits to guide and protect." He turned his gaze to the stars. "Let them feel my spirit reaching out to them." He closed his eyes for a moment and leaned against a tree. He doubted his prayers were heard, but it was all he could do to help.

He pulled out one of his daggers Catherine had managed to bring with her. He stood and twirled it in his hand, stopping it in a defensive hold with its blade pointing inward. He looked at Catherine, watching her soft breathing.

Even after his shift had ended, Aaron got no sleep that night, a regular occurrence for him.

The sun rose, and the next day began. Little was said until midday rest.

"We should be about two days out from Tressona," Klew updated Catherine and Aaron.

65

Aaron scratched the side of his head, his fingers brushing along the tip of his ear. "How do they feel about humans?"

Klew frowned. "I do not know. Tensions are rising due to the ban on trading. Last I knew, the anger was only toward King Hargon, but that may have changed."

Aaron nodded slightly.

"Do not let that worry you too much." Klew placed his hand on Aaron's shoulder. "I will vouch for you."

As they continued their journey, Aaron's only consolation was his arms wrapped around Catherine as they both rode Chestnut. That day was different, though. She leaned into his arms a little more, almost as if she needed it too. Aaron struggled to understand why. All she talked about was possibly finding her family. He decided to stop questioning the small act he didn't understand and just enjoyed it.

Catherine and Klew held conversations about the forest they rode through and about Tressona. Aaron listened but didn't retain much of the information.

That night, as Aaron helped Catherine dismount, she leaned in and kissed him, her hands still on his shoulders and his on her hips. She hadn't kissed him since the journey had started. He pulled her close and held her tight in his arms. He missed moments like that. Aaron kissed her forehead as the embrace ended. That night, they did everything together; Aaron helped her set up her sleeping mat, and she helped him. Klew went to gather food as they finished setting up camp.

While they were alone, Catherine asked, "What has been bothering you?"

Aaron didn't even pretend things were fine. "I'm worried about my parents. What if the guards accuse them or target them? They have no way to fight back."

Catherine took his hands. "Maybe once we find our families, they can help."

Aaron could not crush that joy in her eyes. "Maybe." He held her cheek in his hand and kissed her softly on the lips.

Klew refused to let Aaron take a shift that night, drawing attention to the fact that he knew Aaron wasn't sleeping much. Doubting anything would change, Aaron laid down and attempted to sleep. His mind did manage to leave reality, but Aaron wouldn't consider it a blessing when he woke.

Aaron felt small; the age of five came to mind. The ship rocked with the waves under his feet. Crude and dirty men wandered around the deck, taking part in their various duties.

One grabbed Aaron by the collar of his shirt and said, "You ain't supposed to be up here." His breath smelled awful. "Back down you go." The pirate dragged the young Aaron below deck; all of Aaron's protests were ignored, even when he tried to explain why he was up there. "Captain Alik isn't going to like your behavior." He threw Aaron to the floor and grabbed a whip that hung near the room's entrance. "Let's get the punishment out of the way for him." The whip cracked.

Aaron woke with a cry of pain. Although just a dream, his back felt as though it was on fire. Catherine stirred next to him, and Klew came over.

"Are you alright?"

Aaron touched his back. No blood. "It was just a dream."

"Past or future?"

"Excuse me?"

"The look on your face says it was about you. Was it your past or future?"

Aaron shook his head. "Neither. It was just fantasy."

Klew gave a look of doubt but allowed the lie to pass. He stood and walked back over to the fire.

Aaron's back still hurt as he tried to get back to sleep. Past? Could that have really happened? Aaron then remembered swimming with Catherine several years ago.

She had touched his back and asked about scars he did not remember getting. Pirates. How would a five-year-old half-elf end up on a human pirate ship? Knowing that sleep was lost, he tried to retrace his life, and as always, it stopped at the age of eight in the orphanage. The story was that someone found him bloody and passed out on a road outside of Dovan. Bloodied. Maybe it was true. It didn't make any less sense than a half-elf with an elven mother, or so he thought, in a human orphanage. He wished he could have a dream that just explained everything.

❧

Aaron could not help but stare in awe at the Grand Hall in Tressona. It was much simpler than the Dovan palace, yet it could still take one's breath away. It was built around the base of a large tree. The tree almost seemed to be part of the architecture. The large double doors were flanked by stained glass windows depicting trees.

"I should take you to the Isle Lands," Klew said, observing Aaron's gaze. "Imagine the most beautiful thing you've seen and multiply it hundreds of times."

Aaron looked over his shoulder at Catherine tending to Chestnut and whispered, "I doubt it."

"Alright, lover boy," Klew clapped Aaron on the shoulder, "let's get some rooms in the inn."

❧

69

The three sat around a table in the corner, with a warm dinner in front of them. The tavern was well-kept and well-lit. Everything was simple yet felt like it was in place. There had been no more than a few odd glances sent Aaron's way and he was grateful that's all it was, but he knew they had to keep going, and each city they went to was another unknown.

"Annathalinda said our first stop would hold a clue, but she didn't say how or what." Klew tapped the table with his index finger.

"We can't wait forever," Aaron pointed out.

"I suppose we choose our own path and hope Etienne guides us true."

Aaron turned to his beloved. "What do you remember?"

Catherine sighed, closed her eyes, and said, "Everything was in the trees...other than the stables...It would snow...but there were also hot days..."

Aaron glanced at Klew, who nodded as he wrote things down.

"Anything else?" Aaron touched her wrist.

Her eyes shot open. "Wood!"

"Wood?" Aaron and Klew asked in unison.

"Wood! I was learning to carve! We traded wood goods to traveling merchants!"

Klew's eyes lit up. "I know of just the place!"

"Where?" both Aaron and Catherine asked.

"Soriana."

"Where is that?" Aaron inquired.

"It's in the Galida forest, just south of the Northern Lands."

"How far from here?" Catherine sat up straight, hope twinkling in her eyes.

"If we take the route through Thyla, about a month."

"Is there a path *not* through Tith?" Aaron took Catherine's hand.

"Yes, but it is a far longer path. It doesn't go through Tith, just right by it. It will take us through the Holy Hills."

Catherine sat up straight. "Are the Divine Sisters there?!"

"Um...well...no..." Klew's face contorted in a puzzled fashion. "They were bestowed on the elves a few centuries ago."

Catherine slumped back down. "Oh."

Klew laughed softly. "Not to worry, there are still many things to see there!"

Aaron finished his ale. "Sounds like we have a plan. I think I will retire to the room so we can get an early start."

"I have a few more questions for Klew before. Sleep well."

Aaron leaned over and softly kissed her. As he turned to leave, he saw the face of a fellow patron change from a scowl to a smile. At least not all hope was lost. Now, if there was a way to prove his trustworthiness without kissing Catherine in front of every elf they saw. He wouldn't mind kissing her that much, but it would be rather impractical.

Aaron made his way to the room he was sharing with Klew. He claimed the bed by the window. Aaron lay down, the window open. He removed his mother's ring from his right hand and held it up, stars twinkling in the center.

He heard an echo of what his mother once told him. "This will one day be yours." Before he could reflect on the sweet memory, her cry of pain rang in his mind. His hand closed tight around the ring as he shook his head, foolishly thinking it would help.

Aaron sighed deeply, slipped his ring back on his finger, and said a small prayer, asking for nothing more than peaceful sleep. His prayers were unheard.

Aaron saw nothing, but the sound of clashing blades rang out. Cries of anger and pain also filled the air. When his vision came back, he looked down at his small childish hands with the ring held out.

"Take it, my love," his mother whispered. "Take it and run!"

Aaron opened his eyes. The mostly full moon's light trickled through the drawn curtains. He looked over his shoulder and saw Klew fast asleep. Knowing sleep was going to be hard to find, Aaron got out of his bed and made his way to the tavern. The hall was empty other than a bartender and one patron. Aaron sat down at the bar.

"Is this a wine or ale kind of night?" the bartender asked with a smile.

"Ale. Definitely ale," Aaron responded without hesitation.

While handing Aaron the pint glass, he asked, "If you don't mind, what worries you?"

Aaron shook his head, "A past I wished I wasn't remembering," and took a long drink.

The elf nodded in understanding and poured another pint.

Aaron laughed as it was placed next to a hardly touched glass. "I just might get more sleep if you keep this up," and took another swig.

"That's my intention. And do not worry, these are on the house."

Aaron raised his glass and said, "Thank you."

"I couldn't help but notice you and your companions earlier. What are the three of you doing together?"

"That is not entirely my place to say, but Catherine is searching for something and Klew was told he could help."

"By whom?" he leaned in.

Aaron raised an eyebrow.

"I love hearing travelers' stories. Reminds me of before my daughter and son were born."

The half-elf nodded. "I suppose I could tell you. Annathalinda."

The elf stood straight. "Annathalinda?! What interest would she have in you? No offence."

"None taken." Another gulp of ale was consumed. "I've been asking the same thing myself."

"If I may...what is this past you are running from?"

"Oh, I stopped running a while ago. I just try to ignore it now. All that remains are nightmares of a battle and captors that I do not remember."

"Well, if Annathalinda has anything to do with it, she'll help you solve that mystery."

Aaron nodded solemnly, not fully believing the bartender, while knowing it was true. They were both silent for a moment. Once Aaron finished his first glass, he examined the bubbles in the second glass and said, "Ever since I knew about her, I have wanted to meet Annathalinda. But now that it is a possibility, I wish I had never heard the name."

The bartender took the empty glass. "Etienne be with you, my friend."

Aaron raised the glass in thanks. Once it was downed, he returned to his room. Not with hopes of sleep, but rather to not concern Klew with his absence once day breaks.

CHAPTER 5

C atherine opened her eyes slowly as the sun began to penetrate her eyelids. She was growing accustomed to the ground as a bed. The night before, Klew informed them that they were only two days outside the Holy Hills, but still four days from the capital Avendale.

After blinking several times, getting her eyes to adjust, Catherine rolled over and saw that Aaron was no longer on his sleeping roll; as a matter of fact, his sleeping roll wasn't even there. She sat up and saw Aaron and Klew sitting at the embers from the night's fire.

"How long was I asleep!?" She turned her gaze to the sun and saw it was thoroughly above the horizon.

The two men looked over at her. Aaron smiled and approached her. "You were so restless last night, we decided to let you sleep a while longer." He leaned over and kissed her on the head.

Catherine took his outstretched hand and stood. She gave him a soft kiss on the lips.

"Did you have nightmares?" He brushed some of her hair out of her face.

She shook her head. "Not that I can remember."

Aaron smiled. "At least there is that. Get some breakfast, I'll take care of your things."

"Thank you." She gave him another kiss and walked over to Klew. "Am I putting us behind schedule?"

Klew smiled at her. "No. I always plan for unforeseen events." He extended a leaf full of berries. "Freshly picked this morning."

Catherine eagerly took and ate them. Far better than the rations from the inn. Once she had eaten, they all finished their packing and continued their travels.

She was thankful for an uneventful road, but it did give her time to think, which was not always good. She thought of Aaron's parents and how worried they must be, how heavy this must all be on Aaron, why Annathalinda would care about them, and about her family. What if they could never find them? What if they were dead? What if they did find them? What would that mean for her and Aaron? She couldn't ask him to give up his search just because she found her family. A fair, female face flickered in her mind. Her mother. She knew she had to find the truth. Catherine remembered her sister fighting with her mother. There was so much turmoil.

She took a deep breath and reminded herself to take things as they came. No time to fret about the unknown.

When they paused for the night, Aaron gathered his bow and arrows and went hunting. In what felt like no time, he returned with three rabbits, each with an arrow through the head.

"Impressive," Klew acknowledged.

"I've been hunting since I was little," Aaron replied.

"He rarely misses," Catherine noted.

Aaron shrugged, but Catherine knew what she said was true.

Shortly after the sun had gone down, the three sat around the fire, and Klew announced, "We will not need to keep watch once we reach the Holy Hills." After receiving confused looks, he continued, "Ever since the war, no one has dared to cause harm there. We will need the rest before continuing our journey anyway."

"That will be a nice change," Aaron laughed. "I'll take the first watch then."

Klew nodded.

Catherine perked up and said, "I'll take the second watch."

Klew nodded. "It is set then."

As they ate, Catherine fantasized about the Holy Hills and the White Library. She pictured walls of white limestone, granite statues of wizards and Ainjeal, and a library filled with ancient books and scrolls. She then began to wonder if she could learn to cast spells. Most elves did have magic running through their veins.

"Do you think I could learn some spells while we are there?" she finally inquired.

Klew smiled at her. "Of course." He turned to Aaron. "Would you like to learn as well?"

Aaron sat up straight. "I...uh...yes! I mean..." he slouched slightly, "if I can."

"Why do you think you can't?"

"Well, I've never really thought of it as an option," he rubbed his upper arm in a half-embrace of himself, "I do have human blood."

"That never stopped me."

Catherine turned her attention to Klew and, at the same time as Aaron, said, "You're part human?"

Klew nodded. "My mother is half-elf, half-human."

"I thought you were half-elf, half-wizard," Aaron inquired. "Your ears are pointed, yet you wear the robes of a wizard."

"My father is a wizard. And before you ask, my mother can cast spells as well. It is not just due to the majority of my blood being of magic roots, as a matter of fact," Klew raised a finger, "most halflings can."

Catherine watched as Aaron's eyes lit up. She had never thought about the fact that Aaron might wish to cast spells and not have the ability.

That night, her dreams were filled with magic. The majestic buildings that were filled with spell books. The colorfully dressed wizards designating their specialty. Statues of Ainjeal decorating the city.

⁂

She woke with a smile on her face, she rolled over to look at Aaron, but had to blink out the sun. The sun. Aaron was supposed to wake her up for her shift. She sat up abruptly and looked around. Klew lay fast asleep. But Aaron...

"Klew! Wake up!" Catherine stumbled over to her companion and shook him violently.

"What?" he groggily rolled over and rubbed his eyes.

"Aaron's gone!"

"What?!" Klew sat up and looked around. He looked up to the bright sky and hurried to his feet. "Maybe he...uh... went for water. I'll go to the stream we saw yesterday. You stay here."

Something was wrong, Catherine could feel it, and the panic in Klew's eyes said he felt it as well.

"Aaron?!" She couldn't think of anything to do other than call out his name.

Klew came back; he wasn't at the stream. Aaron was gone.

Catherine wished she knew how to track. Aaron had once tried to teach her, but she could never figure it out. They had spent an entire day searching the area for Aaron, to no avail.

"We can't keep looking forever," Klew stated.

Catherine didn't want to hear it. "He has to be here somewhere."

"Catherine," he took her by the shoulders and looked her in the eyes, "the wizards might be able to help us."

She sighed. She knew he was right. "Promise me we're not giving up, just taking a different approach?"

Klew nodded. "I promise."

⇜∘⇝

Avendale was magnificent. It was surrounded by a blue and gray stone wall with thin silver inlays. The libraries were made of metal that resembled silver and gold and were set with inlays of precious stones. The towers were made of blue and gray stone, but one was of marble. That tower rose above the rest. Its cap was encased in silver and reflected the sun's light. Catherine couldn't see its base, but she couldn't help but already be in awe of it.

As they walked through the giant gates that were made of pure gold, she saw what she had always dreamed of. A blue marble Ainjeal stood before her. His golden breastplate glinted in the sun. He held a golden sword in two hands and was mid-slash. His face looked alive. Hardened by war, but gentle towards allies. His wings were spread wide. Each feather vein was engraved. Creases in his fingers were present. Even the laces on his boots had detail.

Catherine eventually noticed an etched golden plaque on its base. "Jehepsu, bringer of the Divine Sisters."

She looked hastily back up. There, on his hip, was a dagger, and on his finger a ring. The dagger was leaf-shaped, with wing-like designs that extended slightly onto the blade, and three intertwining lines encircling the hilt. The ring had three matching intertwining lines.

The young elf jumped as a hand was placed on her shoulder. She sighed when she saw it was Klew.

"Sorry, I did not mean to startle you." He removed his hand from her shoulder. "We should probably get the horses to a stable."

Catherine nodded.

As they walked through the town, she began to notice all the people. They smiled and greeted her and Klew kindly. Most of them wore white, gold, or silver robes;

some even wore white robes with gold or silver lining and designs. A few were wearing other colored robes, usually gray or blue, but one or two red-robed wizards could be spotted. There were a handful of people wearing commoners' and woodland attire; most of whom were elves.

Once she was able to close her mouth from the feeling of wonder that overwhelmed her, Catherine asked, "What does the gold and silver embroidery signify?"

"Stature," Klew said plainly, "in both ability and socially."

After finding an inn and securing the horses, they headed back out. A tall man, about the same age as Catherine, with blond hair and light blue eyes, approached them with a slight bounce in his step. His blue robes and dark blue cape swayed with his zealous steps. Once he was close enough, he greeted them with a large smile and a drawn out, "Hello!"

"Hello, John," Klew said with a smile on his face. "Would you be willing to tell me where your mother is?"

"Sure. She is with my father at the Fourth Library." The young man waved his hand loosely to the right, an apparent attempt at directions.

"It's been so long since I've been here, could you show us the way?"

"If you introduce me to your friend." John smiled sheepishly.

"My manners! This is Catherine." Klew placed his hand gently on her shoulder.

John bowed his greeting.

Catherine blushed slightly. "It's a pleasure to meet you."

The wizard stood straight and lifted a finger. "Now, to show the way!"

As he led them through the city, John made small talk. "I suppose you've never been here before; have you, Catherine?"

"No. It's beautiful."

"It is. It wasn't always this way, though."

"Oh?" Catherine eyed a door decorated with precious stones.

"My parents showed me some paintings from before the Holy War. You wouldn't see a difference between here and other library cities. Ah...here we are!"

The doors were made of heavy wood with golden handles. The inside was breathtaking. Dozens of full bookcases lined the walls and filled the floor. Long tables were placed between all of the bookcases. Large windows running from the ceiling to the floor brought in the light. There were two windows on each wall. Catherine soon noticed a second area above them. That area also had books and tables, but it was like a balcony that circled the inside of the library. More wizards and elves could be seen wandering above them than could be seen on the floor. Catherine was shocked that the balcony was successfully attached to the windows as if they were walls.

"Hm...I don't see them..." John turned to an elderly wizard, who was wearing a gray robe and sitting at a desk near the entryway, "Have you seen my parents?"

"They left with Clay," he answered, waving his hand dismissively.

"Clay is here?" Klew stood taller.

The old wizard nodded, and John piped up. "He is! Giving his annual report."

"What a pleasant surprise." Klew turned to Catherine. "He may be able to help us."

Catherine simply nodded and said, "I'd love to meet him."

"Thank you." John nodded towards the old wizard.

"You're welcome," the wizard responded.

John led Klew and Catherine back outside.

"Where could they be?" asked Catherine.

"They're probably in the Hall of Libraries."

As they walked through town once again, Catherine continued to take in all the sights. Even the most basic buildings possessed an elegance of their own.

Once they reached their destination, Catherine saw carvings of various birds along the edges of the large, bronze doors. Although the bordering astounded her, the carving of a large phoenix in the middle took her breath away. The Fire Bird appeared to be flying up, wings outspread, and beak pointed towards the sky. It had rubies for eyes, which Catherine felt were watching her every move. The phoenix was also perfectly symmetrical so that it split in half as the doors were opened.

Immediately after entering, the three of them walked down a lavishly decorated hallway. The torch holders were golden and sparkled even though they were unlit. The light of the sun streamed through colored glass that resembled many ancient wizards wearing white robes with gold or silver borders and patterns. Most of the glass wizards held staves or books. Catherine stared in awe as the light reflected off the hanging crystal decorations and danced upon the blue marble floors.

Soon, they went up marble stairs. The flight of steps led to a hallway similar to the one below, but it was not quite as lavish. The floor was a gray marble, the windows were plain, the torch holders were silver, and there were no crystal decorations dangling from above. They then passed through a plain wooden door.

The room was large with bookshelves lining the walls from floor to ceiling. In the middle of the room, there were tables with piles of books and papers on them, and there was a male elf, a woman, and another man standing over one of the tables. The elf had long, blond hair, partially tied back, revealing his pointed ears. He wore white pants with a light blue shirt. When they got closer, Catherine could see shells decorating around his collar. His sleeves were rolled up and his white boots tied up to his knees. The woman had light brown hair, braided so that every hair was in its place. She was clothed in a white dress, which resembled a robe. The other man had a dark black beard and hair, highlighted by gray and white hairs. He had extremely dark blue eyes. He wore a white robe and cape. The robe had a silver lining, while the cape had gold.

"Hello, Mother!" John said as he ran over to the woman.

"Hello, Honey," she responded as she straightened up and wrapped her arms around John.

The elf and wizard did not notice the others enter.

"What are you doing?" John asked, looking at the paper lying on the table.

"Going over a report," said his mother.

John rolled his eyes, "What fun."

"Remember, you will eventually be doing this. Now what are you doing here?" She placed her hands on her hips after speaking.

"Klew wanted to see you." John motioned to Catherine and her companion.

John's mother looked over at them. "Klew! It has been too long." She embraced him. "Now, who might you be?" Her eyes were a light brown with a hint of green.

"Johana, this is Catherine," Klew introduced.

Catherine's eyes widened. "Johana!?!"

John's mother chuckled. "I'm not that special."

"But you...you..." She was in awe to meet the co-leader of the Holy Hills.

"Are just a friend. Anyone Klew trusts is a friend to me."

"Wait...that means..." Catherine looked over at the elf and wizard.

"We'll send aid," Johnter announced as he hit the table and straightened up.

"Thank Etienne," the elf stated while standing tall as well.

"My love?" Johana got the wizard's attention.

The two turned.

"Klew!" the elf exclaimed happily. He walked over, clasped arms with Klew, and embraced him with one arm. "How long has it been? A year?"

"Too long! How have you been?"

"Busy." Clay laughed.

"It sounds like we need to speak in private, but before that," Klew motioned for Catherine to come forward.

Sheepishly, she complied.

"This is Catherine. I am helping her find her family."

Catherine was unsure of how to feel about that announcement. It was something she had held quiet for so long, but surely the most powerful wizard and wizardess could help.

"I don't understand," Clay's brow furrowed.

Johnter walked to Johana's side as she placed her hand over her heart.

Catherine glanced around at everyone staring at her. Finally, she got the courage to say, "I was kidnapped. I have very few memories. And those I have are vague. I..." she swallowed back a tear, "I have been living in Dovan since I was seven and don't know how I got there. And now..." this time the swallowing didn't help, "Aaron is gone and I don't know what happened to him."

"If there is anything we can do," Johana reached out and hugged Catherine.

"I can go with you," John suggested.

Johana let go of Catherine. "Yes! And he can contact us if there is ever anything we can do!"

"I'll go too," Clay chimed in.

"Thank you," Catherine said through sniffs. "I don't want to be a bother, though."

"Not to worry. I have finished my work here and will just send word back to the Isle Lands."

"And I was planning on traveling anyway!" John reassured.

Catherine wiped her tears away and gave a small smile. "Thank you. Thank you, all."

⊷⊶

The night before their departure, Klew, Catherine, and Clay were all staying at the same inn, and a traveling bard had stationed himself in the tavern. Catherine joined the crowd to hear the tales he had to share. He told legends that spanned everywhere from the origins of the Dragon Lady and Lord of Dragons to how the Qualivica Plane once had established trade routes across Eylaour.

Finally, as the night drew to a close, the bard said, "Now I can't tell stories in Avendale without telling the Legend of the Divine Sisters."

Catherine leaned in. She always loved that legend.

"About ten thousand years ago, these hills were known as the Kiltal Hills. That time was a time of turmoil. The portal to Hektom had not been sealed, and Grand Fiends roamed the plane. For the most part, the people of Eylaour maintained control of their lands until the Grand Fiends banded together. The Grand Fiends went into hiding for a few years. At first, everyone thought they had won and driven them back, but they were horribly wrong.

"One stormy night, Avendale was besieged by an army of Grand Fiends. The battle was nonstop for days. The Grand Fiends were slowly pressing further and further into the city, destroying everything as they went. The wizard Zolar led a day-long prayer to Etienne. As they concluded their prayer, the sky opened up and a holy light shone down on the wizards and wizardesses. The Ainjeal came down. Their wings were a multitude of colors. Their armor was shining in the holy light.

"With the Ainjeal by their side, the war was finally won. Once all the Grand Fiends were either vanquished or had retreated, Jehepsu presented Zolar with the Divine Sisters: Jahola, whoever wore the ring would be protected from almost all harm; and Keelhola, the bearer of the dagger would hold the power to bring an ally back to life within a day's time. And thus, these hills were renamed to the Holy Hills in honor of the Ainjeal saving them."

"What happened to the Divine Sisters?" a listener asked.

The bard took a deep breath. "About five thousand years later, the wizards bestowed the Divine Sisters on the elf Leopa in thanks for sealing the portal to Hektom. Leopa felt that the Divine Sisters were too powerful for one being to hold, so she separated the Divine Sisters between two of the elven kingdoms. No one has heard of their presence since."

∾∾

It had been hard enough getting accustomed to traveling with Klew, but their party had changed and there were two other strangers to contend with. She could tell Klew trusted them completely, so it made it a bit easier. However, having more people there made it more evident that Aaron was gone.

The 14th Day of the 3rd Moon of the 35th Year of King Hargon

Clay is determined that Annathalinda can help us find Aaron, especially since she sent Klew on this mission to find us. He's already been missing for half a moon. We took a detour and went back to where he went missing, but Clay could find no remaining traces. I will keep reminding Klew that we need to find him, but it seems they are just putting their main hope in Annathalinda. I know she can help us, but she's all the way in the Northern Lands! It will take at least a couple of moons to get there.

She looked up at the group sitting around the fire. They joked and laughed. She walked over, hoping their joy might somehow transfer to her. John smiled at her, and she couldn't help but smile back, even though her heart still felt broken. She soon was able to immerse herself in the stories and watched in awe as John made various forms out of the elements. He even made mimics of their horses out of the fire.

Catherine had to stop herself from reaching out and touching them.

"Here," John said.

She looked over and saw he held out his hand with a rabbit made of water. Her hand got wet as she petted it. She couldn't help but laugh when she saw its little nose twitch.

"Hold your hands out," he suggested.

"What?" Her laughter paused.

"Hold them in a cup in front of you. Like mine."

Catherine cupped her hands together. John reached over with his open palms and, once close enough, the rabbit slowly hobbled from his hands to Catherine's. Her eyes widened as she felt something surge inside of her. She had never felt anything like it. Her veins felt like rivers, rushing through her body. Her hands tingled. She stared at the rabbit. It stood in her hands, motionless.

Someone said her name, "Catherine?"

She looked up with a start and the rabbit fell apart, leaving water on her hands. She looked down with distress as the feelings left her.

"Sorry," Clay laughed. "Klew just told me."

Catherine pulled her mind away from the puddle of water left on her hands. "What?"

"I think you just cast your first spell." He smiled genuinely.

"But I..." she looked at her hands. "I didn't do anything."

"You maintained John's spell, which took magic."

She looked at John.

He was smiling at her. "How did it feel?"

Catherine's eyes lit up. "Amazing! Can you teach me more?"

"Of course."

⧂⧃

Catherine closed her eyes, took a deep breath, and slowly released it. She felt heat rising within her. She concentrated on what Klew taught her; she imagined the heat in her chest as a flame and guided it up to her shoulder and through her arm, feeling the warmth fill every crevice. Once the internal flame reached her hand, she opened her eyes, extended her arm in front of her, and a bout of flame flew from her fingers to the pile of wood. The kindling caught fire.

"You did it!" John hugged Catherine.

"That was amazing!" She hugged him back.

"Good job, Catherine," Klew congratulated. "You're getting the hang of this."

"I lit a fire, it's not that impressive." She blushed.

"You've only been doing this for a quarter moon. That is very impressive."

"It is," John agreed.

"Really?" Catherine looked into John's eyes.

He smiled at her, "Yes."

She smiled at him and sat down by the fire she started. With magic. As she watched the flames dance, she couldn't help but ask, "Why do sorcerers have to use incantations?"

"Before the portal to Qualivica opened," Klew started, "wizards did not exist on this plane. Once the portal opened, they came over. Now elves, humans, and dwarves all existed here, but sorcerers did not. They didn't exist anywhere. It is believed that once wizards came here, they interbred with humans and passed on their magical tendencies to their descendants. However, the non-magical human blood muddied their abilities and made it so they did not have innate magic, but with a magical item and an incantation, they can cast spells."

Clay added, "We elves are much like wizards in our magical abilities. We have it naturally within us. Do we need to learn and practice, yes. But it doesn't take anything more than just our concentration, practice, and energy."

"Energy?" Catherine inquired.

"Notice how you sometimes get tired after practicing for a while?"

She nodded.

"Just like running. It takes energy out of you. But, like running, the more you do it and the more you practice the more you can do."

Catherine looked down at her hands. She wondered what else she'd be able to do.

Later that evening, once she was in her bedroll, Catherine thought about Aaron and all the possibilities of his vanishing. She wiped away a few tears, thanking Etienne no one could see them. Soon her mind drifted to another place and time. She was no longer in her body, but she saw Aaron standing there, holding the hands of a girl she had never seen. She had black, curly hair, deep brown eyes, and wore an elegant red dress. They were looking into each other's eyes.

"Catherine!" John shook her.

"What? What?" she rolled over, trying to detach reality from dream. It wasn't until after she stood and heard a deep guttural noise that she finally realized they were about to be attacked.

CHAPTER 6

Plunk, plunk, plunk...the dripping of water on the cold stones continued. There was only a dim light, from an unknown source, that allowed shadows to fill the room. The small circular room was made of nothing but black and dark grey stones. The air was crisp and sent chilling bites all the way through Aaron's body.

Aaron moaned, "Ugh! My head! What happened?" He pushed up to a seated position and rubbed his head. "Where am I?" He looked around; his vision was blurred. Slowly, he got up and started rubbing his arms for warmth.

Aaron attempted to walk but soon stumbled from dizziness. He reached out his left hand and placed it against the wall; his right arm was still wrapped tightly around his chest. He slowly began to regain his sight, and his headache began to subside. Shortly, he was walking normally again and could find his way around, but he kept his hand on the cold wall. The room seemed to be a closed circle. But as he looked over his right shoulder, the wall under his left hand ended. There was no door or anything else; it just opened to a hallway. Aaron began to walk through the hallway, stopping every once in a while because of his head. No matter how far he walked, the hallway didn't seem to change any; it was still stone walls, puddles of water, and chilling air. The hallway seemed to be endless. Tired, Aaron flopped to the ground, leaned against the wall, and gave a deep sigh. He closed his eyes. His mind began to drift to happier times.

☙❧

"Aaron!" Catherine shouted with a loving smile.

Aaron turned from the horse he was brushing and reciprocated the smile.

"I found a lovely spot by the lake."

"Thom-" Aaron began to ask.

"Go ahead," responded Thomas. "Work is almost done anyway."

"Thank you!" Aaron jumped over the fence.

As they began to walk away, Aaron took Catherine's hand in his, fingers intertwined. She led him through the forest.

"This isn't the way to the lake," Aaron stated, puzzled.

"It is, but not the usual way." She gave a playful smirk.

As they passed between two ancient willow trees, Aaron held the branches out of the way and Catherine asked, "Isn't it lovely?"

Aaron froze, mouth open.

The trees were full of brilliant green leaves and various colored flowers. The willow trees dipped their branches into the shimmering turquoise water. The sun's rays drifted through the branches and rested on top of the calm water. The light made everything glow. The birds sang sweet songs in the trees.

The love songs continued to be heard as Aaron looked over and smiled at his love. They stood there looking into each other's eyes. Aaron cupped his hand around Catherine's cheek and pulled her closer for a passionate kiss. Once they pulled away, Catherine led Aaron to a fallen tree that rested next to the lake. They sat down, and Aaron wrapped an arm around her waist. He watched as she took in the surroundings.

Soon, Catherine looked to the sky, her lips parted slightly, and she whispered, "Aaron."

"What?" He followed her gaze. A majestic bird flew high overhead. It was large, much larger than Aaron had ever seen. Its deep red wings flickered as they beat.

"Is that..." Catherine didn't finish.

"A phoenix," Aaron whispered.

The bird gave a glorious call and flew off. The trees shifted in the wind, the birds stopped singing, and it seemed as if more flowers bloomed.

☙◦❧

Aaron shook his head, trying to rid himself of sleep, and then sighed deeply. He looked to the left, then to the right. His eyes widened; he couldn't remember which way he came. He rose to his feet.

"I guess I'll go this way," Aaron whispered to himself while turning to the left. He knew the worst thing that could happen was ending up going back to where he came from.

Aaron walked cautiously down the hallway, and once again, it seemed endless. Around the same time that he became weary of walking, Aaron saw a light. He began to mind his steps and became conscious of every movement and noise he made. He soon saw an open archway. Once he reached it, Aaron knelt down. He placed his right hand against the cold stone wall, his left on the wet ground in front of him, and he peered through the archway into a room where two people stood.

The woman was tall. She wore a black robe, with a black rope tied around her waist, and the bottom hem was just high enough off the ground to reveal her black boots. The sleeves on the robe ended where they covered part of her hands. She also wore a black cloak that touched the ground, and the hood was pulled far enough down to cast a shadow over her face.

There was also a man in the room. He had dark skin, brown eyes, and short black hair. He wore a black long-sleeved shirt, black pants, and black boots.

Aaron heard the female say, "Did you remember to create a fake wall to block him?"

"I...I don't...don't know. Why?" the man answered, stuttering as he spoke.

"Because he is out of the room!" Despite not being too much taller than the man, the shadowed woman towered over him in that moment.

"Maybe I didn't-" He shrunk down.

"I told you to check this morning!"

He looked down and to the side. "I don't think I did that either..."

"Xyxthris!" She clenched her fists as she yelled.

He threw up his hands. "I'll go find him!"

"Never mind! I will."

Without hesitation, Aaron stood and turned to run, but just as he began to move someone grabbed his arm.

The female said, "You're not going anywhere."

"Who...who are you?" Aaron's voice shook, and he slowly tried to slide his arm free of her grip.

As she tightened her hold and drops of blood formed on Aaron's arm, she said, "Do you really want to know?"

Aaron pulled his arm away from her, inhaled sharply as gashes formed where her nails scratched into his arm, and backed away. "What do you want with me?"

The shrouded woman reached out, but just before touching Aaron again, an invisible force jolted out.

Aaron was hit by the pulse and fell back. Everything grew hazy. He saw the woman stand over him, then everything went dark.

૭૦૯

"Ugh, my head," Aaron groaned as he sat up and held his once again throbbing head. He leaned against the wall. It was just as icy and wet as the floor. The only light in the small room was a torch near a set of stairs leading up. Aaron reached out and touched the iron bars encaging him. He saw a couple of other cages in the room, but there were too many shadows to see if they were occupied or not. "Where am I?" he thought out loud.

"In her dungeon," a young woman's voice answered.

Startled, Aaron looked to his right. He squinted and saw a girl sitting in the next cage in the farthest corner from him, staring at him. "Who are you!?"

"My name is Sasha." She shifted to sitting on her legs in a kneeling position and asked, "What does she want you for?"

"I don't know...I don't even know who she is..."

Sasha laughed again; her laugh was genuine and had a little high-pitched ring to it. "She's the most powerful and evil person that's ever seen light...If she's ever seen light."

"Do you know what her name is?" Aaron crept to the edge of his cage that was nearest to Sasha.

"Kindraze."

Aaron began pouring through as many memories as he could, trying to grasp where he had heard that name before.

Sasha interrupted his thoughts. "Who are you?"

"Aaron."

Both were silent for a while. Aaron rubbed his arms in a futile attempt to warm his body. One of his hands ran over where Kindraze had dug her nails into him. The blood had already congealed. He moved closer to the door of his cage, running his hands over the bars, reaching through, and feeling the lock. Eventually, the silence was broken by Kindraze.

While running down the stairs, Kindraze yelled, "Which one of you has it!"

Aaron hastily backed away from the door.

"You have it!" She pointed at Aaron.

"I have what?" The half-elf moved to the farthest side of the cage from her.

"Leave him alone!" yelled Sasha.

"Be quiet, girl!" Kindraze shouted, then turned back to Aaron and ordered, "Give it to me!"

"Give you what? I'd give it to you if I knew what it was!" Aaron failed to remain calm.

In rage, Kindraze cast a spell at him. It looked like a black cloud with flames snaking in the middle. The spell forced Aaron against the wall, hard. He felt a burning run through his veins. The heat from the spell was not just on the surface but penetrated his body. His surroundings grew less and less clear until only dark figures could be seen. The figure he believed to be Kindraze entered his cell and reached down. He felt her hands rip his mother's ring off his finger. Aaron tried to close his fist but only managed to get his fingers to twitch. Suddenly, it felt as though all his breath was removed from his body. He began to gasp for air. Kindraze left his cell.

Still gasping for air, Aaron felt someone touch his shoulder. He turned his head and saw a crouched figure reaching through from the adjoining cell. He heard a faint whisper but couldn't make out the words. Pain began to shoot through his body, but shortly after the chanting stopped, he felt a relaxing warmth take over. Air returned to his lungs, and his sight began to clear.

Sasha kept her hand on his shoulder. "Does that feel better?"

Aaron nodded. Still feeling weak, he whispered, "How did you heal me?"

She showed him the palm of her hand. There was a crescent moon with stars that seemed to glisten tattooed on her hand. "There are magic crystals embedded in the stars. No one can take my magic away from me."

"I didn't know that was possible."

"We didn't either. Until Saro tried it on me." Sasha sat back on her heels.

"Saro?!" Aaron's mind was clearing just enough for him to recognize the famous sorceress.

"Yes. Who else would I trust with such an experiment?"

"That makes sense. I just..." He pushed himself to a seated position. "I wouldn't imagine her helping just anyone."

"You think I'm just 'anyone'?"

Panicked at his blunder, he tried to explain, "No! I just...you just...I didn't know you were..."

He was cut short as Sasha began to laugh. "Sorry, I couldn't help myself."

"You're not...you're not mad?"

"No. I will admit, however, I don't understand where that statement came from. Saro is a leader of the people, just like your royals."

"About that..." Aaron knew she sensed the elven blood in him and assumed that's where he's from. "I'm from Bellmora."

"But you have-"

"I know. It's a long story that I don't even know the entirety of."

"We have time." Sasha leaned into the cage bars.

Aaron shook his head. "No. We have to get out of here." He crawled over to the door, stuck his hand out, and began feeling the lock again. Both were quiet for a moment. "Are you able to unlock this with a spell?"

"No. I focused on healing magic. I'm now regretting that choice."

"I'm not. You saved my life." He paused and looked over at her. "Thank you."

Sasha smiled at him. "You're welcome...So, why was she so upset over your ring?"

Aaron looked longingly at his finger. "I don't know. It was my mother's. That's all I know." He sighed deeply, then returned his focus on the lock. "Do you happen to be wearing a hair pin?"

"You can pick locks!?" She bounced with enthusiasm.

"Shh! Not so loud," Aaron whispered.

"Sorry! Here..." she reached into her hair and pulled out a small silver pin. "Will this work?"

Aaron took the pin from her. "We shall see." He reached through the cage and carefully put the pin in the keyhole. He carefully fished around the mechanisms. He felt the first pin lock in place. He slowly moved the pin to the next one. He thanked Etienne for the fact that, as a child, he got bored and taught himself how to pick a lock.

Shouts came from upstairs. Aaron pulled the pin out of the lock, knowing he was halfway there. He slipped the pin back through the bars, and Sasha put it carefully back in her hair.

"Intruders!" echoed through the halls above.Sasha stood up. "They're here!"

"Who?" Aaron wasn't sure if her excitement was good or bad.

"Trinity and Tilen! My family!"

"How do you know it's them?" Aaron stood up and positioned himself to see up the stairs as best he could, which was still poor.

"We promised each other that if one of us was taken captive, the others would come to rescue them."

Aaron let his pessimism stay in his head. She looked so hopeful.

CHAPTER 7

৯৯৯

Catherine's brown hair moved in the wind at the same pace as the leaves in the trees. "What was that?" she asked, looking at the pile of dust, claws, and teeth the monster created when it died.

Clay placed his hand gently on Catherine's shoulder. "A Grand Fiend."

"Aren't those from..." She stopped talking, unable to utter the word out of fear.

"Hektom?"

She nodded.

"They are the opposite of Ainjeal. What do you think?"

John shifted as he wrinkled his forehead. "But how did it get here?"

"Someone must have opened the gate. Let's get moving again. Where there is one, there is likely more."

Catherine did not like the thought of encountering more of them.

৯৯৯

The fight kept playing over and over in her head. The three men did a good job protecting Catherine, but she couldn't help but still be afraid. Grand Fiends had not been seen in Eylaour since the portal was closed. Why were they appearing again?

At one point, while Catherine continued to dwell on her fears, the horses became restless. Clay drew a sword while steadying his horse. "Take caution. I think more are near."

Immediately, Catherine went through all of the skills she had in her head. She had a dagger by her side which Clay gave her. Klew and John had been teaching her to cast spells, although she wasn't very good at it. Slight panic began to set in.

A low growl came from behind some trees. A large being stepped out in front of their path. The horses reared and neighed loudly; everyone barely held on. The monster's red skin contrasted with the green around it. Its long-clawed hands dripped with blood, of what Catherine didn't want to know. Its wings were nothing but a slightly skinned bony outline. This one was larger than the last.

The first instance of seeing this creature drew on for a bit in Catherine's mind, then suddenly Clay jumped off his horse and unleashed both of his swords, lunging at the Grand Fiend. Klew began casting spells, not even bothering to dismount. And Catherine felt John leave their horse to aid Klew. Unsure of what else to do, Catherine backed

Chestnut up, creating a larger distance between them and the Grand Fiend. The flurry of spells, blades, and claws began to blur her vision.

Her heart stopped as she heard Clay cry out as claws slashed across his chest. He continued to fight, but blood was beginning to flow from the wounds. She watched, helplessly, as her three companions continued to fight the vile beast. Finally, Klew cast a spell that froze the beast for a few seconds, and Clay slashed his right sword through the Grand Fiend's neck, decapitating it. John ran over to Clay as he fell to his knees. Catherine, still too scared to act, simply watched as John gripped Clay and his hands began to glow. She saw the bleeding slow.

Klew got off his horse and joined the other two. He helped John lift Clay to his feet. "We should be close to the next town, let's get you back on your horse and there as quickly as possible."

Catherine just sat there helplessly as John and Klew assisted their injured friend onto his horse again. Clay was regaining color in his face, and the blood had stopped flowing, but he was still slightly hunched over in pain. John mounted the horse behind Clay, leaving Catherine alone on Chestnut.

The rest of the ride was done in relative silence. Catherine was not even sure she heard many animals. She kept an eye on Clay and was reassured as he slowly sat up straighter and straighter as they rode.

The sun had barely moved further across the sky by the time they reached the nearby town. It was in a flurry of activity as they approached.

Klew dismounted as he grabbed the attention of a local. "What's going on?"

"Grand Fiends! They are attacking the northern edge of town!"

Clay, who appeared to be much better than he was previously, and John dismounted and in unison said, "Lead the way."

Klew turned to Catherine and said, "Help where you can," before turning and joining the others on their way to the fight.

The local noticed Catherine's uneasiness. "I think I know where you could help."

Catherine got off Chestnut. "Of course."

The local led her to a medical station, which wasn't more than an open area with paddings on the ground where the injured could lie. "Here, they could use all the assistance they can get."

The young elf instantly began helping in any way she could. Getting supplies, helping with wounds, and anything else anyone mentioned needing.

She began to lose track of time and became in sync with those around her when she heard someone yelling as they brought someone in. "Dark magic! There's a spell caster out there somewhere!"

Catherine helped carry the injured man onto the padding. There were no visible wounds that she could see. One of the healers came over and began mumbling to herself. A soft light began to glow between her hand and the patient. Catherine jumped a little when the patient began to gasp for air. Soon, more healers were calling out for Catherine's assistance, and she obeyed.

More and more injured were coming in without visible wounds. Catherine began to feel increasingly helpless. The medical area was divided into two sections: one for physical injuries and the other for magical injuries. Catherine's heart would sink as she watched fighters come in injured, be treated, get up, and go out to fight again – only to end up back at the infirmary. It was a never-ending cycle.

Finally, Catherine's body forced her to sit down for a moment. She looked up at the sky and saw the sun starting to set. With this moment to breathe, she fought back tears. She had never seen anything like this. It was a constant barrage of injured. Catherine feared looking towards the battle. She knew they were fighting Grand Fiends, but how many were there? How could this fight be taking so long with so many people defending the town? Right as she began to collect herself again and take one last sip of water before beginning the tasks again, she gasped. "John!"

A pair of fighters carried the unconscious wizard to the padding. Catherine rushed over with another healer.

"No visible wounds," the healer said as they assessed the situation. A light glow emitted from their hand that was placed on John's chest.

Catherine took John's hand. It remained limp. The glowing stopped, and the healer pulled their hand back, not moving otherwise. Catherine ran her hand over John's cheek. No response. The healer placed their hand back on John's chest, and the glowing resumed. Again, nothing. Catherine looked at the healer.

The healer backed away. "Nothing's working!" they called to another.

Only a few other medics heard over the now common-place commotion and looked over.

"Stay with him," the healer commanded Catherine, then turned and rushed away.

Catherine turned her gaze back to her friend. She watched his chest; it did not rise or fall. Beginning to panic, she placed her cheek in front of his mouth, holding her own breath. No air brushed against her cheek. "He's not breathing!" She turned, still holding his hand, desperate to find someone to help. Tears began to stream down her face. No one seemed to hear, but she couldn't leave his side. Catherine turned her gaze back to John. "Please, please don't leave me." She gripped his hand with both of hers, holding it close to her chest. She closed her eyes and began to weep uncontrollably.

After what felt like an eternity, she jumped as she felt a hand get placed on her shoulder. She looked up to see one of the lead healers.

"Don't stop," they whispered.

Catherine looked back down and saw a glow between her hands and John's. She felt a warmth enter her shoulder and flow through her arm to her hands, and the light began to glow brighter. She felt another hand on her other shoulder, and again, warmth spread from her shoulder to her hands, and the light grew even brighter. Soon, John gasped for air as his entire chest lunged upwards.

"John!" Catherine cried and flung her arms around him.

The healers who assisted in the healing pulled Catherine back as John continued to cough. "Give him some space," one whispered.

Tears of joy were streaming down Catherine's face as it took every ounce of willpower to remain seated.

Finally, John's breathing became normal, and he opened his eyes. When he made eye contact with Catherine, he paused, and she could see confusion on his face.

"You were injured," she said softly, while leaning in and cupping the side of his face in her hand.

His eyes widened, "Necro-ah!" He cried in pain as he tried to sit up.

Catherine gently helped him lay back down. "Shhhh..." She tried to calm him. "Don't rush it."

"No," he winced in pain. "Have to warn-" he winced again.

"John?" Catherine's concern raised. "What's going on?"

"Necromancer," John took a deep breath. "There's a necromancer out there."

Catherine turned and yelled as loud as she could, "Bayla!"

The head healer came over again, "What's wrong?"

"He's reporting a necromancer's presence."

Bayla gasped. "We need to alert everyone." They then hurried away.

Catherine turned back to John.

He smiled a weak smile at her. "Thank you."

She stroked his cheek, and he closed his eyes again.

❧

The sun had almost fully set, and the moon was starting to show. Catherine was granted leave to get some sleep. She wanted to remain by John's side, but both John and the healers insisted she go somewhere less busy to get some restful sleep. There was a small setup just outside the infirmary where healers and medics were taking their naps. Catherine chose an empty bedroll and lay down. At first, she wasn't sure if she was too tired to sleep, so exhausted that the adrenaline from the day wouldn't matter, or if her thoughts would keep her up. But soon, sleep overtook her mind.

Catherine found herself running through the streets of Dovan. She held onto her box, knowing Aaron's life depended on it. Once she reached the infirmary area, an elven nurse wrapped an arm around Catherine's shoulder as she took the box with one hand and guided Catherine to Aaron's side. They had stripped him of his armor, and his teeth were clenched around a rag as another medic stitched a wound in his side. Catherine took Aaron's hand, and his eyes opened for a brief moment. In that moment, Catherine saw his face relax and relief fill his eyes. That moment was harshly ripped away from them as he winced once more in pain.

Catherine jerked as she heard loud screams of panic.

Catherine opened her eyes. The screams were not part of her dream. She sat up and looked around. She saw people pointing to the sky. As she turned her gaze upward, she heard someone say, "Dragons!" At that moment, she saw a large, winged figure glide in front of the moon. She could not tell what color it was. As she looked back around, everyone else seemed to notice with her that the dragons were not attacking. For some reason, that didn't comfort her, but she knew it at least meant they didn't need to fight dragons at the same time. For now.

She sighed as she realized she was far too awake to sleep again, so she went back to the medical area.

"John!" Catherine realized she got there just in time. Her friend was sitting up, and it appeared as though he was getting ready to leave.

He smiled at her. "I'm doing much better." He took her hand in his. "Thank you."

Catherine kissed him on the cheek. "Don't die."

At that, they parted ways once again. Catherine regained her rhythm and did her best to help in any way she could.

As dawn approached, Bayla called Catherine over to a patient. "We need assistance healing."

"But I-" Catherine was unsure of how she could help. She was not very good at spell casting. She honestly felt that what happened with John was a fluke.

"Just try!"

Catherine did as she was commanded. She reached out to the injured warrior. He looked young. She placed her hand on his shoulder and closed her eyes. She imagined a light starting in her chest. It grew warm. She then led that light up through her arm and out her hand. Her arm and hand also grew warm. Slowly, she felt her body get weaker and weaker. She had to concentrate more and more on pushing the light outward from her center. She finally caved and opened her eyes. Only Bayla remained with their hand on the warrior. Their eyes were open though, looking at the man's face. Catherine finally dropped her arm, too tired to continue trying. The light underneath Bayla's hand stopped glowing.

Bayla leaned over the warrior's face for a few moments, then shook her head. "He's gone."

Catherine sat down next to the warrior.

Bayla placed a hand on Catherine's shoulder. "You did what you could. Take some time." Then they walked to someone else.

Catherine sat there in silence, staring at the young man. She struggled to hold back tears until she saw the ring on his finger. He had a wife. Did he have children? She could no longer hold back the tears. Her chest began to ache. Her jaw tensed, and pain ran up the sides of her face. Why was this happening? Who in their right mind would open the portal to Hektom?

She cried until she had no more tears to cry. The pain remained, but the tears dried up. She looked around. There was still so much to do. Her muscles ached. It was almost as if they were screaming with the pain in her heart. But she knew she was needed. If pushing through the pain meant one less person died, it was worth it.

The battle continued until midday. That was when the tides finally turned, and fewer and fewer people were being brought in. Finally, what they had all been waiting for. Cheers of victory began to echo through the town. Catherine gave a sigh of relief, but knew the work wasn't over. People began to flood in with more minor injuries.

"Catherine!" She looked up as Klew entered the area. He came over and embraced her. "Where am I needed?"

Catherine spread her arms. "Anywhere there is someone injured."

Klew squeezed her shoulders, nodded, and went to assist where he could.

The young elven woman paused for a moment and looked around. She saw John enter the area, but head straight to healing people. She grabbed a moist towel and handed it to someone in need, and brought bandages to another. She heard a familiar voice say, "Careful," and turned her attention back to where the injured were flooding in.

"Clay," she whispered as she watched her friend limping in with his arm slung over another man's shoulder. She hurried over to him. "Are you alright?"

Clay smiled. "I'm fine, just a sprain."

"Here, sit down." Catherine pulled a stool over. She knelt down and gently removed his boot.

Clay chuckled slightly. "Look at you."

"What? You thought a girl who spent her whole life alone wouldn't learn a bit of healing?"

"Fair. Ow!"

Catherine began wrapping his ankle. "There," she slipped the end of the cloth in on itself to hold it in place.

Clay picked up his boot and began putting it on.

Catherine stared at his foot, while not really looking at it, for some time. She slowly looked up at his face as she asked, "Why were there so many Grand Fiends and a necromancer so close to the Holy Hills?"

He paused, hung his head, and replied, "I really don't know." They were both silent for a moment. He looked up at her. "But we have a mission. You're missing from your family, and we need to find them and discover what happened." He placed a hand on her shoulder.

Catherine forced a half smile and whispered, "And find Aaron."

He nodded. "And find Aaron." Clay smiled a tight-lipped smile.

The moment of calm made her think. She wondered about her dream. Why was she in Dovan? Why was Aaron injured? What was happening there? Why did the weight of the world rest on her shoulders in that dream? She finally voiced her thoughts, "Do you have the same bad feeling as I do?"

Clay laughed slightly and resumed putting on his boot. "I have a lot of bad feelings, which one are you referring to?"

"That we're involved."

His boot slipped on, but only out of muscle memory. He looked at Catherine with slight confusion, "What do you mean?"

"Clay!" Klew came over to his companions. "Couldn't make it out clean, could you?"

Clay's emotions seemed to shift quickly as he smiled at his long-time friend. "You know me. It's not fun if you don't get hurt."

Catherine stood. "Excuse me. I need to continue helping."

Klew patted her shoulder as she walked past. She resumed helping the injured, but her thoughts were finally free to wander. That dream felt real. More real than the dreams she had been basing her entire past on. Could it have just been a dream and nothing more? Perhaps it felt real because her feelings were genuine, but not necessarily the situation itself.

Catherine jumped as she felt a hand being placed on her shoulder and turned around.

"Catherine," Bayla repeated. "Rest. You have done so much. Go. Be with your friends."

Catherine composed herself. "But there is still so much to do."

"And you've done enough. We have more hands now."

She reluctantly nodded and put down the cloth she was washing. The young elf rinsed off her hands and left the area to join her companions, who were not far off.

"Why are you no longer assisting in the healing?" she asked quizzically as she approached Klew, John, and Clay.

The three turned to her, and John answered, "They are down to basic injuries. They want to save their spellcasters' energies in case..."

He did not need to finish his statement for Catherine to know what he meant. She simply nodded. With a slight shrug, she asked, "What do we do now?"

"The inn seems to be on the other side of town, so it's still in good condition," Klew answered. "I say we take rest until we're ready to continue."

"I second that," Clay chimed in.

⤎✦⤏

They had been in town for a few nights. Catherine and Clay sat at a table in the inn's tavern, while Klew and John ordered drinks.

"I've been thinking about something," Clay started.

"What is that?" Catherine inquired.

"What you said."

She crinkled her forehead. "What did I say?"

"That you think you're involved with everything going on."

Catherine relaxed her face, color almost flushing out. She had forgotten she had voiced those feelings, but she had had the dream again the night before. "Oh."

"What did you mean by that?"

She sighed. "I don't know entirely. I just have this feeling that...that...we're somehow involved or will be involved. I mean...how does an elf just show up in a human town all alone? And then on top of that, meet a half-elf with the same history?"

"But what makes you think these are related at all?"

Catherine looked down at her hands, which rested on her lap. "I've been having dreams."

Clay leaned in.

"I...I can't quite describe it. But there's a battle. In Dovan." She closed her hands gently.

"Dovan?"

Catherine nodded. "And for some reason, Aaron and I are pivotal."

He looked down at the table. They were both silent for a while.

She shook her head. "They're probably just dreams."

Clay shook his head. "Maybe, but let me know if you have any more of these dreams."

Klew and John returned and placed the wine on the table.

"I feel like we're interrupting something," John noted.

Catherine shook her head. "Nothing important." And forced a smile.

Both Klew and John raised an eyebrow each but said nothing and sat down. Catherine took her glass and began to drink, praying it would make the dreams stop.

"I think we're all ready to head out again tomorrow morning," Clay stated.

They all nodded in agreement.

"What path are we taking?" Catherine inquired between sips.

Clay and Klew glanced at each other. Catherine straightened up.

"Ah…" Klew looked back at Catherine. "We're taking a detour."

Catherine's expression dropped. "What do you mean?"

"We've been talking with some of the leaders here, and they would like to send a message to Thyla but have no one going that way at this moment."

She looked down at her glass. It was mostly empty. Her hopes were dashed.

"Catherine, I'm sorry." Klew reached out and placed a hand on her shoulder.

She shook her head. "I understand."

"Wait," John interrupted. "Isn't that near the Ehath Forest?"

"Yes," Klew answered.

"My father got reports that a war has broken out between Tith and Ehath."

Klew nodded. "Yes. Tith is trying to reclaim their lands. But this message needs to be delivered to Saro."

"What about my father? Shouldn't he be alerted?"

"They have already sent messengers that way."

John settled down.

"So," Catherine raised her mostly empty glass, "to Ehath we go."

CHAPTER 8

A male voice called out, "Run!"

Both Sasha and Aaron looked up. At that moment, a young man ran down the stairs, jumping the last fourth of the way down. He had short brown hair, his eyes were a greenish hazel, and he wore basic commoner's clothes: a cream-colored, loose shirt, brown pants, and black boots. He also had a dagger in his right boot and a small, brown, cloth pouch hanging by his left side. The man slid into a kneeling position in front of Sasha's cage and started to pick the lock.

"Tilen!" Sasha cried happily.

"Yes, it is I," the young man responded, his voice was different from the voice they heard yelling earlier.

"Is Trinity here?" She moved to kneeling on the other side of the cage door.

"Yes, she is. I tried to make her stay, but she refused." Tilen flashed a quick smile at Sasha.

"Where is she?"

"Right up the stairs." He motioned his head towards where he had come from. "She's holding back the

Ehathians that stayed to fight. In other words, the dumb ones." Tilen opened Sasha's cage, with a mischievous smile. He then turned his head and made eye contact with Aaron. He shifted over to Aaron's cage.

"Aaron, this is Tilen," Sasha informed, as she stood up and climbed out of the cage.

Once Sasha entered more light, Aaron could make out more of her features. She had curly black hair, tied in a messy bun, and caring brown eyes. She wore a long-sleeved red dress that probably sparkled when it was clean. Aaron turned his attention back to his rescuer, "Thank you for your help."

"You're welcome," he responded without looking up from the lock.

As she ran up the steps, Sasha shouted down, "I'll go help Trinity."

"What kind of lock is this!?" Tilen shouted angrily while pulling out his broken pick. He looked up at Aaron. "I'm going to look for the keys." He continued to have care in his voice as he spoke, then ran up the stairs.

Sasha came back down. "What's wrong?" she asked, while kneeling down next to Aaron's cage.

"He can't pick the lock," Aaron's voice drifted off as he thought for a moment. "Do you still have that pin?"

Sasha reached into her hair and handed it to Aaron. "Tilen is the best lockpick in Tith."

"I have no doubt, I just want to try." He began to pick the lock again. The pins he had depressed before were still depressed, but when he reached the last pin and pushed it down, he felt static, and the hairpin snapped. "It's magic," he whispered.

Tilen shouted, "Found them!"

There was a slender sorceress with long brown hair that was loose and brushed against her back as she ran down the stairs. She rushed to Aaron's cage and searched through a ring of keys. "Got it!" she shouted joyfully as the lock opened. She placed her hand on Sasha's shoulder, "Are you well enough to help?"

Sasha nodded and placed her hand over her fellow sorceress's. "Always, sister."

The two went back up the stairs. Aaron crept up the stairs, doing his best not to be noticed. What he saw was visual mass confusion. Spells of all forms were flying, and dark shadow figures flung themselves at the sorcerers and sorceresses. This verified what Aaron heard Tilen say. The Ehathians were on Kindraze's side. He backed down the stairs again, looking around, but finding no weapons.

He waited until the pulsing of the spells' powers stopped and the noise of battle died down. Unsure of what to expect, he crept back up the stairs. Not too far from the top of the stairs lay a sorceress motionless on the ground. Suddenly, Aaron's memory covered his surroundings with the vision of his mother lying dead on a wooden floor, covered in blood.

"Aaron!" Sasha called, jolting him back to the present.

Aaron shook his head and looked at her as she walked over to him. He watched her gaze go down to the floor.

"Oh," she looked back up at him. "Is this the first battle you've been in?"

Aaron looked back down at the woman. She looked nothing like his mother and there was no blood. "It is not. But it's been a long time."

Sasha wrapped an arm around his shoulders.

"We have what we came for," Tilen proclaimed, then looked around, "And lost too many to go any further. It's time to go back to Thyla."

The militia muttered in agreement.

Aaron's hand instinctively reached for his ring and his natural tendencies were suddenly disrupted by the fact that the ring was no longer on his hand. "I..." he started before trailing off.

Tilen looked over. "Yes?"

"I cannot join you."

Sasha, Tilen, and Trinity exchanged glances. "We're your best chance of getting out of here alive," Tilen stated frankly.

"I know." Aaron looked down at his bare hands. "I can't leave without my mother's ring."

Tilen's shoulders slumped. "Your mother's ring?"

Aaron's hands closed into fists.

"Yes," Sasha said, stepping between Tilen and Aaron.

Tilen straightened up in surprise.

"Kindraze wants it. She's furious that Aaron had it. It's important."

Tilen looked around. "I can't risk any more lives."

Aaron gently stepped around Sasha, "I'm not asking you to. I'm not even asking for your assistance. *I* can't go with you."

"There is no way we are leaving you here alone," said Trinity. "It's a death sentence."

Before anyone could say another word, they heard the distant sound of whispers.

"Reinforcements," Tilen muttered. "Okay, Sasha, Trinity, you're with us. The rest of you get back to Thyla and inform Saro what we're doing."

As the larger party started to head out, Tilen guided Sasha, Trinity, and Aaron down the hall.

Once they snuck into an abandoned room, Tilen turned to Aaron. "Okay, what's the deal with your mother's ring?"

Aaron shrugged. "Honestly, I have no idea."

"It must be magical," Trinity suggested.

Aaron began running as many memories as he could conjure.

∂∞⊝

"Now, Aaron," his mother said sweetly. "One day this will be yours," she held out the silver ring with intertwining lines. "You will hold the responsibilities it comes with."

∂∞⊝

"Must we go looking?" young Aaron heard his father implore his mother.

"It's my duty as Bearer of the Ring to find the Dagger," his mother said stubbornly.

∂∞⊝

Aaron clung to his dying mother, unable to see clearly through the tears. Blood was everywhere.

"Take this," she gasped while sliding a ring into his small hand. "It will keep you safe."

"No! You need it!" the young boy cried.

"There he is!" a gruff voice called as a large man wielding a sword ran in his direction.

Aaron stood and ran for his life, clinging onto the last piece of his mom.

绋―绖

Aaron shook his head. "All I can remember is it was my mother's, something about it keeping me safe, and a dagger."

"A dagger?" Tilen asked with confusion.

Aaron shrugged. "She mentioned needing to find a dagger because she had the ring...I'm sorry. I just..."

"You just what?"

Aaron sighed, softly said, "I was just so young when I last saw her," and hung his head.

Sasha reached out and placed a hand on his shoulder.

"Okay," Tilen inhaled deeply. "I'm guessing the ring has some sort of protection enchantment. I'm not sure the dagger will help us find it here. Where to start?"

"I'd say, let's start somewhere we haven't been," Trinity suggested and began to leave the room.

绋―绖

Aaron was beginning to lose hope. They had been searching for what felt like forever but were getting nowhere. There were no clues, and there always seemed to be another place to look. "I'm sorry," he said.

The other three looked at him.

"This is a waste of time. We should leave."

"Aaron," Sasha reached out and touched his arm, "if it's important, it's important. Besides, I have a feeling we don't want Kindraze to have that ring. If it really is as powerful as she made it out to be."

Aaron opened his mouth to contest, but then they heard a voice in the distance getting closer. "That voice..." Aaron approached the doorway.

"What is it?" the three inquired.

Aaron waved his hand at them, indicating for them to be quiet and listen.

"My lady, they have escaped," Xyxthris spoke softly.

"They what?!" Kindraze boomed.

"They have escaped. They had help."

Kindraze growled. "Never mind. They aren't as important as this."

Aaron peeked around the corner and saw her holding up a ring. He knew in his heart it was his ring. He quickly slid back into the room as the two approached.

"Are you going to wear it, my lady?" Xyxthris inquired.

"No. I want to see if we can destroy it. Come, let's bring it to Mohan's lair."

The four watched as Kindraze and Xyxthris walked past.

"That's my ring," Aaron whispered. "I'm going to follow them. You do not have to join."

"You can't do it alone," Tilen whispered. "We're coming with you."

They slowly followed the evil sorceress and her henchman through the halls. Almost losing them a few times out of caution. The hallways were eerily quiet for how many Ehathians were summoned to fight earlier, but they just took that to their advantage and decided to worry about it at a later moment. Something about Kindraze did not sit right with Aaron. She seemed to almost float as she walked, and her walk seemed almost familiar. The more he analyzed it, the more familiar it seemed. Suddenly, it dawned on him. She walked almost the same way Catherine walked.

Kindraze and Xyxthris abruptly stopped at a door, and their followers ducked into a room. Xyxthris shuffled through some keys and opened the door. The two stepped inside, closing the door behind them.

Aaron pressed his back against a wall and sighed.

"What now?" asked Trinity.

Tilen sat down. "We wait to see if they come back through."

Aaron slid down to a seated position and closed his eyes. The image of Catherine filled the black. He worried about her and whether she and Klew were alright. Aaron lost track of time as they all waited quietly. But eventually, the door opened again, and they could hear Kindraze and Xyxthris speaking.

"Yes, my lady," Xyxthris replied.

"Good, now go see if you can summon more Ehathians. I think it's time for another raid on Thyla." Aaron could hear the wicked smile in her voice.

The two passed by without noticing them.

Aaron and his companions waited for a few moments, letting the two get out of view. Tilen then approached the door. He tugged on it slightly, but it was locked. He pulled out his picks and began to silently work. Aaron, Trinity, and Sasha maintained watch. In a matter of moments, Tilen successfully picked the lock, and they all slipped in.

The corridor they entered was much darker than the others. The torches were spread further apart, and it almost seemed as if they didn't glow as brightly. Tilen led the way. There were no turn-offs or doors until they reached a room. It was small with only one other way out. A large black cauldron sat in the middle of the room. The cauldron was filled with fire. Aaron approached the cauldron; the fire burned hot, but he saw no source. The flames danced a hypnotic dance. Aaron almost thought he could see the shadow of figures in it. He watched, trying to make them out. He soon began to hear whispers in a language he had never heard, but that sent a shiver down his spine. The longer he stared at the flames, the louder and more all-encompassing the voices got.

Aaron jolted to his senses as Tilen turned him around.

"Are you okay?" Tilen asked, his hands on each of Aaron's shoulders.

Aaron looked around, and all three of his companions were looking at him with concern. "Yeah...I just...I saw and heard something."

"What?"

"I'm not sure. It was just figures that I couldn't quite make out, and I've never heard the language before. But it was unsettling."

Trinity knelt by the cauldron, investigating the side. "Shadow touched."

"What?" the other three said in unison while looking down at her.

"There's an engraving here. It's in the shadow touched language."

"Can you read it?" Aaron knelt next to her.

The sorceress shook her head. "No. I don't know shadow touched. I just know this symbol is theirs," she said while pointing.

"How old is this cauldron?" Sasha circled it while examining it.

"Haven't the shadow touched been gone for centuries?" Aaron asked.

Trinity nodded.

Aaron felt a chill go up his spine, and he shivered. "I don't like it in here."

"I don't see the ring in here either. Let's continue," Tilen added.

They gathered again as they continued down the next hallway. The ground in the hallway was uneven, and the walls were unfinished. They continued down the hallway until they reached another opening. The area was larger than the room housing the cauldron, so they all knelt by the entryway, trying not to be seen if anyone was there.

Aaron looked around. No one was visible, but there was another exit off to the right. The room was full of metalworking equipment, and an anvil sat in the center, but there was no forge. Something small was sitting on the anvil. "My ring," Aaron whispered. Aaron slowly crept forward, trying to keep to the shadows, which was easy with how many shadows there were. He reached the anvil. There sat his ring. As he took it and slipped it on his finger, he heard that foreign language again, but it sounded closer. He slowly turned and saw a figure standing in the other doorway. He couldn't see the figure's eyes, but somehow knew they were making eye contact.

The figure raised its arms, and instinctively, Aaron stood and shouted, "Run!" as he began running back the way he had come. Just as he was reaching the hallway, he felt a hot pain surge through his back and spread to every limb. He cried out in pain and collapsed under its magical weight.

Sasha and Trinity reached out and lifted Aaron to his feet. Aaron felt pain with every step but knew he had to push through. The four of them ran for their lives. Sasha began to chant softly as they ran. Aaron felt a calming warmth come from where she touched him. Slowly, the calm overtook the pain, and he was able to hold himself up. Static lightning crackled along the walls as a spell missed them.

"Hold your breath!" Tilen yelled as a green mist began to form in front of them.

Aaron inhaled deeply before entering the fog. The air burned his skin as he ran through, but they all made it through. They continued to run, ignoring the cauldron as they entered that room and quickly exited. A large bolt of fire crashed into the wall of the room as they ran out of it. Tilen paused briefly, turned around, said a quick chant while clutching a pendant around his neck, and then turned back to join them in running. Aaron glanced over his shoulder after that and saw a force field go up in the hallway behind them. The quartet finally made it through the original door and closed it behind them.

"No time to wait, let's get out of here," Tilen said between breaths.

Tilen and Trinity guided them through the halls. Aaron knew he wouldn't be able to find his way around again. but did not care; he wanted out. The hallways were eerily quiet, but they simply took advantage of that and quickened their pace. They left through a side entrance.

Aaron paused as they exited. They were in a forest that seemed dead. The trees' bark was black, and there were no leaves. The branches were tangled together, blocking the sky. The trees were also larger than Aaron had ever seen. He had to climb to get over some of the roots and none of the lowest branches were within reach. The canopy was so thick that Aaron could not tell if it was day or night.

"Ehathians!" Tilen called out.

Shadowy figures began to emerge from behind the trees; their shadow weapons drawn. In a matter of moments, the four were outnumbered. They began to run, as best they could, through the forest. The three sorcerers threw spells behind them as often as they could without sacrificing their progress. Aaron had nothing he could do, so he just ran. Soon, Aaron felt a sharp pain in his right shoulder. He glanced over and saw a shadow arrow, which was embedded in his shoulder, fade away. The pain did not. Blood began to flow from the wound. Knowing he did not have much time, Aaron simply continued to run. Every movement of his arm caused sharp pain. Slowly, his vision began to blur, and he started to stumble. He heard his name being called, but it was too late. His vision blackened.

೫∘ஆ

Aaron heard a fire crackling. He slowly opened his eyes. He was in a room. He moaned as he tried to roll to his side.

"He's awake!" he heard Sasha say.

He looked around. Sasha walked over to him. She looked much cleaner. An older woman stood up from a chair against the far wall, next to a small table.

"Where..." Aaron leaned on his left elbow while grasping his throbbing head.

"You're in my tower," the woman said as she approached the bed Aaron lay on.

Aaron looked up at her, while caving into his body and lying back down. Her face was soft but contained slight wrinkles that hinted at a life well lived. Her hair was a silvery gray, braided over her shoulder. Her eyes were a deep brown that somehow showed a caring heart that was strong.

"Who are you?" he managed to ask.

She smiled. "My name is Saro."

Aaron's eyes widened. "I...Thank you." He stumbled over his words.

Saro laughed. "No need for formalities. Sasha has filled me in on your adventure. You are a welcomed guest. It appears the Ehathians have a target on you, so please, rest up." Saro turned to Sasha and nodded while leaving the room.

Sasha took Aaron's hand. "I'm so glad you're okay."

"What happened?" he asked.

"I'm not quite sure, but I saw you collapse, and then the Ehathians didn't stop. They ganged up on you. We managed to fight them off you and get you away from them. Thankfully, the rest of the search party hadn't truly left; they just camped a safe distance away and came to help. We healed you the best we could, but you remained unconscious for the three-day travel."

Aaron looked into Sasha's eyes. "Thank you."

"For what?"

"Not leaving me."

Sasha smiled. "Of course. Now, get some rest. I can tell you're still weak." She patted his hand and left the room.

Aaron looked at the ceiling and watched the shadows from the fireplace dance around. After a while, he decided to close his eyes once again and try to get some rest.

❧

Aaron sat at a large table, set up in an even larger tent, with paper scattered across it. Catherine sat to his right, and Klew stood across from him.

"Annathalinda will be here tomorrow," Klew informed.

Aaron nodded. "It will be good to have her back."

Catherine placed a hand on his shoulder.

"And ah...someone has some even better news for you," Klew stepped to the side.

A beautiful, young woman approached. Her hair was like gold. She wore a long, flowy white dress with a sword hanging at her side. "The dracona have responded," she said with a sweet voice.

Aaron straightened his back. "Oh?"

"They are sending some members to help with this war."

❧

Aaron opened his eyes quickly. Who was that? What do dracona have to do with anything? What war?

"Good, you're awake," an unfamiliar voice said.

Startled, Aaron looked over to someone carrying a tray of food.

They came over to his side. "You should be well enough to sit up at this point, so..." They placed the tray down and began to help Aaron sit up.

He required more assistance than he would have liked to admit. "Thank you," he said quietly.

They picked the tray up and brought it over to Aaron. "Here you go. Eat up," and then left.

Aaron took this moment to look around. The room was simple. It had the bed he sat in, a chair, a small table against the far wall, a dresser, a fireplace in the corner, and a nightstand that was covered in creams and ointments. There was a window with the sun shining in. The scent of the food slowly wafted its way into Aaron's nose, and his stomach began to grumble. He suddenly realized he had no idea when the last time he ate was. And so, he ate.

He ate in peace. Contemplating his dream and everything that had happened to him on the journey. He slowly twisted his ring. Once he finished eating, he decided to try to stand. The food gave him energy. He slowly scooted himself to the edge of the bed, with his legs hanging off. His feet touched the ground. He pushed himself up, leaning heavily on the bed. Every muscle in his body screamed in pain. He swallowed, pushing the pain down. He took one adventuresome step, followed by another. It became easier with each step. Finally, he made it to the door. He opened it up and peeked out into the hallway.

It was a simple hallway. Stone walls and wooden floor. There was a mix of windows and torches to provide light, no matter the time of day. He heard people talking in the distance. He followed the voices. The voices led him to an open reading room. There was an entryway on the opposite end of the room, and bookshelves filled to the brim covering the other two walls. A wooden chandelier with candles hung from the ceiling. Tilen, Trinity, Sasha, Saro, and an older man sat in cushioned chairs talking.

"You're walking!" Saro said pleasantly as she looked up at Aaron.

The rest of the sorcerers there turned to look.

"Aaron!" Tilen and Trinity said in unison as they stood up.

"Hello," Aaron said sheepishly. "I apologize if I'm interrupting."

"Oh no, please, you're welcome to have a seat." Saro motioned to an open chair.

The half-elf sat down as instructed.

"Aaron, please meet my husband, Valex." Saro indicated the older gentleman.

Valex had black hair that was more gray than black, a thin beard, and dark green eyes. "Pleasure," he nodded.

Trinity spoke. "I hope you don't mind, but we were discussing your ring."

Aaron closed his right hand and touched the ring with his thumb.

Valex leaned forward, "May I see it?"

Aaron looked down, twisted it some, then slipped it off and handed it to Valex.

"Mhmm." Valex nodded while looking at it closely. "Definitely enchanted. Do you mind if I borrow it for a bit? I'll give it back. I just would like to figure out its powers."

"You can do that?" The half-elf straightened his back.

Saro laughed, "He can. I am not sure anyone else can."

Valex added, "I should have it figured out by the end of the day."

Aaron looked at the ring in the sorcerer's hand. He had always wondered. Finally, he nodded. "That is fine."

"Perfect!" the older man stood up, "I should get started then," and left the room.

Saro looked at Aaron. "Maybe we can figure out why they are targeting you now."

"Targeting me?" Aaron's attention was snapped back to reality.

"Well, yeah," Tilen agreed. "The Ehathians that were following us when we left were targeting you. They only attacked us when we got in their way.

"What?" He looked back and forth between all of them.

Trinity and Sasha nodded.

"What do I have to do with anything?" He felt his chest tighten.

Saro looked into Aaron's eyes, "That's what we're going to find out."

☙❧

Aaron followed Sasha outside. The sun felt warm on his skin. Saro's Tower rose high into the sky, far above all other buildings. The layout and architectural styles reminded him of Dovan.

Sasha led him to a large town hall. "There is someone I would like you to meet," she stated.

The town hall was a large stone building, filled with wooden benches and windows that covered a large portion of the walls. The hall was nearly empty, but someone caught his eye. She stood in the far corner. Her golden blond hair hung loose. She wore a flowy white dress and had a sword hanging from her waist.

"Nissela!" Sasha called out.

The woman from Aaron's dream turned to them. She smiled and came over.

"Aaron, this is Nissela. Nissela, this is Aaron."

"A pleasure to meet you." She reached out.

Aaron lifted her hand and bowed slightly. "I apologize for this, but have we ever met before?"

Nissela cocked her head. "I do not believe so."

Even her voice was the same as his dream.

"Sorry. You just seem so familiar."

She laughed slightly. "That is the first time I've ever heard that."

Sasha interjected, "Introduce him to your friends."

Nissela smiled mischievously. "Come."

The three left the hall and walked towards the edge of town. They were still a ways off, but Aaron soon saw a large beast with grand wings and golden scales glistening in the light. Its snout was pronounced with large nostrils and sharp, visible teeth. It had long, golden spikes extending back from its head, almost like hair. A pair of wavy horns that protruded back as well. Its eyes were a deep green. It was sitting on its back legs with the front legs straight and its massive wings folded at its sides. Its scales lay flat all the way to a spiked tail. Its underbelly even had scaling. Nearby were similar beasts, but with green scales.

"Dragons," Aaron whispered. He had never seen one up close.

Nissela guided him to the dragons. "This is Ov," she said while placing her hand on the gold dragon's leg.

Aaron was speechless.

"We have been assisting Tith with the war against the Ehathians."

"We?" his words suddenly rushed back. He knew who she was, but had never met her before.

"I think he just figured it out," Sasha stated.

Nissela laughed. "Yes, we."

"You're the Dragon Lady?" Aaron could barely get the words out.

The golden-haired woman nodded and Ov brought her head down next to her. Nissela placed her hand on Ov's neck.

Aaron's dream ran through his head. "Are dracona real?"

Nissela straightened, and Sasha cocked her head and furrowed her brow.

"Why do you ask?" Nissela questioned.

The inappropriateness of his question came flooding to the forefront of his mind. "Oh...I...I've just always wondered. I loved the legends."

"What makes you think I would know?"

"I mean..." Aaron motioned towards Ov.

"Dracona aren't of this plane. How would I know if they are real?"

The tone Nissela used indicated to Aaron that she was hiding something. But how would admitting to a dream assist in this situation, so he tried to fumble his way out of it. "I just thought since legends say they are related to dragons that if anyone here knew, it would be the Dragon Lady."

Ov looked at Nissela and Nissela made eye contact with her. Nissela's face scrunched in confusion. She shook her head. Ov huffed. Nissela sighed and looked back at her two humanoid companions. "Sasha, could you give us a moment?"

Sasha straightened up, "Um...okay," and then walked away.

Aaron watched as she looked back at Nissela. His fingers twitched, unsure of how to react or what was about to happen.

Nissela crossed her arms and leaned on Ov. "Time for both of us to be honest, but you first. Why do you want to know?"

Aaron sighed. "I had a dream."

She let her shoulders slump and her head dipped to the side. "You had a dream?"

Aaron nodded.

"You dreamed of dracona so now you want to know if they are real?" She seemed unamused.

"No."

"No? Then what is it?"

Aaron raised his hands in front of him in reassurance. "It was a dream. But it was of you."

Nissela's arms dropped, and she stood up straight. "Of me?"

"Well, you were in it."

"What was this dream about?" she spoke slowly.

"I'm not entirely sure," he scratched the back of his head, "but you told me that some dracona were being sent to assist with the war."

"This war?"

Aaron shrugged. "I have no idea, but you were reporting to me for some reason."

Nissela's eyes narrowed as she turned her gaze back to Ov. Ov huffed again. Nissela threw her hands slightly as she rolled her eyes. "Fine," she mumbled and then looked back at Aaron. "Ov trusts you for some reason. Yes, dracona are real, but they are on the Qualivica plane. The majority of them are allies, but they tend to stick to their own needs. I do not plan on asking them to help in this war." There was a harshness to her tone.

"I didn't...I don't..." Aaron couldn't find the words.

Nissela sighed. "I'm sorry. This is just not something I freely share, but Ov is insisting I tell you."

"Insisting?"

Nissela nodded. Ov huffed again, somehow Aaron thought it sounded satisfactory.

"Can you..."

"Speak telepathically? Yes. Much easier than learning draconic."

Aaron made eye contact with Ov but spoke to Nissela, "I'm sorry."

"For what?"

"Forcing you into this uncomfortable situation." Aaron looked deep into the golden eyes. "I don't understand my dream and I don't expect you to trust me or even believe it yourself. So, thank you for trusting me."

Ov closed her eyes slowly and opened them again. Aaron heard nothing but felt a comfort flow over him.

Nissela sighed. "Ov has always been a good judge of character. But know, if you betray us, you will have all of the gold and green dragons after you."

༄৵

Tilen, Trinity, and Sasha were joining their families for dinner, so it was just Saro and Aaron at the table. Saro was a kind woman and did what she could to make Aaron comfortable. She regaled him with stories of her family and how her father reestablished Thyla after having to flee due to the Ehathians. Valex entered the dining hall as the story was winding down. He had a stoic expression. Aaron put down his utensil.

Valex walked over to Saro and whispered something in her ear. Her eyes widened, and she dropped her utensil. They both looked at Aaron. He shifted uncomfortably.

"Where did you get this?" Valex asked, opening his hand to reveal Aaron's ring.

"My mother gave it to me." Aaron began to fear he would not get his ring back.

"How did your mother get it?"

Aaron's fear melted into agitation. "It was a family heirloom."

"Who was your mother?" Valex's tone started to grow harsher.

"I..." Aaron started to speak with anger, then calmed down, "I don't know." He looked down at his almost finished plate, then back up at Valex. "Why?"

The couple looked at each other, then back at Aaron.

"Your mother was an elf?" Saro asked gently.

Aaron nodded.

She took the ring from her husband, stood up, and walked to Aaron. "Then this is yours." She handed Aaron his ring.

He took it, slipped it on his finger, and nodded a thank you. The half-elf looked back at Valex, who still stood there in wonder. "What did you find out?"

Saro returned to her husband, wrapped one arm around him and placed her other hand on his arm closest to her.

Valex finally spoke. "That's Jahola."

Aaron stared at his ring. Jahola. One of the Divine Sisters.

After they were all silent for some time, Valex inquired, "Who was your mother?"

The half-elf shook his head. "I don't know. I only have small moments in memory. Most of my life I spent as an orphan in Dovan, until I was adopted." He looked up at his hosts.

"How did you end up in Dovan?" Saro spoke gently.

"I don't know." Aaron looked back down at his ring. "I remember pirates killing my parents, but I do not remember how I escaped them. It's all a blur."

Saro and Valex looked at each other. Aaron twisted his ring and watched as the intertwining lines weaved in and out.

"So," Saro turned her gaze back to Aaron, "you do not know where you came from?"

Aaron shook his head.

Valex sighed. "This should be a joyous occasion. A Divine Sister has been found. But, Kindraze knows about it now. We have to keep her from getting it."

Aaron stopped twisting the ring and whispered, "The Dagger."

"What was that?"

Aaron looked up. "I remember my mother mentioning needing to find a dagger. She meant *the* Dagger, didn't she?"

"Keelhola," Saro said, just loud enough for them to all hear.

"So, she didn't know where it was," Valex inferred softly.

So many thoughts flooded Aaron's mind that he stood up instinctively and said, "I have to find it."

"Whoa," Saro raised her hands in front of her. "Do you even know where to start?"

Aaron's thoughts paused finally. "No." The image of his mother's face danced in his head. "But it was her mission. I have to complete it."

CHAPTER 9

*T*he 9th *Day of the 4th Moon of the 35th Year of King Hargon*

I have been having this dream, where I am running through Dovan, riddled with battle, in order to save Aaron's life. I know this sounds weird, but I think it is going to happen. Or at least something like it will happen. I just cannot shake the idea that something very bad is about to happen. The fact that Grand Fiends are on the plane again does not help.

We're traveling to Thyla, which is on the border with the Ehath Forest. Klew says we are only a few days away. All this traveling is tiring. I miss Aaron. I hope he is alright. I've spoken with Klew about finding him. Klew thinks we should travel to the Northern Lands and seek counsel from Annathalinda. If anyone could help, she could.

Catherine put down her quill and looked around. Clay was preparing himself for the night watch. John and Klew were settling in for the night. She then looked up at the moon; it was almost half full. She put her journal and quill away and snuggled into her sleeping bag.

Catherine found herself running through the streets of Dovan. She held onto her box, knowing Aaron's life depended on it. Once she reached the infirmary area, an elven nurse wrapped an arm around Catherine's shoulder as she took the box with one hand and guided Catherine to Aaron's side. They had stripped him of his armor, and his teeth were clenched around a rag as another medic stitched a wound in his side. Catherine took Aaron's hand, and his eyes opened for a brief moment. In that moment, Catherine saw his face relax and relief fill his eyes. That moment was harshly ripped away from them as he winced once more in pain.

"We're under attack!" Clay cried, waking Catherine up.

Catherine sat up, still slightly shaken from her dream, and saw Clay, swords drawn, fighting with someone, but all she could make out was a shadow. Klew jumped to his feet and began casting spells that flung bolts of different colors towards the attackers, as did John. Unsure of how she could help, Catherine scrambled to her feet and hid behind a bush.

Four people were attacking, but in the dark of the night Catherine could only make out their silhouettes. Her three allies were quickly gaining the upper hand. She then noticed movement past the combat. Unsure of whether it was a good idea or not, she crept around the camp, remaining in the shadows to get a closer look. Once she got to the other side, she noticed a fifth individual. This person was crouched, watching the battle. She waited to see what they would do, holding her breath and praying to not be seen.

Once the last adversary fell, Catherine watched as the person began to slink away. Right when she was about to point them out to her companions, she caught a glimpse in the moon's pale light. The person had silver hair, not silver like an elder, silver like the metal, and blue skin. Catherine gasped. He turned his attention in her direction, then began to run away.

"Shadow touched!" Catherine yelled as her thoughts finally formulated the words.

The other three came running to her, but the shadow touched was gone by the time they got there.

"What's going on?" Clay asked, looking around.

"Shadow touched." Catherine turned and grabbed hold of Klew's arms. "There was a shadow touched here."

"Shadow touched?" Klew held steady, but concern flooded his face.

"That's not possible," John stated in disbelief.

Catherine shook her head. "I know what I saw!"

Clay wrapped an arm around her shoulders and began to lead her back to camp. "Let's not stay here tonight."

Shadow touched have not been above ground in centuries; what would make them leave? Catherine let her mind run wild with worry. She knew what she saw. She rolled up her bed spread and began to put it all away when she made a sudden realization. "Where are the bodies?" She looked around at where the fighting took place.

"Ehathians," Klew said while also picking up camp.

"This far away?" Catherine inquired.

"At this point, anything is possible," Clay responded with a sigh.

They continued their journey to Thyla. The woods grew thicker. It was about midday the next day when they were finally forced to stop due to exhaustion. This time, they only slept two at a time.

Once it was Klew's and John's turns to sleep, Catherine sat by Chestnut, listening to the birds as the sun slowly crept down the sky.

Clay was tending to his weapons, when he finally asked, "Are you still having those dreams?"

Catherine sighed. She had partially hoped he had forgotten that conversation. She felt so silly being as concerned as she was, but she couldn't shake it. "Yes," she finally resigned. "Just last night even."

The two of them stopped what they were doing and looked at each other.

"Why do you feel that you are somehow involved?" Clay inquired.

Catherine looked down at a purple flower near her knee. "Why would an elf and a half elf be in a human city with virtually no memory of their pasts? How could everything everywhere we go fall apart? And where on the plane is Aaron? Who took him? I know he didn't just leave us. He would never do that." Catherine unconsciously spoke louder to almost a yell.

Clay put his weapons down, went to her side, and sat down. "I understand."

Shocked, Catherine looked at him, "You do?"

He nodded. "I don't have a feeling you are connected, but things are definitely taking a turn. I have a feeling something very catastrophic is going to happen. You would have to be blind to not see it coming at this point."

They were both quiet for a moment.

"Why do you feel your dreams will come true?" Clay finally asked.

Catherine looked up at him. "I feel it in my gut. But also...I've seen a phoenix."

Clay perked up. "You've seen a phoenix?"

"Yes. It was far away and just flew overhead. But yes."

"That does add a twist to this." Clay turned his gaze to the sky. "Let me know if you have any more of these feelings or dreams."

"I will."

"I do think visiting Annathalinda would be the best path at this point." Clay looked back at her.

Catherine nodded.

"It's a long journey though."

"We've come this far," she said with a shrug.

Clay smiled, patted her shoulder, then went back to where he was working on his weapons. Catherine turned her gaze to the sky and watched the leaves dance. She began to go over the last two moons in her head. How did she even end up here? Where was Aaron? Would she ever see him again? So much evil was loose in the plane. Does finding her family even matter that much to her? She was no longer the same woman she was before. She wasn't even sure her old self would recognize her new self. She broke the law by helping Aaron escape prison. She was on a grand adventure with stranger. She can cast spells. She assisted with medical treatments in a battle. Never in an elven lifetime did she imagine any of that would happen to her or that she would be capable of doing any of it.

Her thoughts were disrupted when she heard an unfamiliar voice. She looked around. She saw Clay had stopped what he was doing and looked around as well. She heard it again. Faintly, as if in the distance, whispers in a language she didn't know.

"Time to get up," Clay said as he stood up and shook Klew and John awake.

Catherine instantly gathered the few things she had out. "Who is that?"

"I do not know," responded Clay. "But that's shadow touched."

Klew and John got up quickly after Clay identified the language. The four were back on their horses and continuing their journey in moments.

஬

The sun had set, risen, and was setting again, but they dared not stop for too long. Catherine distracted herself by trying to imagine what it would be like to be in the Northern Lands and meet Annathalinda. Granted she was pretty sure she would not actually meet Annathalinda just get word from her in the best-case scenario.

"Is there an easy path through the mountains to the Northern Lands?" Catherine inquired.

Klew rubbed his chin. "There is, but it is far out of our way at this point."

She sighed an audible sigh.

"Now, now, don't be too discouraged. Elencka is before the mountains and has some ports. We can take a ship from there to the Northern Lands. It should take a quarter of the time."

Catherine perked up. Sea? She had never been to the sea before, at least from what she could remember. And the talk of it being a faster route sounded nice. She then began to daydream of the Northern Land coast. Crystal blue water caressing a black sandy beach, with a light snow on grass just out of the water's reach. She knew this wasn't true, but she couldn't help but imagine a castle made of ice. The sun glistened through the halls.

"There!" John called out and pointed ahead.

Catherine blinked several times to bring her vision back to the present. A soft glow was in the distance and a tall tower rose above the trees.

"Saro's tower."

If it weren't for the impressive height, it would be a simple tower. Plain stones were placed on each other with mortar in between. As they drew closer, a town came into view. Simple buildings with cobble pathways. Lamps were lit along all the streets, lighting the way. Klew led the way to the local inn. Without hesitation, they boarded their horses in the stable, purchased rooms, and went to sleep.

The four met in the dining room in the morning, finally feeling rested.

"I think we'll take a break here before continuing," Klew took a bite of food. "We'll meet with Saro and Valex today but spend a few days in town to regain our energy."

"I say we stick to major paths as well; more traffic and less trouble," Clay suggested before taking a swig of his cider.

"It will also take us through Soriana." Klew smiled at Catherine and whispered, "I didn't forget."

Catherine perked up and suddenly no longer wanted to stay longer than necessary. She wanted to go and find her family. She knew they needed to rest though.

After they finished breakfast, they made their way to Saro's tower. The large, wooden, double doors were unbarred, so they entered. The main entrance served as a gathering area for the entire city, with hallways branching off to the sides. The hall was empty other than a single servant walking from one end to the other. They stopped and looked at the party. "Can I help you?"

Klew responded, "Yes, we're looking for Saro and Valex."

"They are visiting the infirmary. There was a large battle two nights ago."

"Where is it set up?"

"Northeast edge of town."

"Thank you." Klew nodded to the servant and motioned for the rest of the group to follow him as he turned to leave.

As they made their way through town, Catherine heard a loud, deep growl. She turned to where it came from and saw a large green dragon leaping into the air. Its broad, muscular wings flapped rhythmically. Its front legs were curled in close while its hind legs pushed off the ground. She cried out. She had never seen a dragon up close before. She watched in awe.

"What are dragons doing so far west?" Catherine asked.

Clay watched the dragon as well. "Probably assisting in the war with the Ehathians."

"The dragons care that much?"

"The Dragon Lady cares that much."

Catherine kept looking over her shoulder, where the dragon originated from to see if she saw any others as they continued on their way. Without seeing any more dragons, they reached a large tent. As they approached, three people exited the tent.

Catherine's heart stopped, then began to beat faster than it ever had before. She didn't know if time was moving slowly or quickly, but she ran towards them and cried, "Aaron!"

Aaron turned to them. His eyes twinkled as he embraced her and lifted her off the ground. Catherine kissed him passionately. She had missed the feeling of his arms around her and his lips against hers. Tears of joy streamed down her face. After too short a time, Aaron put her back down on the ground, cupped her face in his hands, and they leaned in with their foreheads touching.

"I'm so glad you're alive," Catherine whispered.

"I love you," Aaron whispered back, then pulled her in tight again.

Catherine wanted this moment to last forever, and her heart ached a little as he pulled back, but she knew reality required a pause in their reunion.

"Aaron!" Klew shouted joyously.

Aaron smiled at him, and they clasped arms. The half-elf then turned his attention to their newer companions. His smile faded. Catherine watched a look of puzzlement go over both Aaron's and Clay's faces.

Clay finally asked, "Do I know you?"

"I..." Aaron started, then paused. "I don't think so."

"Clay," Catherine started, then noticed Aaron tilt his head slightly. She looked back at Clay, then spoke slowly, "This is Aaron. Aaron, Clay."

The two men shook their heads and then clasped arms.

"I'm John," John said as he extended his arm to Aaron. "Pleased to finally meet you." They shook hands.

Aaron turned to his two companions, "I'll need to go for now."

"Actually," Klew interjected. "We were looking for them."

Saro smiled. "Hello, Klew. What news do you bring now?"

"Not good," he glanced around, "Here may not be the best place to discuss it, though."

"Right this way," Valex motioned for them to follow him as he led them through the streets and back to Saro's tower.

Catherine leaned into Aaron as they walked with his arm wrapped around her.

Valex led them through a side door that opened to an entryway leading to a hallway. There were windows throughout the hall and regularly spaced doors. He finally opened one on the right, and it was a room with a large table surrounded by chairs.

"Come, sit. Let us discuss this matter." He motioned for them to take a seat in the chairs.

Aaron pulled a chair out for Catherine to sit in and slid it closer to the table as she sat down, and then sat down next to her, his hand on hers.

Once everyone was settled, Klew began to speak. "We are bringing news that not only are Grand Fiends back on the plane, but they have a necromancer on their side. And..." he glanced at Catherine, "Shadow touched have been spotted."

Valex and Saro furrowed their brows as they looked at each other.

Saro spoke this time, "This is troubling news. We had heard rumors of the Grand Fiends, so we have been preparing for their coming. We are not wholly surprised at the necromancer news either. It is troubling that they are joining forces with the Grand Fiends, though. Neither are ones to really have allies. But shadow touched? That is unexpected."

Catherine was caught off guard when Aaron turned and asked, "Where were the shadow touched seen?"

Klew nodded toward Catherine, "Only a couple of days' travel from here."

Aaron looked her in the eyes. There was a softness in them. "You saw them?"

Catherine nodded, and Aaron squeezed her hand. "We also heard someone speaking in the shadow touched tongue about a day's travel," she added.

Aaron looked at Saro and Valex. "The cauldron."

They nodded in return. Catherine shook her head shallowly.

Clay spoke up this time, "What cauldron?"

Aaron turned his attention to Clay. "In Kindraze's fortress-"

Catherine's mind filled with the sound of her mother angrily shouting, "Kindraze!" That name had a meaning to her, but what? She suddenly realized she had missed part of the conversation.

"The Dark Wars were fought in this area?" Aaron questioned.

Clay nodded. "They took place everywhere, really. But it is believed there were fortresses built by the shadow touched that are still standing today."

"So, they may not be related."

"It's best we plan for either option to be possible."

Catherine began to listen in awe as they strategized and the way Aaron kept pace with the different plans and ideas. She had always seen the way he organized the farm, but that was just with his parents; this was planning and organizing an army. Something had changed in him.

The sun had moved a noticeable distance across the sky when they finally decided to stop discussing matters for the time being. Valex and Saro offered them rooms in the tower, so they did not have to spend coins on the inn for any more nights. Catherine and Aaron were granted permission to take time for themselves.

Catherine felt a familiar tingle go up her spine as Aaron smiled at her and told her there was something he wanted to show her. He led her through town, then started leading her out of town. Suddenly, she realized they were headed to where she saw the dragon launching from. Soon, the dragons came into view. The scales of the golden dragons glistened in the sunlight. There were dozens of gold and green dragons. Many were sleeping, some were eating a large amount of fresh meat, and others, Catherine wasn't quite sure what they were doing. They just seemed to be sitting there with their eyes open.

"Shival," Aaron called as they drew close.

A comparatively small green dragon lifted its head and began to amble over.

Aaron looked over his shoulder at Catherine and smiled, "You'll love her, she's a sweetheart."

Catherine had not expected Aaron to describe a dragon as a sweetheart. Frankly, she had never expected Aaron to know a dragon well enough to call them anything.

Aaron reached back, wrapped his arm around Catherine's waist, and gently pulled her forward. Shival came close; close enough that Catherine could feel the hot breath coming from the dragon's nostrils. Aaron took Catherine's hand and reached it out. Shival sniffed a few times, then placed her nose under Catherine's hand.

You are much like him. Catherine heard the kind voice in her head.

Catherine jumped slightly.

Aaron laughed. "Sorry, I forgot to mention. They can speak telepathically."

Do not worry, the voice reassured her, *we are here to help. You are a brave and gentle soul. I think I like you.*

Catherine wasn't sure if she should speak out loud or not, so she tried just thinking, *Thank you.*

Shival moved her nose away from Catherine's hand. *You will do great things. Never doubt yourself.* There was silence for a moment. *Your beloved missed you greatly. Your presence is filling him with a joy he thought he had lost. You two have much to discuss. It was a pleasure meeting you.*

Catherine was still speechless as Shival backed away.

Aaron pulled Catherine close. "What did she say?"

"That I will do great things," Catherine finally spoke.

"I could have told you that."

Catherine made eye contact with Aaron. "And that you missed me."

Aaron stroked her cheek. "Of course I did." He leaned down and kissed her.

She felt the hair on her arms stand on end. His lips sparked life inside of her; a life she thought was gone forever. When their lips parted, they touched foreheads and remained close with their eyes closed for a moment.

"I have something I need to tell you," Aaron whispered.

Catherine looked into his deep, brown eyes.

Aaron pulled his ring off and showed it to Catherine. "This is no ordinary ring."

Catherine took it in her hands. She had played with it on his finger so many times. She watched as the three lines intertwined while turning it over.

"It's Jahola."

Catherine froze. Jahola. A Divine Sister. "How..." Catherine was unable to continue her question.

"Valex identified it."

"You..."

"My mother gave it to me before she passed away. She said it would protect me."

Catherine finally moved her gaze from the ring to Aaron. "Are you sure?"

Aaron sighed and shrugged. "I still question it. But it makes sense. Kindraze was the one who captured me, and she wanted this ring for some reason."

That name again.

"I remember my mother mentioning wanting to find a dagger."

"*The* dagger?" She felt her chest tighten.

"I can only assume."

Catherine looked back down at the ring in her hand as she remembered the statue of Jehepsu in Avendale.

"Catherine."

She looked back up at her love.

"They don't know how I'm still alive."

ಶಿ•ೕ

The 11th Day of the 4th Moon of the 35th Year of King Hargon

I do not know what to think. Aaron was captured by an evil sorceress, whose name I can't get off my mind. His mother's ring is really Jahola. I met a dragon. And I'm staying in Saro's Tower as an honored guest. I am very confused right now. One minute, life was dragging on, and now it is moving so fast I can barely keep up. Aaron is now set on trying to complete his mother's mission, which he just realized even existed. Honestly, I don't know if he'd leave me behind to complete this mission. His determination to find Keelhola is one I've never seen in him before.

Apparently, he has been helping Thyla with the war. He said Valex took him under his wing and was teaching Aaron about battle strategies. Who would have thought, Aaron, the poor farmer boy, would become a warrior? Well, I suppose I could have told you that. I always did see his leadership skills; I don't think he did. Until now, at least.

Catherine put her quill down. She looked around the simple room, then out the window at the town below. Streetlamps flickering in the night. She saw a fire in the distance where the dragons were. She looked back at her journal and flipped through the pages, back through time. Her life had changed so quickly. She wasn't sure whether to look forward to or fear the future. But only approaching it head-on would give her that answer.

❧

Catherine woke up to a loud horn echoing through the town. She looked out the window; it was still night. She quickly slipped on an outer dress and her boots and went into the hall.

Aaron emerged from his room, quiver on his back and bow in hand. He looked at her, cupped her face with his free hand, and said, "Ehathians. Stay here."

Defiantly, Catherine protested, "I can help."

175

Aaron was taken aback by her statement but relaxed quickly. "Then follow me."

Klew, Clay, John, Valex, and Saro all joined them as they exited the tower and ran through town.

"Take me to the infirmary," Catherine called to Aaron.

He simply nodded and led her to the large tent where they were reunited. "Stay safe, my love." He gave her a swift kiss, then headed off in the direction everyone else was going.

Catherine introduced herself to other aids and began helping where she was needed. There wasn't much to do initially, so she prepped bandages and supplies. Eventually, the injured began to arrive, and the pace of everything accelerated. Catherine cleaned wounds, stitched gashes, sterilized tools, washed bandages, and attempted to help heal, among other things.

After a fair amount of time, Catherine wasn't sure of the exact duration, but she grew tired. One of the sorcerers assisting someone to the infirmary called out for help.

Catherine overheard the conversation.

"We need help bringing the injured back," the sorcerer told the healer.

"Is it that bad?" the healer asked.

"Yes."

The healer called Catherine over. "Help them."

She nodded and followed the sorcerer. After passing about two buildings, Catherine could see the fight. There were so many Ehathians that they seemed like just one large, black mass surging and flinging arrows at the sorcerers. Sorcerers and sorceresses cast a wide variety of spells, glowing in all different colors, and taking all different elemental forms. Then there were those fighting with physical weapons. The weapons were all magically enhanced in some fashion; the most common one was flaming swords, but she did spy an axe that threw sparks every time it hit something.

She couldn't help but look for Aaron. Her gaze halted for a moment when she finally found him. He stood a fair distance away from the front line. She watched as he skillfully shot glowing arrows into the black mass. There was a calm concentration on his face. A young sorcerer was next to him, creating the arrows. Catherine blinked quickly as she returned her thoughts to the task at hand.

The sorcerer led her to where they were gathering those too injured to fight. She assisted one to their feet and led them back to the tent. Catherine then turned around and made the trip again. After making a few trips, Catherine laid a sorcerer down on a cot and then heard shouting from the battlefield. It did not sound good. She hurried out to see what was happening.

A large number of Ehathians had pushed their way through and were attacking the ranging warriors, including Aaron. Catherine gasped as she saw an Ehathian swing its shadowy sword at Aaron. He caught the blade with his bow, pulled out a dagger from his boot, and stabbed the Ehathian. The sorcerer who was by his side cast a fiery spell, and the Ehathian vanished. With only a few moments available, Catherine watched as Aaron presented two daggers to the sorcerer. The sorcerer pointed a closed fist at them, and, for a brief moment, they glowed blue.

Catherine heard her name being called; she was being summoned back to assist with the healing. She said a quick prayer that if that ring was really Jahola, it would do its job and keep Aaron safe, then turned back to her duties.

As the night went on, she was reassured that the Ehathians usually retreated once the sun rose. That night was no different. As the sun's rays began to stream through the forest, the Ehathians retreated. As with the previous battle Catherine assisted with, despite the battle being over, there were still injured coming in, just less severe.

While she was cutting more bandages, she heard a woman say, "Aaron!" She turned and saw a black, curly-haired sorceress, who looked familiar, approach Aaron as he walked into the tent.

His left sleeve was cut, providing the bloodsoaked fabric that he had wrapped around that arm.

"Aaron!" Catherine called and rushed to her beloved.

The sorceress was sitting Aaron down once Catherine reached them. He smiled up at Catherine.

"Are you okay?"

"I'm fine," he reassured. "Just a scratch."

Catherine was not convinced due to the amount of blood she saw on the cloth. The sorceress unwrapped the wound, and it confirmed Catherine's intuition. But before she could do anything, the sorceress was placing her hand on it.

Aaron took the sorceress's hand in his. "Sasha, don't waste your energy on this."

"That's going to need stitches," the sorceress said.

"Then so be it. Go help others." Aaron smiled at Catherine. "Looks like I have the best seamstress in town to do it."

Sasha turned to Catherine. "You must be Catherine. I'm Sasha." She extended a hand.

Catherine shook it. "I can take it from here."

The sorceress nodded. "Let me know if you need anything."

Catherine looked carefully at Aaron's arm. "What happened?"

"An Ehathian's sword slid off my dagger when I blocked."

"Let me get supplies." Catherine watched Aaron out of the corner of her eye. He closed his eyes tight as she walked away. He was always good at hiding his pain. As she came back with a needle, thread, clean bandages, and a rag, she saw his face relax as he opened his eyes. "This is going to hurt." She handed the coiled rag to him.

"I've had worse." He smiled at her.

She couldn't help but smile, remembering the time she had to stitch his cheek. She looked him in the eyes; somehow, the stress of the night diminished ever so slightly with him there. "Stop forcing your toughness. I brought you the rag for a reason."

Aaron looked at his wounded arm, sighed, placed the rag in his mouth, and closed his eyes.

Catherine straightened his arm across a small table in front of him. She carefully began to stitch the bloody gash closed. Aaron barely let out a sound but was biting down hard on the rag. Catherine always admired him for the pain he could endure. Once she finished closing the wound, she wrapped it tightly with a clean bandage. After he removed the rag, Catherine leaned over and kissed him.

"I'd give you all the warnings about what to and not to do, but I know you won't listen to any of it."

Aaron smirked. "You know me so well."

Catherine wanted to stay by his side, but she knew she was still needed elsewhere. "Rest up." She gathered her supplies and turned to put them away.

"Catherine," Aaron said softly.

She looked at him.

"Is there any way I can help?"

She smiled. It seemed he didn't want to be far from her either. "I have some cloths that need washing."

The sun was fully in the sky once the infirmary finally calmed down.

Catherine was washing cloths with Aaron when Sasha came back over to them. "I apologize for my abruptness earlier."

The elf looked up from her task. "We were in the middle of a battle. Abruptness is to be expected."

Sasha smiled at her. "Once you've rested. Join my sister and me for a meal. Aaron can show you the way."

Catherine nodded a thank you as Sasha left.

Aaron wrapped his good arm around Catherine's waist. "Come on. I'll get you back to the tower for rest."

അം

"And then," Sasha put down her utensil, "and *then* he jumps down from the ledge onto an Ehathian, stabbing their back."

"That's not what happened," Aaron corrected. "I didn't land *on* the Ehathian, I landed behind them."

Catherine's head was swimming. Aaron recanting war stories? She thought back to watching Aaron shoot his bow in battle. Aaron, a war leader? She would have never imagined him as that. A leader, yes. A war leader? Well, she never imagined being in a war. She glanced between these friendly faces. There was camaraderie there. Much like what she felt with Klew, Clay, and John. She watched Aaron closely. He'd changed. She no longer saw a farm boy when looking at him. She saw the man she knew he could be.

Trinity interjected, "Then there was the brilliant plan you had to ambush the Ehathians coming to attack."

"That was brilliant. It worked, didn't it?" Aaron angled his head to the side.

"It did work, but you almost died in the process." She wagged her full utensil at him.

Catherine leaned towards Aaron. "You almost died?"

"That's beside the point." Aaron waved his hand in her direction.

"No, that's exactly the point. What happened?"

"It's not that exciting of a story."

Catherine glared at him.

Aaron sighed. "Okay, so the Ehathians hadn't attacked for a couple of nights, so I knew they were due to attack soon. So, I had the idea of having a heavier-than-average watch that spread slightly into the forest, waiting for them. Obviously, it was my idea, so I was one of them. We managed to climb into the trees and waited. Thankfully, I was right, and they did come that night."

"Thankfully?" Sasha rolled her eyes.

"Hey, there would have been a lot of lost sleep for nothing if they didn't come. Anyway, the Ehathians start climbing through the forest towards Thyla, and we attack. It was going beautifully."

"Until..." the black-haired sorceress tilted her head toward her shoulder as she leaned forward.

"*Until* the Ehathians began climbing the trees." Aaron smiled. "And, *of course*, my tree was one of the first ones they climbed."

"They were climbing so fast," Trinity added.

"What happened?" Catherine found herself tightening her grip on her utensils.

"They pulled me out of the tree." Aaron mimicked a move one of the Ehathians did to pull him down.

"They must have known it was your plan, because they swarmed you as you hit the ground." Sasha laughed.

Aaron stopped looking at Catherine for the first time when telling the story. Catherine followed his eyes. They were on his mother's ring as he twisted it with his thumb.

Aaron looked back at Catherine. "And that's where my side of the story ends."

Catherine reached out and placed her hand on Aaron's. Something else was on his mind.

"Oh, but it gets better," Sasha stated. "Valex saw this and cast a massive light spell on the cluster of Ehathians. Honestly, I have never seen anyone cast a spell that large. It lit up the forest."

Trinity laughed slightly, "That plan might have failed if it weren't for Valex."

Aaron turned his attention to Trinity. "Hey, even Valex gives me credit for that idea. I was the only one pulled out of a tree."

"Fair enough. You *were* the only person who almost died that night."

Catherine could sense that something had shifted in Aaron. She could also tell that it was not the time to bring it up. They finished their meal and conversations.

Once out of the home, Catherine leaned into Aaron, took his hand, and asked, "What's bothering you?"

"What do you mean?" He rubbed the back of her hand with his thumb.

"Ever since they talked about the ambush, you've been...distant."

Aaron sighed. "My ring."

"Jahola?"

Aaron nodded. "I feel like it's a beacon for them. Ehathians seem to always know where I am and target me."

"Maybe Annathalinda can help."

He looked at her with a furrowed brow. "What do you mean?"

"Well, we were planning to travel to the Northern Lands to speak with Annathalinda. Maybe she could help you, too."

Aaron paused for a moment. "She might have an idea about Keelhola as well."

CHAPTER 10

⤨

Aaron found it hard to leave Thyla. He felt a kinship there. He learned so much during his time there. Once Valex accepted that Jahola was his, Valex took him under his wing and taught him all about military strategies. Aaron's bow skills came in handy, and he perfected his dagger skills. He thanked Etienne that the Ehathians were nothing but shadows. He didn't know if he could kill someone with a face.

It felt amazing to be back with Catherine, though. Feeling her lean in when he wrapped his arms around her. The softness of her lips against his. Seeing her bashful smile that could light up a moonless night. He was thankful the others looked after Catherine and protected her.

He couldn't help but wonder if Catherine really supported his search for Keelhola. What if it took them in different directions? What if she found her family? He didn't want to lose her again, but he also finally felt like he had a purpose since leaving Dovan.

He watched Catherine assist with prepping their dinner. She was always resourceful when it came to meals.

He then looked down at his injured left arm. It still hurt, badly, Catherine and John had tried to use magic to heal it, and it helped only slightly. Ehathian weapon wounds tended to resist magic healing.

Aaron remained relatively quiet that night. He took in what he could and observed. He felt distant. He offered to take the midnight shift with Klew and so went to bed early. He fell asleep quickly.

Aaron's adopted parents' house was still in the distance. He didn't know what to expect. He didn't even know if they knew he was still alive. As he approached the edge of the wheat field, he saw nothing but scorched earth. The field had been burned. Fear shot through him, and he began to run to the house. The stable gates were open, but no horses could be found. Aaron ran to his home.

"Mom! Dad!" Aaron grew desperate. "Tammy! Thomas!"

The front door was unlocked. Aaron froze in his tracks after opening the door. Furniture was overturned and smashed. All the cupboards were open and emptied onto the floor. Aaron knelt as he picked up pieces of a vase his adopted mother had made. Deep in his heart, he knew they weren't there, but he had to check. He walked through every room. It was all the same. Disarray. No crevice had been left unturned. He prayed his parents were alive.

As he stood there, taking in the view of the absolute destruction of his home, he heard a sly, unfamiliar female voice come from behind him, "I knew you'd return."

Aaron felt someone gently push him as Clay said, "Aaron. Your shift."

Aaron opened his eyes. Midnight. It was a dream. He was still in the Elencka forest. He sat up and rubbed his face, trying to encourage wakefulness. He looked over at Klew doing the same, and John and Clay who were lying down for the night. He sighed, stood, grabbed his canteen, and took a drink of water. Aaron put his boots on, picked up his daggers, and went to sit at the fire. Klew joined him.

They sat mostly in silence as the moon traveled across the sky. As their shift was starting to draw to an end, Aaron heard a twig snap. He quickly turned his attention to where he heard it. Klew did the same. Aaron drew his daggers and slowly stood. He began to walk towards the sound. Klew stationed himself to wake the others if necessary.

Suddenly, a large, red-skinned creature lunged out of the surrounding forest. Its claws slashed at Aaron. He raised a dagger, cutting its hand. A blue bolt flew past Aaron and struck the beast. It howled in a way Aaron had never heard before. The creature was terrifying. It was taller than any man Aaron had met, its skin a deep red, its claws warped the human-like structure of its body. Its eyes were red, its stringy hair jet black, and it had what appeared to be charred wings. It wore metal armor. It turned towards Klew. Aaron was struck across the chest. Apparently, there was also a tail.

Aaron drove a dagger into the beast's back, in the gap of the armor right between the base of the useless wings. It arched its back, forcing Aaron to pull his dagger out or release it from his hand. He pulled it out. A black ichor began to spill from the wound.

It turned back towards Aaron and slashed. Aaron jerked back, dodging the swipe. He instinctively swung in retaliation. The creature caught his right hand. It hissed, released his hand, and backed away.

Clay swung his swords at the creature. One dented the armor, the other glided off. An arrow made of fire zipped between Aaron and Clay, piercing the beast. The creature growled deeply and then caught Clay off guard by swinging an arm, knocking him over.

It made eye contact with Aaron. All he could see was rage. Voices started to flood his mind; he couldn't understand a word that was being said, but it sent fear through every fiber of his being. It became increasingly difficult to breathe. Suddenly, the Grand Fiend turned away from Aaron; he gasped for air. He took a step back. Aaron felt warmth fill his lungs, and breathing became easier.

Clay had only one sword in hand and was fighting the beast from the ground. Aaron quickly grabbed the other sword, took it in both hands, and winced as he slashed through the Grand Fiend's neck, decapitating it. The creature turned to ashes. Aaron dropped the sword and pulled his left arm closer to his body. That had hurt more than he anticipated.

Catherine assessed everyone's injuries. Once satisfied with the degree of healing, they all sat down around the fire. Aaron stared at the fire for a bit, then felt eyes on him. He looked up and Clay, Klew, and John were all staring at him.

"Yes?"

"Why did that Grand Fiend recoil from you?" Clay inquired.

Out of the corner of his eye, Aaron saw Catherine look up at him. He knew what she was thinking. She was surprised he hadn't told the others. He looked down and twisted his mother's ring. After a moment of silence, Aaron pulled the ring off and held it up, not saying a word.

"A ring?" John asked, unconvinced.

"Not just any ring," Catherine added.

Clay and Klew both stood.

"Could it be?" Klew whispered.

Aaron sighed. "Jahola."

John suddenly stood as well.

Aaron brought the ring back down and turned it over in his hands, watching the intertwining lines snake around the ring. "Valex identified it."

Klew timidly approached, "May I?" and held out his hand.

Aaron gently placed the ring in his hand.

Klew carefully turned it over in his hands. "It just feels like a ring."

"What do you mean?"

The part wizard laughed. "I don't know. I guess I always imagined it would be radiating with power that you could feel just by touching it. It's beautiful." He extended his hand back to Aaron. "This must be why Annathalinda sent me to help you."

Aaron took his mother's ring. "And now I must see her. My mother was on a mission to find Keelhola. I must complete that mission."

Clay cleared his throat. They all turned their attention to him. "Do none of you know the prophecies?"

Aaron and Catherine shook their heads. Klew and John sighed.

"This isn't good."

"But I thought once they were found again the Ainjeal would return?" Catherine innocently asked.

"The prophecies don't mention that. They do, however, mention that the return of Jahola and Keelhola will be during a time of great war. Once they are found again, it's because they will be needed."

Aaron glanced over his shoulder at the pile of ashes. "I think we need them."

"Yes, the opening of the portal to Hektom is devastating, but if we truly find both, this is just the beginning. Some legends even say that the Divine Sisters might not be enough to win the war."

The half-elf turned his gaze back to Clay as Catherine placed her hand on her beloved's hands. "Do you suggest I go into hiding?" He didn't like that thought.

Clay shook his head. "No. We continue our path and speak to Annathalinda. She will know what to do. She was one of the ones who gave a prophecy."

Aaron slipped the ring back on his finger and encased Catherine's hand in his. Never in his life did he think he, a farmer's adopted son, would be part of legends.

❦

Catherine couldn't sleep the night before. They would reach Soriana before day's end, and things just felt right. This forest felt comfortable, almost familiar. She felt as though Aaron could feel her excitement, as he held her a little tighter.

As they drew closer to the town, Catherine said, "Stop."

They stopped their horses.

"What is it?" Aaron asked.

Catherine dismounted Chestnut. She walked over to a tree and placed her hand on it. Visions of her sister leaving flooded her mind. She looked back up the path. The town was close enough to run to. She couldn't help herself. She began to run. The others were saying something, but she paid no attention to them and just kept running. She ran until she entered the city of Soriana, where she stopped dead in her tracks.

The stable was just off to the side of the road. It was large enough to house dozens of horses. Past the stable was a wooden stairway leading into the trees. High off the ground was the town. A large platform was constructed among the trees, with all the structures built on top of it. Rope bridges connected trees that were a considerable distance apart. Catherine turned her gaze slightly further down the road. There was a small market there, on the ground. Her father's stall used to be there.

She thought she heard her name being called but ignored it. She began to run again. So many memories were rushing through her mind as she ran towards the marketplace. She slowed as she approached it. There were not as many people there as she remembered, but the layout seemed to be the same. She slowly made her way through the crowd. She froze and tears welled up in her eyes. There before her was the most beautiful elf she had ever seen. Long brown hair, loose over one shoulder, and caring blue eyes.

Catherine timidly approached the woman. She looked up from the intricate carvings with a loving smile on her face. Their eyes met. The smile left the elf's face.

"Mom?"

Tears instantly flooded and overflowed from the elf's eyes as she ran from behind the table to embrace her long-lost daughter. Catherine began to cry as well. The feeling of her mother's arms once again around her felt strange, yet wonderful.

Catherine was startled when her mother pulled away from her. She looked up and saw her mother looking past her, and then heard her name being called. She turned. Aaron and the others stood nearby. She saw the gentle question on Aaron's face and smiled. "Aaron," she turned back to her mother, "this is my mom!"

"Catherine!" her mother gasped. "We must tell your father you've returned! Lothro," she addressed the elf at the table next to her, "watch my stall. Catherine has returned!"

Lothro nodded slowly, slightly in shock.

Catherine's mother took her by the hand and guided her through the market to a nearby stairway. They climbed the stairs and wandered through the treetop pathways. Catherine followed her mother to a familiar structure.

Her mother opened the door. "Love?!"

A male voice came from another room. "Yes?"

"There's someone you'd love to see here."

A tall, male elf with long blond hair and blue eyes walked through the doorway and stopped. A look of disbelief crossed his face.

"Dad?" Catherine asked timidly.

He rushed to embrace her and picked her up off the ground slightly. Words of disbelief and love flooded from his lips, until finally he said, "I'm so glad you're home."

They finally broke the embrace and sat down in a communal area where they began to catch up. Catherine told them all about growing up alone in Dovan. Until finally she said, "I also couldn't have survived without Aaron's help," and she suddenly realized, "Aaron!"

Catherine's parents looked confused, then her mother said, "That man in the market."

"Yes! My friends. I completely forgot about them. Please," she stood up, "come meet them."

The three of them went back down to the market. Standing on the edge of it were her friends.

"Aaron! Klew! Clay! John!" Catherine waved at them to get their attention.

The two parties united.

Catherine turned to her parents, "Mom. Dad. This is Aaron, Klew, Clay, and John," she motioned to each of them as their names were said. She turned and smiled at her friends. "These are my parents!"

No one seemed sure how to react for a moment, then Aaron extended an arm in greeting. "Pleasure to meet you."

Catherine's father clasped Aaron's arm, then pulled him into a hug, "Thank you for taking care of her."

৵৽

They all sat around a table with Catherine's parents. There was a pause in the stories being exchanged to catch the family up on all the happenings in their lives.

"What happened?" Aaron asked.

Catherine was caught off guard; for an unknown reason, she hadn't even thought to ask.

Catherine's father took her mother's hand, and they looked at each other. They finally looked back, and her mother said, "Kindraze took her."

"Kindraze?" Aaron questioned. "The sorceress down in Ehath?"

Tears began to well up in Catherine's mother's eyes. Her father's brow furrowed as he said, "Yes, but she is no sorceress."

Catherine's heart sank as she whispered, "Kindy." Not once in her parents' tales did they mention her sister. Her sister never came back.

Aaron turned to his love. "What was that?"

Catherine had a lump in her throat and stones in her stomach. "Kindy," she said more clearly.

"Oh, my dear!" Catherine's mother rushed to her daughter and held her close.

"Kindy?" Aaron said in thought. His eyes widened. "That was your sister's name."

"Her sister?" Klew questioned.

Catherine's father nodded. "Kindraze was our daughter. When Catherine was five years old, Kindraze began to dabble in dark magic. Two years later, she left. No notice, no warning. She just up and left. Then one night, we woke to Catherine screaming. We rushed to her room, but it was too late. We watched as Kindraze vanished with a limp Catherine in her arms. We honestly didn't even know if Catherine was alive." He turned his attention to Catherine and placed his hand on her arm. "We are so happy she is."

Catherine couldn't believe it. It was her sister. Her sister was the one who kidnapped her and took her from her parents. "But why?" Her voice shook.

"We always assumed revenge." He spoke plainly with a shrug.

"Revenge for what?"

"Trying to prevent her from going down the path she is on now."

"But why Dovan?" Aaron asked gently.

Catherine's father shrugged. "We don't understand any of it."

"None of that matters now," Catherine's mother stated, "We have Catherine back," And pulled her daughter in for another hug.

⌘

"How could you ask me that?" Catherine snapped.

"Catherine," Aaron raised his hands.

"No! I *just* found them, and now you want me to leave?" Her hands were clenched in fists.

He placed his hands gently on her shoulders. "That's not-"

She violently shrugged them off. "That's exactly what you just asked!"

"*I* can't stay. I'd love for you to come with me."

"You want me to just leave what I've been looking for my whole life?" She turned slightly away from him.

"If it's your choice to stay," he looked towards the ground, "you have that choice."

"But then you're just going to leave?"

"Catherine." He hung his head.

"I can't believe..." She turned back to him. "Why would you make me pick between my parents and you?"

"You did the same to me in Dovan. Before I got arrested."

"But I changed my mind. I chose you." She pointed at him and then flung her arm out as she said, "And now you're going to choose some random mission that you have no clue what you're even doing over me?"

"That's not-"

"Yes, yes, it is." Catherine looked him dead in the eyes. "I thought you loved me."

"I do!" It felt like someone stabbed Aaron in the chest.

"Then don't you want me to be happy?"

"Catherine."

She shook her head, "I'm done with this conversation," and walked away.

Aaron stood there, speechless. She never let him explain. He would come back for her.

❧

"Something doesn't add up," Aaron tapped his finger on the tavern table they all, minus Catherine, sat around.

"What do you mean?" Klew looked to him.

"Why would Kindraze kidnap her sister to deposit her in Dovan, when she could have easily just taken her captive?"

"Maybe Kindraze hadn't taken over that fortress yet?" John suggested.

Aaron shook his head. "Then why kidnap her? I mean, why not kill her?"

"Well, there has to be *some* good in her," Clay replied.

"I don't know." Aaron turned his gaze to his food. "Something doesn't feel right about all of this. Why would Kindraze kidnap her sister, deposit her in Dovan, where she would end up meeting me, who would then become a target of Kindraze?"

"You know, sometimes weird things just happen," Klew stated.

Clay leaned in and spoke softly to Aaron. "You also might be reading into things since Catherine isn't leaving with us tomorrow."

Aaron sighed. "I had these feelings before."

"You're smart. You probably unconsciously saw this coming."

Aaron knew he was wrong, but had no way to prove it, so he remained quiet. Clay patted him on the shoulder. The rest of the meal was spent in relative silence, with only brief discussions of plans for the next day before they continued their path to the Northern Lands. Once the most basic of plans were set, Aaron called it a night and headed to his room.

Catherine had been refusing to speak to him ever since he approached her to see if she would join them on their travels. He knew finding her parents was the one thing she had always wanted the most. But he had hoped she had known that he had finally found what he was meant to do and that she would want to be by his side. She had been by his side for over half their lives. The hopes of joining with her again were what kept him going while they were apart. And now, she chose her parents over him and didn't want to have anything to do with him for thinking there was even a chance she would pick him over them.

As it had been for the last few nights, Aaron had trouble falling asleep, and once he had fallen asleep, his dreams were restless.

Aaron stood, frozen in fear, as an all too familiar pirate, although significantly older than he remembered him, strode toward him with a cutlass in hand and a snarl on his face. Aaron drew his daggers; he barely noticed the commotion around him of the other pirates fighting with his friends and crew.

The old pirate spat on the deck. "You look familiar."

Aaron had to hold back all the vulgar things he wanted to call this man.

"Funny. I don't usually leave survivors." The pirate's eyes lit up. "Oh yeah. You're the boy we took prisoner."

Aaron lunged forward and swung his blades.

⋖∘⋗

"I had a dream," Catherine told her parents. "I was with Aaron and the others. In Dovan. We were all gathered in a large tent, around a large wooden table. There was a map of the city with different markings on it. They were all talking about strategy and about different units going to different places. Eventually, Aaron took my hand without looking at me. Once decisions were made, everyone else left the tent. Aaron looked at me and thanked me for trusting him. He said there was no one he'd rather have by his side."

"That's quite the dream," stated her father.

"It was just a dream, though," Catherine tried to convince herself.

"What is this mission Aaron is choosing over you?" her mother inquired.

"Oh, uh..." Catherine wasn't sure if she should share. They were her parents, however. "Aaron is looking for Keelhola."

Her parents both put down their utensils and looked up at her. Catherine began to feel uncomfortable. Did she say something wrong?

"There's something we should tell you," her mother said gently. "Kindraze was training with Annathalinda when I became pregnant with you."

"What?!" Catherine was taken aback.

Her parents nodded.

"Kindraze decided to take a break from studying to be home and help care for you. Annathalinda came to visit after your birth."

"She came to see me?" Catherine was in shock.

They nodded. "The night you were born, Annathalinda had a vision. About you."

Catherine was growing increasingly more incredulous.

"She didn't share the details of the vision but told us you were destined for great things." Her parents looked at each other, and her mother continued to speak without losing gaze with her husband, "And to never get in your way." They looked back at Catherine. "You should go."

The young elf didn't know what to say or do.

"Catherine," her mother took her hand. "We love you. We always have and always will. But you have developed a life. You are being called to something far greater than Soriana. We'll always be here when you need a rest."

Aaron's face flashed in her mind. The thought of being with him again caused her heart to flutter. But how could she leave the family she had been longing for for so long? She then thought about her reoccurring dream of running through Dovan to save Aaron's life. If that was a vision of the future, if she didn't go with Aaron, who would save him? Tears began to well in her eyes.

"I'm going to miss you," she whispered.

"Oh," her parents wrapped their arms around her, "we'll miss you too. But we'll be right here, waiting for you to come home again."

She didn't have much time. Her friends were leaving town that day by midday. She hurried to her room and gathered her things. She said her farewells and then rushed through town, making her way to the stable, praying they hadn't left yet.

"Aaron!" she shouted as she approached just in time. They had all mounted their steeds.

Aaron's crestfallen face lit up. "Catherine!"

The others turned their attention to her.

"I'm...I'm sorry." She looked into her beloved's eyes. "I want to go with you."

Aaron dismounted his horse, and he wrapped his arms around her. "There's no need to be sorry. You had to make a hard decision."

He kissed her forehead and she felt at home.

☙◦❧

They were only a day away from Fintal, where they would meet a ship to take them to the Northern Lands. Klew had sent a messenger bird ahead of them in hopes that it would speed the process.

Catherine was growing tired. If they were not in a town, there was a high likelihood they would be attacked. Aaron really did seem to be a beacon to the Ehathians.

The 10th Day of the 5th Moon of 35th Year of King Hargon

I finally found my family! My parents are alive and well. My sister...well, my sister is now the evil sorceress that captured Aaron and is terrorizing Thyla. She apparently was Annathalinda's student at one point. After my birth, Annathalinda told my parents I was destined for something great. What could that be? I'm no longer an orphan but have been my whole life. There is nothing special about me. Aaron, on the other hand, he's the Bearer of Jahola. He's on a mission to find Keelhola. Even if he fails, he's already filling the feet of one of the greats. However, he still has no idea who his parents were and why his mother had Jahola.

I thought leaving my parents after finally finding them would be harder than it has been. It helps that Aaron has encouraged me to write them letters regularly to stay in touch. Even though I can only send them once I reach a town at the same time I send Thomas and Tammy their letters, it does help. Aaron is far more understanding than I thought he would be. He will just listen when I talk about them. Really listen.

Catherine looked up at Aaron and the others. He smiled at her when he saw her looking at him. She could tell something was bothering him, but she didn't know what. It started after they left the last town two nights prior. She put her journal down and pulled some bandages from of her bag.

"You don't need to do that right now," Klew insisted.

Catherine put her hands on her hips as she approached him. "Yes, we do."

Klew pulled his left shoulder out of his robe with a grimace, revealing bandages.

Catherine knelt next to him. "It hasn't bled through, that's good." She unwrapped the injury. It was still glistening with the healing fluid his body was producing.

She took a cloth and gently dabbed the slash an Ehathian sword inflicted on her friend, then wrapped it with new dressings. "You should be healed soon."

Klew nodded a thanks and slipped his arm and shoulder back into his robe.

Catherine put the leftover cloth in her bag and sat down next to Aaron. Without hesitation, he wrapped his arm around her.

"Any word on a ship?" Clay asked.

Klew shook his head. "I wasn't expecting any, though. We'll know when we get to town."

"Midday?" Aaron asked.

Klew nodded. "If things go well, we should be on a ship and sailing the next morning."

"I've never been on the water before," Catherine added. She wondered what it would be like to be surrounded by water and on a ship. She closed her eyes and tried to imagine what it would feel like with the deck rocking back and forth beneath her feet. She had no idea what it would smell like, but she heard that it had a distinct smell. She wondered if the birds sounded different. Back in Dovan, she could identify the various types of birds by their songs, so she expected that they would sound different by the coast. Her eyes opened as she thought of Water Birds. She knew it was extremely rare to see a Water

Bird as they tended to be invisible, but the idea of the possibility excited her.

"I'll take the first watch," Aaron stated, pulling Catherine's consciousness back to the present.

Good. She could stay up a little later and talk to him about what's been bothering him.

Slowly, their companions all went to sleep.

"You should really be getting sleep," Aaron told her softly.

"Not until you tell me what's wrong," Catherine replied.

He turned his gaze from the fire to his beloved. "What do you mean?"

She looked into his eyes. He knew what she meant. "Something has been bothering you since we left town."

Aaron sighed. "I'm just not looking forward to the voyage."

"Oh? Why?"

"Bad memories."

Catherine knew that's all she would get from him. She wished he would just open up to her about his past. She understood now that she had information from her past that she wished she could ignore. But it hurt. She could be trusted, and there was no way she could help him if she didn't know what was really bothering him.

She took a breath. "If you want to talk, I'm here for you." She then made her way to her bedroll and lay down for the night.

∽•∾

"Ah, the smell of the sea," Clay said while taking a deep breath in.

"That's the smell of the sea?" Catherine asked with a scrunched nose.

Klew laughed. "That's the smell of a coastal town mixed with the sea. It's much better once you're away from shore."

Aaron didn't know why, but the smell was rather comforting.

"Let's head to the docks to see if we have a ship for tomorrow, then we'll head to the tavern to see if there are rooms for the night."

Aaron stopped walking when he heard the waves caressing the shore. In his mind, he saw his mother walking hand-in-hand with his father on the shore. She held the edge of her light blue dress just off the white sand, revealing bare feet and a shell anklet. His father's light tan, almost cream pants brushed against his bare feet and the sand.

"You coming?" Clay asked with a laugh.

Aaron nodded his head. "Yes, sorry. It's just so breathtaking." He saw Catherine look at him with a questioning look and just shook his head. She looked away. He needed to tell her. But that meant he had to admit it was real.

They continued through town towards the dock. The town was a wonderful blend of forest elves and coastal elves. The larger buildings were made of tan and brown granite, while the smaller buildings were made of wood. Some of the elves wore the traditional forestry browns and greens, while others wore the light tans and blues of the Isle Lands. The sea birds could be seen flying around, landing to peck at the ground for morsels of food. The sounds of the docks could be heard as they approached: people shouting from on deck to down below, large bells ringing, sea waves splashing against the ships, wood creaking with the waves, and ropes twisting under the weight of boxes and barrels.

The crow's nests, masts, and sails started to peek above the building tops as drew closer. Once the large ships towered over them, Aaron's attention skimmed over the various flags flapping in the wind. There was a cream flag with a grand tree in the center. Then a flag divided into red, black, green, and white bands. A bit further away was a dark blue one with a golden star on one side and golden rays extending to the other side. But one caught his eye in particular; it was a light blue with a pink conch shell in the center and golden rays extending towards the edges. He had a flashback to a large version of that flag over a large mantel, only his memory also had a gold outline of the shell.

"Where is that flag from?" Aaron asked as they passed by the ship bearing the familiar flag.

Clay smiled. "My homeland. The Isle Lands."

The Isle Lands. Is that where he was from?

They approached the walkway to the ship with the dark blue and star flag. A man with a dark blue cloak and scruffy beard stood in front of the boarding ramp.

"Hello, Rehalik," Klew said as they approached the man.

"Ah, Klew, glad you made it safely," he said with a deep voice.

"We did. These are my companions." Klew motioned to the others.

The man nodded. "Pleased to meet you. All the arrangements are set. We should be casting off right after sunrise."

Aaron heard his mother whisper to him, *We can watch the sun rise over the sea waves while casting off.*

"Perfect!" Klew turned to the group. "Let's find some rooms for the night and return here before dawn."

∂∘⊘

Catherine walked down the hall to the tavern area. Just as she thought, Aaron was still sitting at the table they had all eaten dinner at, alone. He looked up, startled, when she approached.

"I thought you were in bed for the night?" he asked.

"I did that to encourage the others to follow so I could talk to you," she said gently as she sat down next to him.

Aaron sighed and looked down at his mostly empty mug.

"What is bothering you?"

"Memories." He took a drink.

"Of what?"

"The last time I saw my parents."

Catherine wasn't sure how to respond, so she just remained quiet, hoping the silence would portray the numerous questions in her head.

Aaron sighed once again. "Do you remember how I told you my parents died when I was five?"

"Yes."

"I saw it happen." He looked into her eyes, and there was anguish.

All the muscles in her body relaxed as compassion flooded over the tension.

"We were sailing, I don't know where to, but pirates overran our ship. I'm the only survivor."

"But...how? You were five?"

Aaron shrugged and looked back down at his mug. "They took me as a slave. Why, I don't know."

"How did you get to Dovan?"

Aaron leaned back. "That's even more of a mystery. I have no memory between being on the pirate ship as a slave and wandering through the streets of Dovan, bloodied, at night. Clare found me and brought me to the orphanage."

Catherine reached out and placed her hand on his arm. "Why didn't you tell me before?"

"I didn't want it to be real. I wanted it all to be a bad nightmare that my childish imagination came up with while in the orphanage."

"How do you know you didn't?"

"More memories are coming back." Aaron looked back at his beloved. She could see pain in his eyes. "Everything here reminds me of them."

Catherine wrapped her arms around him; she let his forehead fall against her shoulder. She had always assumed Aaron didn't know what happened to his parents.

But she realized how silly it was to think that wasn't a concern either. Aaron was a half-elf living in a human city. Clearly, something traumatic must have happened to get him there, even if he couldn't remember it. She kissed the top of his head, just as he always did for her when she was upset.

He watched pirates murder his parents. The horror of those memories the trip must be bringing up for him. Catherine hugged him a little tighter.

છ૰ઙ

The dock was just as busy as the day before, even before sunrise. Catherine watched as they guided the horses up the ramp.

Rehalik approached them. "Good morning. Ready to set sail?"

"How long is the journey?" Catherine asked.

"About a half moon."

Catherine felt Aaron take her hand. She knew it was for comfort, so she squeezed it in acknowledgement. They then began to follow Rehalik up the ramp. Aaron paused at the top; Catherine paused with him.

"Not sea-sick already, are you?" Clay laughed as he patted Aaron's shoulder.

Aaron forced a laugh. "No, just getting my bearings."

Catherine's heart sank. What was this trip doing to Aaron? However, this was the trip he was wanted to go on. It's his mission. She saw the smile fade from Aaron's face as the others walked past them. That's how much this mission meant to him.

As they began to walk again, Catherine lost her footing as it felt like the ship was moving out from under her. Aaron wrapped his arms around her as she stumbled into him.

"Sorry," she said sheepishly.

Aaron smiled down at her as he helped her regain her footing. They then continued again. Walking on a ship was much harder than Catherine had expected. Aaron assisted her to the railing on the starboard side. She crossed her arms in front of her and leaned on the railing, watching the waves splash against the next ship over. The sun's rays started to peek over the horizon. It was actually quite beautiful. Aaron leaned his right side on the railing, his body facing Catherine, but his gaze was out to the water. Catherine opened her senses as more people boarded the ship and commands began to be shouted.

Finally, Aaron whispered, "We'll be casting off soon."

Catherine looked at his distant gaze and reached out to him. He turned his attention to their joined hands and squeezed.

Klew approached the two. "Have you ever been on a ship?"

Catherine shook her head. Aaron didn't respond.

"It's quite calming when out in the middle of the water." They were all quiet for a moment, then he continued, "It will be good to be home for a bit."

Catherine turned her attention to Klew. "What's it like?"

Klew smiled in a way that Catherine didn't think she had seen on his face before. "It's cold, for one." He chuckled slightly. "But the snow somehow makes things warmer. The grass and trees are green year-round. The beach is covered in black sand. A beautiful contrast to the green grass and white snow. The capital is farther inland. We will head there after landing, so that we may meet with Annathalinda."

"Do you think she can help us?" Aaron asked, still looking down at Catherine's hand in his.

"If anyone can, it's her. Besides, she's the one who told me to find you. She must know something."

A loud bell began to ring as shouts came from portside. They were casting off. Catherine looked up as they raised the sails and the wind took hold. She watched as they slowly moved through the docks and out to sea. The sun was high enough that she didn't need the lanterns that were lit, but it was still dark enough that she could watch the lights from shore slowly fade away.

Finally, Aaron sighed. "I suppose we should take a look around and get used to it here." He then turned his back to the sea and tried to pull his hand free. When Catherine didn't let go, he looked at her.

"I love you," she said softly with concern.

Aaron gave a small smile. "I love you too."

Catherine released his hand, but followed him, losing her footing a few times. Aaron was always more surefooted. They made their way across the main deck to the stairs leading to the lower levels. Catherine held tightly to the railing as they stepped downward. The first deck was the living quarters, but they continued down to where the mess deck was. Half of that deck was the dining area. There were dozens of long tables surrounded by chairs, with one side of the mess hall lined with where the prepared food would be served; the kitchens lay beyond that. The other half of the deck was the bathing area, divided into men's and women's sections.

The next deck down housed the animals. There were several stable stalls and a gated area filled with goats. Catherine paused to stroke Chestnut's neck as he shifted nervously in his stall. Aaron and she then made their way back to the stairs. Further down was off limits to passengers, so they headed back up to the living quarters deck.

"I suppose we should check out our respective areas," Aaron suggested.

Catherine nodded. It would be good to determine where she would be sleeping for the next several nights. Their rooms were across the hall from each other, so they parted ways. Catherine quietly opened the door to the room she would be staying in. It was a bunk room with about six bunk beds. One elf was already lying on her bed, fast asleep. There was a key hung by the foot of each bed that matched one of the two chests that sat on the floor at the foot of the bed. There were a couple of communal tables in the room.

Catherine found the pair of beds furthest from the door. Both keys still hung by the beds. Catherine picked the bottom bunk. Opening the associated chest, she placed all but her journal and quill inside. She went and sat down at one of the tables and began to write.

The 12th Day of the 5th Moon of the 35th Year of King Hargon

Aaron had never told me this before, but he watched his parents get murdered by pirates. That is why he's been so uneasy about the sea voyage. I know how intense my memories were, but they were nothing compared to watching your parents die a brutal death.

I'm now understanding why this mission means so much to him. It might have been the mission that killed his parents. He feels he owes it to them to finish it. I was so hard on him about it, too. I need to figure out how to make it up to him. We'll be on this ship for almost a full moon, so that should give me time to figure it out.

Despite all the emotions this trip is bringing, it is rather exciting to be on a ship. I've never traveled over water. And Klew said we should be able to meet Annathalinda! I've heard the Northern Lands are beautiful. I can't wait to see it.

CHAPTER II

❧

They had been on the ship for several days. They were all settling into their routines. Clay put his Isle Land skills to use and helped around the ship. Klew, John, and Catherine studied spells. Aaron kept to himself; he occasionally listened in on the spell casters, wondering if he'd be able to learn any, but not feeling adventurous enough to ask. He knew people were beginning to wonder what was up, but it hurt too much when bringing it up to Catherine before they left, and trying to recall happy memories of his parents was all that was keeping him from losing his mind. If he had to relive everything once again, he didn't know how he'd make it through.

Aaron leaned on the railing at the bow of the ship, watching the waves in the distance. His curiosity was piqued when he saw a splash. He turned to one of the crew. "Do you have a spyglass I could borrow?"

"Of course," the crew member went and retrieved a well-used spyglass.

Aaron focused on where he saw the splash. He didn't see any large sea creatures. The water was calm for a few moments, then suddenly a large splash happened again.

"Catherine!" Aaron quickly turned to find his beloved. He found her sitting on deck, chatting with a few women she was quickly becoming friends with. "Catherine!"

She looked up at him with curiosity. "Yes?"

"Come, you must see this!"

Without giving her much time, he grabbed her arm and pulled her back to the bow of the ship. He handed her the spyglass. "Focus out center."

Catherine did as she was told. "And?"

"Just wait." Aaron eagerly watched the water's surface. Another splash.

Catherine lowered the spyglass. "What just happened?"

"Did you see the splash?"

"Yes. But there were no creatures."

"Oh, but there were."

Catherine just looked at him with confusion.

"Water Birds."

Quickly, she lifted the spyglass back up and looked back out over the water. "How do you know?"

Aaron leaned in next to her. "The size of the splash is much too large for a fish that is not visible from this distance. And, if you watch the water as it comes back down, you can see the outline of the bird." He watched over her shoulder, waiting for another splash. He didn't have to wait long.

Catherine squealed with joy. "I did! I did see the outline!" She lowered the spyglass, flung her arms around Aaron, and kissed him.

It surprised him. He knew she would be excited, but the kiss was not expected. He smiled at her as she stepped back a bit and blushed sheepishly.

"Sorry about that." She brushed some of her hair behind her ear.

Aaron reached out and touched her cheek. "Never apologize for something like that." He leaned in for another one.

Once their lips parted again, she eagerly asked, "Can I show the others?"

He nodded. He watched as she ran to share the news. For a moment, he felt happy. But then, his mind began to wonder how he knew to look for the outline, and it probed until he remembered his mother and another female elf standing on a balcony with him. He did not know his age.

"His eyesight might not be good enough," the elf *warned.*

"Have faith," his mother reassured. "Aaron, look through the spyglass. Wait for the splash. Then you'll see it."

His mother had to help him hold the spyglass up, but he waited patiently. Then he saw the splash, and the water fell around the beautiful outline of a large bird. It almost seemed to shimmer behind the water.

"I saw it!" the young half-elf exclaimed excitedly.

His mother wrapped her arms around him. "Maybe one day they'll grace you with their full display of beauty."

Aaron swallowed hard as he held back tears. But he couldn't help but smile as Catherine brought with her Klew, Clay, John, and a handful of other passengers. Aaron began to walk past them, but someone touched his shoulder. He turned.

"Let's have a chat," Clay said as he motioned off to the side.

Aaron didn't know what spurred this, but knew it was coming at some point. The two walked off to the right, far enough away from the crowd that they wouldn't be heard.

"How did you know that?" Clay asked.

That was not the question Aaron was expecting. "Know what?"

"That you can see the Water Birds in their splash. Dovan is not on the coast."

Aaron glanced out to the water. "My family is from the coast."

"You know where your family is from?"

Aaron shook his head and looked down at the deck. "Not exactly. I just have memories of beaches and coasts and ships." He looked up at Clay. "I remember my mom showing me how to identify a Water Bird splash."

"What do you remember? Maybe I can help you."

Aaron's heart skipped a beat. His parents were no longer alive, but maybe he had other relatives. He twisted his ring. Maybe one of them knew more. "White, fine sand. There was a dock in the city. I feel like our house oversaw the water, or at least I frequented somewhere that did. My mother regularly wore light blue dresses." He paused. "Much like your shirt."

Clay's head tilted very slightly. "Did your mother wear shells?"

"An anklet."

A smile came across the elf's face. "I think you're from the Isle Lands. We should go there after we visit Anna-thalinda."

Aaron's hope rose, then fell. "What good would that do? How would I find anyone?"

"I have connections. Besides, with your mother having borne Jahola, she must have been important."

Aaron looked down at his mother's ring.

"Now that we have that mystery solved, on to the next."

The half-elf looked at Clay, puzzled.

"Why have you been avoiding everyone?"

"Oh." He cast his gaze downward.

Clay raised an eyebrow.

"I just...I don't have fond memories of sailing."

That seemed to confuse Clay. "What do you mean?"

Aaron looked back out to the sea. "My parents were killed by pirates."

"Pirates?" There was almost a shake in Clay's voice.

Aaron looked at him. His emotions shifted to worry. "Yes. Why?"

Clay shook his head. "No reason. I just...My betrothed has family who were lost at sea, and they believed it to be pirates as they found the ship adrift. No one survived."

"Unfortunately, I'm sure many are lost to pirates." Despite what he said, Aaron wasn't sure if he believed the statement or what it might indicate for his family.

Clay nodded, then turned to join the others. Aaron watched as he spoke to Klew. Aaron shifted and pretended not to notice when Klew glanced in his direction. He then turned his attention back out to the water, leaning on his arms folded in front of him. After a few moments, someone wrapped their arms around him from behind. He turned to see Catherine embracing him.

"Thank you," she said.

He kissed the top of her head. "Of course."

❧❧

Aaron lay on his bed, feeling the ship rock back and forth beneath him. They were halfway through the journey. He was starting to come to terms with his memories. He was considering talking to Klew and John about teaching him some spells, if he could learn. The pain was still there, but he just felt like he could ignore it for a bit. It helped watching Catherine enjoy her time. She had changed since finding her parents. There was a glow about her that he had never noticed before. He liked it.

He closed his eyes, focused on the rocking, and slowly drifted to sleep.

He was startled awake, unsure of how long he'd been asleep.

Clay held his arm. "Get up and grab your weapons."

Aaron flung his feet over the edge of the bed and hopped down. "What's going on?" He pulled on his boots, opened his chest, and pulled out his daggers.

"Pirates."

Aaron's heart stopped, and he froze for a moment. Clay did not appear to notice the faltering and turned to leave. Aaron realized he was supposed to follow and did. They made their way through the bunk room; others were also preparing to fight, while a few cowered in the back of the room. Aaron paused briefly when he saw a father comforting a young boy. He was not going to let history repeat itself. They made their way to the deck.

Aaron stood, frozen in fear, as an all too familiar pirate, although significantly older than he remembered him, strode toward him with a cutlass in hand and a snarl on his face. Aaron drew his daggers; he barely noticed the commotion around him of the other pirates fighting with his friends and crew.

The old pirate spat on the deck. "You look familiar."

Aaron had to hold back all the vulgar things he wanted to call this man.

"Funny. I don't usually leave survivors." The pirate's eyes lit up. "Oh yeah. You're the boy we took prisoner."

Aaron lunged forward and swung his blades.

Captain Alik caught the blades with his cutlass. "I knew we should have killed you on the spot."

"That mistake will be your downfall." Aaron kept his left blade locked with the cutlass but slid his right blade out and cut the pirate's arm.

The older man took a step back, growled, and then lunged at Aaron.

The half-elf stopped the cutlass with his left blade and swung his right but missed.

Captain Alik laughed. "Time I fix my one mistake: leaving a survivor."

Their blades clashed again and again. The sound of metal on metal slowly faded, and Aaron began to hear almost nothing but his own breathing. His jaw was tight, with his mouth tied in a grimace. The pirate slashed his arm, but he did not feel a thing; he just kept swinging his blades. Memories of the pirate killing his parents and so many others flashed in his mind.

Aaron stopped the pirate's overhand swing with crossed daggers above his head. He quickly straightened his weapons, causing the pirate's sword to twist out of his hand.

With a grunt, Captain Alik thrust his heel forward into Aaron's leg, causing the half-elf to fall to the ground. Aaron let go of one of his daggers as he hit the deck but maintained grip on the one in his right hand. The pirate pulled out a knife from his belt and drove it into Aaron's left shoulder, just missing his chest due to Aaron attempting to roll to the side. That injury hurt. The half-elf gave a cry of pain, but it didn't stop him. Aaron could have sworn the world grew a reddish tint as he cut through the pirate's upper wrist, causing Captain Alik to release the knife. Aaron quickly shifted his dagger to his left hand and pulled the knife out of his shoulder with a grunted cry of pain. Without much more thought, Aaron kicked the feet out from under the pirate and slammed the blade of the knife into the pirate's hand, pinning it to the deck.

Captain Alik screamed in pain. Aaron stood over him.

"It was your biggest mistake." Aaron then thrust his dagger into the pirate's chest and pulled it back out.

The pirate's eyes grew wide with the impact; he gasped and then went still.

Aaron dropped his dagger. Captain Alik was dead. Aaron had killed him. He killed a man. People began shouting new things all around him, but he didn't hear a word. He just stood in place, staring at the person he killed.

Aaron did not snap out of it until someone was pulling him away. He suddenly realized that the person had their hands on his shoulders and was guiding him away. He looked over his right shoulder to see Clay. He then realized that there had been a fight other than his and Captain Alik's happening and looked around. The other pirates were fleeing. People were cheering for Aaron. Yet it felt wrong.

"Aaron!" Catherine cried as she ran to her beloved's side.

The half-elf suddenly became very aware of how injured he was, and the pain began to creep into his body.

The world spun slightly as Catherine and Clay sat him down. He winced as Clay put pressure on his shoulder.

Catherine held Aaron's hand tightly in hers. He felt a gentle warmth flow from her hand to his and slowly spread throughout his body, concentrating on his injuries. Slowly, the pain began to subside. He looked in Catherine's eyes. There was nothing but love and compassion in her eyes.

"I killed him," Aaron whispered, unsure of what else to say.

Catherine's expression dropped. She looked up at Clay.

Clay knelt. "That's a good thing."

Aaron shook his head.

"He's taken hundreds of lives. Who knows how many more he would have taken if you hadn't killed him."

Aaron looked at Clay.

"He would have killed you. You had no choice."

Aaron turned his gaze to the deck boards between his feet. Clay said something to Catherine, but he did not hear what it was. He had defeated dozens of Ehathians, but this was different. There was a body. There was a soul that left the plane. He snapped out of his numbness when he felt Catherine twisting his ring. He squeezed her hand.

Catherine looked up from his ring and into his eyes. "Was he the one who killed your parents?" Her question was gentle.

Aaron nodded.

She let go of his hands and wrapped her arms around him. He held her close. Somehow avenging his parents' deaths wasn't as satisfying as he thought it would be.

Clay, Klew, John, and the captain eventually came over. John and Klew hung back a bit, turning people away who tried to come over.

The captain walked straight up to Aaron. "We owe you a huge thanks."

Aaron didn't say a thing but looked at him.

"That pirate has been terrorizing the sea for decades." He paused for a moment. "He doesn't leave survivors."

Aaron looked away quickly, knowing the truth.

"Something caused him to misstep, and you took advantage of it. Thank you. We probably all owe you our lives."

Aaron looked back up at the captain and remembered the kids below deck. They were not on a battleship or a cargo ship. They were on a passenger vessel. His family's vessel was also a passenger vessel. "What did he want?"

"Excuse me?"

Aaron glanced around. "This...this is a passenger vessel. What did he want?"

The captain sighed. "No one knows, but it's his style. He targets passenger vessels and kills everyone aboard then either burns the ship or sets it adrift."

Aaron turned his attention to the fleeing pirate ship and wondered if anyone would pick up where Captain Alik left off or if they would retire.

The captain offered to let Aaron stay in his quarters that night to avoid the commotion, but Aaron politely refused. He saw people whispering and looking at him when he walked into new areas of the ship. Clay stayed by his side.

Once in the bunkroom, the small boy, who had been comforted by his father when the ordeal started, timidly came up to Aaron. "Excuse me," he said softly.

"Yes?" Aaron looked down into the young eyes.

"Thank you for saving us."

Aaron's mind was transported back to when he was this boy's age, and he stood on a deck of death for a moment. When his mind returned, he knelt by the child and hugged him. Aaron had to hold back tears. This child did not have to go through what he did. Maybe it was worth it.

∂∾ᔆ

The 30th Day of the 5th Moon of the 35th Year of King Hargon

It's so dark at sea when there is no moon, but I kind of like it. There's something soothing about the waves rocking the ship back and forth while watching the stars dance in the sky. It almost makes me forget about everything that has happened.

Pirates attacked the ship. Not just any pirates. The pirates who murdered Aaron's family. Aaron killed the captain. In honesty, he saved our lives, but he does not always see it that way. He's taken it hard. I don't blame him. I've never taken someone's life. But I had just assumed, with how many battles he had been in, that this wouldn't have been a big deal. I'm trying to support him as much as possible.

We were told we would make land in a couple of days. It will be good to be on land again, but I have quite enjoyed this trip. Other than the attack, it's felt like all my worries were left on shore. Hopefully, they don't all come flooding back the moment I get off the ship.

Catherine placed her journal back in her bag and lay down. She closed her eyes and focused on the gentle swaying of the ship. Soon, she drifted off to dreamland where she stood in a small room, looking at herself in a mirror. *She wore a white and gold dress and a gold circlet on her head. The dress opened wide at the floor, trailing behind her slightly. The sleeves were golden and clung tight until her elbows, where they draped down loosely, revealing white underneath. The corset of the dress was gold, with intricate flower designs. The golden fabric continued past her waist and opened to reveal a white underskirt. The gold circlet was composed of three intertwining lines that dipped down to a point at her forehead, with a clear crystal that seemed to catch every color of the rainbow hanging down.*

A female elf with curly, dirty-blond hair walked in. "You look gorgeous."

Catherine turned. "Thank you."

"Are you ready?"

Catherine woke. She felt happy. She got up, dressed herself, and met the others in the mess hall.

"My, don't you look happy," Klew remarked.

"I had a good dream," Catherine informed.

"About what?" Aaron glanced up from his food.

She frowned. "I actually don't know. But all I know is I was exceptionally happy."

"I'd love some exceptionally happy times myself," John added.

They all mumbled their agreements.

As they were finishing their breakfast, Catherine looked up at Aaron. "Want to learn a spell today?"

Aaron almost spit out his drink. "What?"

"Want to learn a spell today?" she repeated herself matter-of-factly.

"I..." Aaron stumbled through his thoughts. "I don't know if I can."

"Let's try."

They made their way to the deck and found a secluded area. Catherine sat down on the deck, cross-legged. Aaron followed in suit.

"Hold out your hands," she commanded.

Aaron opened his palms in front of him, resting the backs of his hands on his knees.

Catherine hovered her hands over his and closed her eyes. She envisioned a star forming between their hands as she grasped at a small warmth in her chest and drew it through her arms and to her hands. When she opened her eyes, there was a light between each of their hands.

"Do you feel that warmth?" she asked.

Aaron nodded. She could tell he was focused as he didn't make eye contact and just stared at their hands.

"Grab it with your mind. Feel the warmth enter your hands and up your arms and to your heart."

The half-elf closed his eyes. Catherine watched him carefully, then closed her eyes as well. They sat there in silence for a while. Catherine peeked every once and a while, but only saw Aaron with his eyes closed, brow cutely furrowed. The sun was growing warm as it rose higher in the sky.

The young elf jolted her eyes open as she felt a tug at her magical light. The light was flickering. She watched as it dimmed with the tugs. Finally, as the sun was hitting its high for the day, she felt a drawn out pull, the lights dimmed slightly, and Aaron snapped his eyes open. The lights began to grow again, and the tug ceased.

Catherine smirked slightly. "How'd that feel?"

Aaron's shock melted away, and he began to smile. "Good."

"You have magic running through your veins." Catherine released the chain of warmth, ending the lights, and pulled her hands back.

Aaron turned his hands over and rubbed them gently against his legs.

"Let's pause for now and get our midday meal."

The elf could see pure joy on her beloved's face. He can cast spells.

As they ate, their companions asked how it went. Aaron could not stop talking about how it felt. He was ecstatic.

When there was a pause in the conversation, Klew caught Catherine off guard. "How did it feel for you?"

"What?" Catherine was not expecting someone to address her in the conversation.

"This is the first time you've had someone draw from you, correct?"

She thought about that. She had added to others when healing at times, but no one had ever drawn from her. "I suppose you're right. It...it felt like something was tugging at the magic. I noticed the lights grow dimmer."

Klew nodded. "It does require more magic to maintain the same level of spell when someone is drawing from your power." He turned back to Aaron. "How far did you draw it?"

Aaron looked down. "Only to my elbows."

The table grew silent.

Aaron looked back up at everyone, confused. "Is that...bad?"

"No!" Klew broke the silence. "That's excellent. Honestly, most would only get it to their wrists after a few days of trying. You have some powerful magic in you."

"He is, well..." John glanced around, "You know."

They all knew. They did their best to keep Aaron being the Bearer of Jahola a secret. They didn't want unnecessary attention.

After their meal, Aaron was eager to continue practicing, and Catherine was keen to continue teaching.

Their previous spot had been taken by a family playing a game, so they found another secluded spot. They sat back down in the way they were before. Aaron placed his hands on his knees, palms up, and Catherine hovered her hands over his, summoning the lights. Almost instantly, there was a slight tug. She smiled to herself and closed her eyes.

Soon, the tug became a background feeling, and her mind began to wander. She wondered what the Northern Lands would look like especially with the snow from it being winter. The already cold air had been getting colder even with the sun high in the sky. She wondered about her dream the night before. What had she been getting ready for? All she knew was she was happier than she had ever been.

Suddenly, the warmth in her heart exploded, and her thoughts were ripped from her mind. All she could see was light but heard the clashes of war from all around her. Just as quickly as it had come, the vision ended. She quickly opened her eyes and found herself gasping for breath. Her heart still felt an extreme heat, but she had ended the spell in shock. She realized her hands were no longer above Aaron's; they were holding onto his. There was a tingle there, though. She looked at Aaron. He was breathing heavily as well.

"Was that..." he struggled to catch his breath, "normal?"

"I don't think so," Catherine admitted.

They both sat in silence for a while, calming their breaths. Catherine looked back down at their hands. They still tingled.

"What happened?" she finally asked.

"How am I supposed to know?"

Catherine released Aaron's hands and drew hers back to her lap. The tingling stopped. "I was just thinking about my dream, then suddenly all I saw was a bright light and heard the sounds of fighting."

"I saw the same thing. Only, I was pulling the warmth like you instructed, and right when it reached my heart that's when everything happened." He looked down at Jahola. "And my ring got exceptionally hot."

"I think we need to talk to Klew. No one has ever mentioned seeing joint visions when doing this. It didn't happen when I would draw from others either."

Aaron stood and reached out to help Catherine stand. She hesitated in taking his hand, but nothing happened when she did. No visions. No tingling sensations. Just her beloved's hand. They made their way around the ship, looking for their allies. It wasn't until close to dinner that they found Klew and Clay near the helm.

"How is the training going?" Clay asked with a smile as they approached.

"We have some questions," Catherine stated simply.

His smile faded. "Let's find somewhere we can talk."

The four of them found a secluded area.

"What do you want to discuss?" Clay asked.

Catherine suddenly realized she had not let go of Aaron's hand since he helped her stand, but she wasn't about to let it go. "Something happened while we were training." She looked up at Aaron, and he looked down at her. "We had a joint vision." She looked back at the other two.

"What do you mean?" Klew inquired.

"Once I drew the magic to my heart," Aaron explained, "we both had a vision of white with the sounds of fighting."

"That's rather...unusual. Anything else?"

"It felt like all the air had been removed from my lungs," Catherine added.

"Same," Aaron replied.

Klew and Clay looked at each other. Catherine couldn't tell what they were thinking.

Suddenly, Clay's brow furrowed, and he looked at Aaron. "Did you say you brought the magic to your heart?"

Aaron nodded.

"Already?"

The half-elf shrugged.

"Did you do it a second time?" Klew asked, ignoring his companion's confusion.

The couple shook their heads.

"That's where we'll start. Honestly, I've never heard of this happening. We may need to discuss this with Annathalinda as well. But we can start doing some testing to see if we can recreate it."

Catherine felt Aaron squeeze her hand. Hopefully Annathalinda had all their answers.

᷒᷒᷒

Catherine leaned over a railing as the coast slowly approached. Storm clouds loomed overhead, and a cold wind blew. She was impressed at how beautiful the blue waves caressing a black beach were. She pulled her cloak tight against her arms. Crew members were bustling about, preparing the sails for docking. Aaron came up behind her and wrapped an arm around her waist. She leaned into his embrace.

The sounds of the dock grew louder as they drew closer. The buildings were all made of dark stone and hardwood. There were not nearly as many ships as at the wharf in Fintal. Soon sailors started shouting down to the dock workers, and ropes were being tossed down. The ship came to a halt, and boarding planks were hoisted.

Passengers began to gather at the planks, but Catherine and Aaron hung back, waiting for their companions. Once Klew, Clay, and John approached, Aaron removed his arm from around Catherine's waist and offered her his hand. She paused, her hand floating just above his, remembering the day before.

"It hasn't happened since," Aaron whispered, seeming to know exactly what she was thinking.

She took his hand and, as he promised, nothing happened. They approached their friends, made their way down the planks, and gathered where they would retrieve their horses.

"The capital is only three day's travel from here," Klew informed. He glanced at the sky. "But if the weather does not favor us, it could take longer."

"We will gather supplies and head out in the morning," Clay announced.

Once they had their horses, they began making their way down a road that followed the coast. At one point, Klew stopped, tapped Clay's arm with the back of his hand, and pointed at a ship that was separated from the others. Catherine saw the blue flag with a pink conch shell outlined in gold with golden rays extending towards the edges.

Clay straightened up. "What is she doing here?" Catherine caught a hint of excitement in his voice.

"What is who doing here?" she asked.

"My betrothed."

"You know, you don't talk about her much." Catherine pointed out.

He smiled. "She doesn't like me to brag."

"Are you going to try to meet her before we leave for the capital?"

"Oh, she's most likely already at the capital," Klew answered for his friend.

"Then we shall finally meet this mysterious betrothed." Catherine smiled. Something happy to look forward to.

They continued on their way to the inn. In a very short amount of time, it became apparent that Klew knew most of the people in the town. That night it began to snow, which Catherine wasn't surprised about since it was winter in a land that gets year-round snow.

After they ate dinner, Catherine stood outside, watching the snow fall. Eventually, Aaron joined her. They were the only ones out there.

After some moments of silence, Aaron softly said, "Klew wants us to try to recreate it tomorrow night. Once we're out of town."

"Do you think it will happen again?"

He shrugged. "I have no idea. I've never done this before."

"I suppose we should get some rest then."

Aaron nodded. They brushed the snow off their cloaks and headed inside for the night.

⊱⊰

They sat around the fire; the snow had calmed to just a flurry. They hadn't traveled as far as they would have liked due to the weather, but Klew said they were making good progress and so far weren't even a day behind schedule.

Catherine gently took Aaron's hand.

He looked up at her and said, "I suppose we should try now."

She nodded. They turned towards each other. Aaron held his hands face up in front of him. Catherine hovered her hands above his. Aaron watched as she closed her eyes, then felt a warmth in his hands. He looked down, and there was a slight glow between them. He silently sighed and closed his eyes.

He imagined a channel going from his heart, through his chest, through his arm, and to his hands. He had to push to the point that it almost physically hurt. When the channel finally reached his palms, he envisioned a soft light starting to fill the channel, and he felt a warmth creeping into his blood. He tugged and pulled at the light, dragging it through the channel he had created. He knew the air was cold but felt a few droplets of sweat on his brow. He had to fight the urge to wipe them away. The distraction cost him some progress. He refocused his mind on pulling the light and warmth through the channel and towards his heart. He lost track of time, but once the light reached his shoulders, he felt like giving up. How had he done this before? But he knew he couldn't stop. They needed to know what would happen when he succeeded. He took a deep breath, trying to relax his muscles slightly. The light retreated a bit, and then he pulled on it once more.

He wasn't sure if it was only a few moments that felt like eternity, or if it truly had been eternity, but the light and warmth were intense and right by his heart. He paused. He opened his eyes and saw Catherine across from him. Her eyes were closed, and she looked calm. Without closing his eyes, he gave one final tug on the light, and he felt the heat overtake his heart. In that same instance, a blinding light overtook his vision. All of the air was pushed out of his lungs as if his chest was crushed. Wings. He saw a faint image of large, feathered wings. Just as suddenly as it had all started, Aaron was thrust back to their camp and his vision returned.

Once again, Catherine's hands were clutching his, as if clinging on for life. They both were panting and struggling to breathe. Catherine's eyes met his. She looked scared. His ring burned to the point he wanted to take it off, but he did not want to let Catherine's hands go.

"Are you both okay?" Klew asked.

They turned their attention to their companions. Both nodded.

"Did it happen again?"

Aaron looked at Catherine, and she looked at him. She saw something different too.

CHAPTER 12

*T*he 4th Day of the 6th Moon of the 35th Year of King Hargon

Last night, Aaron and I practiced magic again and had visions. The last time, we both saw only white and heard fighting, but this time we saw different things. He saw large, feathered wings. I saw what looked like a hammer striking an anvil. I hope Annathalinda can tell us what this means. None of us know what it could mean.

Aaron and Klew tried sharing their magic tonight, but Aaron was unable to bring it to his heart.

Klew said even though the snow has been slowing us down, we're only about half a day behind, so we should still reach the capital tomorrow night. He's sent word ahead. Hopefully we can have an audience with Annathalinda the next day.

The next day, Catherine was thankful for Chestnut. The snow, although lightly falling, had piled high overnight. Thankfully, they had acquired tents for the journey. It snowed in Bellmora, but never this much. The most she had seen was ankle-deep and by midday most of it would melt away. As they traveled, the snow was up to their horses' knees, and the snow continued to fall even into midday. Catherine could tell Aaron was just as concerned as she was about the visions they were having. What could they mean? Why were they having them?

The sun was setting when they reached the capital. The capital was surrounded by farms growing hardy plants such as pumpkins and squash. The palace slowly came into view. If Catherine had not been riding Chestnut, she would have halted in her tracks. Somehow, it was more beautiful than she had imagined. It was not made of ice like she had imagined, but glass. The setting sun's rays glistened off the glass walls. The stone path led through the city and towards the palace. There was a glass passageway leading towards the front gates. The center of the palace towered above the edges. Dozens of towers climbed high as they drew closer. They were still a distance off once they reached the inn, but Catherine could tell the frame was made of a white metal. She couldn't wait to get closer to it the next day. The glass almost looked like ice.

After they ate, but before parting ways for the night, John asked, "Should we go over what we need to discuss with Annathalinda?"

"These visions stemming from Aaron's magic," Klew stated.

"How do we know it's Aaron's magic?" John questioned.

"What do you mean?"

Catherine perked up with curiosity.

"Catherine could be the cause of it," the wizard suggested.

"But she's drawn from us before without anything happening."

"But we've never drawn from her."

Catherine suddenly became uneasy as everyone turned to at her.

"Would you be up for trying?" Klew asked her.

Aaron placed his hand on her shoulder. She nodded. Everyone was quiet for a moment.

Aaron slowly removed his hand from Catherine's shoulder and broke the silence, "Keelhola."

They all nodded.

"Why everything seems to be out to get me," the half-elf added.

They were all quiet for a few moments, then softly Catherine said, "My sister."

"You think Annathalinda might know something about what happened?" Aaron asked gently.

Catherine looked down at her mostly empty wine glass. "She knew Kindy. She was Kindy's teacher."

Aaron touched her wrist, and she looked up at him. Concern covered his face, and she realized she had tears in her eyes.

"We'll find out what happened." He spoke softly. "I promise."

҈∞҈

Aaron was nervous. Annathalinda had sent Klew to find him. His mother's ring was Jahola. Catherine's sister was the one who kidnapped her and captured him and had been trained by Annathalinda. Something weird was going on with his magic. When Klew drew magic from Catherine, nothing happened.

The snow was only in small piles at the edges of the streets. It melted quickly upon hitting the road. Aaron barely noticed the town going by as they approached the palace. But eventually, he couldn't ignore the towering structure. The walls were made of crystal-like glass with many angles. The entry to the glass archway leading to the main gate featured a stained glass, round emblem of dark blue with a golden star on the left and golden rays extending to the right. Once they were under the arch, the temperature increased, and Aaron instinctively loosened his grip on his cloak.

White stone ramparts surrounded the base of the palace. As they walked through the gate, Aaron was forced to squint as the sun glistened off the palace walls. The moment they entered, Aaron felt warm. So warm, he wanted to take off his cloak. As they continued in, he noticed that not all the glass was clear. Some of the panels were vibrantly colored images depicting elves of the past. The inner walls and floor were made of white stone. The doors of redwood. The floor had a deep blue runner rug with red edges leading through each pathway.

Klew guided them through the outer edge of the palace. Finally, they reached large double doors with guards standing on either side. The guards wore black pants, red tunics, and light mail. One had a sword at his side; the other held a redwood staff, it was simpler than Klew's.

Klew spoke to the guards, but Aaron didn't listen; he was examining the carving on the doors. It was of a female elf, in a flowy dress with both arms extended outward. She was looking up, and there were flames in each hand. Her hair and skirt were being tousled as if a wind was billowing through. The doors suddenly opened, and Aaron flinched slightly with surprise.

The room was a grand hall with a raised area at one end. There were two large tables on either side of the raised area with a row of chairs facing the rest of the room. Tapestries hung on both sides of the room. The runner rug led straight down the middle of the room to a large redwood chair, where a regal elf sat. She had fiery red hair and wore a red robe with blue borders. She was leaning to one side, resting her chin on a closed fist, speaking to an elf standing just to the side of her. The other elf had curly, dirty blond hair and wore a light blue dress. Her back was turned to the entryway.

Aaron couldn't move for a moment. There she was. Annathalinda. Her hair was just as red as people described. Yet, something about her seemed soft. He had heard so many legends about her visions and spell-casting abilities. If they were true, then she had ended a war by calling down stars from the sky onto the battlefield. But as he looked at her, he saw a furrowed brow. He saw fine lines around her eyes and mouth.

The half-elf started when someone placed their hand on his back and guided him forward. It was Clay. The five approached. Annathalinda's green eyes shifted to Aaron, and she sat up straight. The elf standing next to her turned around, catching Aaron's eyes. They made eye contact.

A flood of memories enveloped his mind. He remembered this elf picking him up when he was just a boy. He remembered her teaching him to skip stones across the sea. He remembered sleeping on the beach as she told him legends of the stars.

"Emma." Aaron was unsure of how loud he spoke, but he was compelled to.

"A-" the elf swallowed. "Aaron?" Tears were welling up in her eyes. "Is it..."

Aaron felt his heart drop to his stomach. He nodded. Emma ran down the steps and embraced Aaron, crying. He began to cry as well. He never thought he would see family again. But there she was.

Finally, their tears subsided, and they pulled back from each other. Emma began to laugh slightly. The two of them looked over as Clay approached and placed his hand on Emma's shoulder.

"Emmyana?" Clay simply said her name.

"Aaron!" Emma shook the half-elf's arms in excitement. "Aaron's alive!"

Clay's eyes widened, and he looked back at Aaron. "I thought..."

"They never found his body! I had lost hope! But..." she looked back at Aaron, laughing through tears, "but here he is." She cupped the side of his face with her hand.

"Aaron?" Catherine asked softly.

He turned to her and reached out an arm, pulling her closer. "Catherine, this is Emma. My cousin."

"Your cousin?" Klew asked.

Emma and Aaron nodded.

"But your aunt and uncle were..." Klew's eyes widened.

John gasped and fell to one knee. Clay elbowed him, and he stood again.

Aaron furrowed his brow and looked at Emma. "What was that about?"

The corners of Emma's mouth dropped. "Do you not remember?"

He shook his head.

"Your parents were the king and queen of the Isle Lands. You're the heir to the throne."

Suddenly, Aaron felt faint. He was not expecting to hear that. No memories were flooding his mind. The world around him began to disconnect. It didn't feel real. There was some fussing going on around him, but he just focused on staying conscious and trying to decipher all the thoughts rushing through his head. He had family. He knew where he was from. He knew his past. His parents were royalty. He's a prince. Does this mean he has to rule the Isle Lands? He's not fit to do that. He knows nothing about the Isle Lands. He knows nothing about ruling a kingdom. He grew dizzier and placed a hand on his forehead.

He felt gentle hands on his arms, softly pushing him down. He obeyed the guidance, not feeling sure enough to fight much of anything. He found himself guided to a chair. So many thoughts and questions still swirled in his mind.

Finally, his thoughts began to calm down and drew him back to his immediate surroundings, when he heard Catherine saying his name. His vision began to come into focus and he saw Catherine, Emma, Clay, and Klew crouched around him.

"Aaron?" Catherine repeated.

He nodded.

"Are you okay?"

He didn't know how to answer that. He just looked at Emma and asked, "I'm a prince?"

Emma nodded. "I'm sorry. I thought you knew. I didn't mean to take you by surprise like that."

"I don't remember much. Honestly, I didn't remember you until I saw you." Aaron saw sadness cross his cousin's face. "I have so many questions."

An unfamiliar voice came from behind his friends, "I don't mean to be rude."

Everyone turned to look at Annathalinda, who had risen from her chair and was standing not too far away.

"Mind filling me in?" she asked with a small smirk.

"Did you know?!" Emma asked.

Annathalinda raised her hands in defense. "I did not know he was alive. I just knew someone from Dovan needed to meet you."

"Dovan?" Emma looked back at Aaron. "That's where you've been this whole time?"

Aaron nodded.

"So," Annathalinda exclaimed, "it seems as though Aaron needs to fill us in on some missing history. What we know is that he was on a voyage with his parents. Somewhere along the path they were ambushed, and everyone but Aaron was killed. And now he is here with us."

"I only have bits and pieces of my memory," Aaron admitted.

"That is fine. Just tell us what you know."

Aaron told them how Captain Alik took him prisoner, but he didn't remember much from his time on the pirate ship. Then his memory skips to the outskirts of Dovan, where he was placed in an orphanage and adopted by Thomas and Tammy. He admitted that most of his memory had been coming back during the journey with Klew.

A serious look came over Annathalinda's face. "Do you have it?"

Aaron knew what she was asking and took off his mother's ring and handed it to her. "My mother gave this to me shortly before she was killed."

"Wait, your family are the keepers of Jahola?" Clay asked with sudden realization as he turned to Emma.

"They were sworn to secrecy," Annathalinda stated as she took the ring and looked at it closely. "When I heard the ring was not found, I was so worried it had fallen into the wrong hands." She looked at Aaron and smiled. "Your mother knew it would keep you safe." She handed it back to Aaron, who quickly slipped it back on his finger. "Now, I know there is much to talk about, let's move somewhere more comfortable. Are you okay with walking?"

Aaron felt embarrassed but nodded. He rose to his feet and followed Annathalinda as she guided them out a side door. It led to the interior of the building, with solid white stone walls. They then entered a room with a large, round, redwood table, surrounded by chairs. Annathalinda motioned for all of them to join her around the table as she went to the far end. Catherine sat down next to Aaron and took his hand under the table. He appreciated the silent support.

"Aaron. You and Emma have much to talk about, but we will not address that here." She skimmed over the party, then paused when she looked at Catherine. Some of the color of her face faded away. "Who might you be?"

"Oh," Catherine fidgeted in her seat. "My name is Catherine."

The redheaded elf looked like she had seen a ghost. "I feared she killed you."

Aaron squeezed his beloved's hand.

"I...She abandoned me in Dovan."

Annathalinda seemed to compose herself quickly as color began to fill her face again. "Dovan?" She glanced at Aaron, then back at Catherine. "I'm assuming that's how you two met?"

They nodded.

"We...I actually had questions about it," Catherine said timidly.

Annathalinda sighed. "I really wish I had the answers, but I don't. I have no idea what happened to your sister. I have no idea why she kidnapped you. And I especially don't know why she would abandon you in Dovan."

"My parents said you had a vision about me."

Annathalinda spoke tenderly. "It was less of a vision and more of a feeling. When I met you, as a baby, there was a presence about you. There still is." She glanced at Aaron. "Much like what I feel with him." She looked back at

Catherine. "I don't know how you play into all of this, but you are destined for great things."

"What do you mean 'play into all of this?'" Klew questioned.

Annathalinda sighed and leaned back in her chair. "There is evil stirring through the realm. I've heard many rumors and had some visions. I do not know all the details, but I fear there will be attacks from multiple angles." She looked at Aaron and Catherine. "You two are key, though. I have a mission for you, but I want to help you first." She turned to Klew and leaned forward onto her arms with her fingers intertwined. "You said you had many things to discuss."

"What?" Aaron interjected, trying to wrap his head around everything that was said. "You're just going to change the topic like that?"

She made eye contact with Aaron and simply said, "Yes."

"You can't just say that we're key to something and then change the subject."

"I just did, didn't I?"

"And I'm not letting you do that." Aaron felt Catherine squeeze his hand; it was an attempt to calm him down.

Annathalinda smirked a little. "I like you. You have a fire in your soul." The smirk faded slightly. "Like your mother. Granted, you also seem to have inherited your father's stubbornness. That may come in handy. But for right now, I'm going to out-stubborn you. I promise we will discuss what I said further. I would like to address all of your other concerns first. Who knows, they may be connected."

Aaron saw a sternness in her eyes. He wasn't going to win the argument.

Annathalinda, satisfied with the silence from Aaron, turned back to Klew, "What do we need to discuss?"

"Honestly, it's about these two," he motioned to Aaron and Catherine.

"Mhmm."

"When Aaron was at Thyla, all the Ehathians seemed to target him."

Annathalinda furrowed her brow. "Interesting. I wonder if they sense Jahola. Fascinating. Next?"

"Uh....you didn't answer anything," Aaron pointed out.

"I don't have an answer to that just yet. I need to look into it more and possibly go to Ehath with you."

Her statement took Aaron aback. She'd travel with them?

"Next."

"We've been trying to teach Aaron spells, but a peculiar thing has been happening when he connects with Catherine."

Annathalinda perked up.

"Once the magic from Catherine reaches his heart, they both have visions."

She turned back to Aaron and Catherine. "Does this happen at any other time?"

"The only time it happens to me is with Aaron," Catherine answered.

Aaron shook his head. "I've only ever successfully done it with Catherine, so I do not know."

Annathalinda stood, walked over to Catherine, and held out her hands. "Draw from me."

Catherine's eyes widened, but she obeyed. Aaron watched a red light glow between their hands. Catherine closed her eyes, while Annathalinda watched her carefully.

After several moments, Annathalinda said, "Release it."

Catherine relaxed her shoulders and opened her eyes. The red light vanished.

"Let me draw from you."

The young elf shifted in her seat, then opened her hands, palm up, and created a much dimmer white light.

She closed her eyes. Annathalinda placed her hands above Catherine's and once again kept her eyes open.

After what felt like the blink of an eye, Annathalinda removed her hands and said, "Thank you." She turned to Aaron. "Your turn. Let's start with the easier one, draw from me." She opened her hands in front of her and created the same red orbs.

Aaron wiped his hands on his pants, hoping no one noticed the sweat, hovered his hands above hers, and looked her in the eyes. He read no emotions. He sighed deeply and closed his eyes. The warmth he felt was much hotter and stronger than Catherine's or Klew's. He slowly carved the channel from his heart to his hands, then began to draw the red light through it. Annthalinda's magic seemed to flow much easier. It was smoother and faster. He didn't have to strain nearly as much; although, he did have to strain some.

Aaron felt it was taking an embarrassing amount of time compared to Annathalinda and Catherine. He had to remind himself that he was new to this. Then he began to wonder if he would succeed. His power faltered. His doubt began to take over his ability, and he was losing grip on the magic. Suddenly, Annthalinda's magic pushed forward without him doing anything, and he regained a hold of it. He pulled it once again toward his heart. Once it reached the outer edges, he faltered. Worried that something would happen. He pulled the red magic into his heart. An almost burning warmth filled his body. But no visions. He held it there for a moment. It felt good.

"Release it," Annathalinda finally said, and he let it go, opening his eyes. "Now let me draw from you."

"I..." Aaron glanced around nervously and shifted in his chair. "I don't know how."

"It's very similar. Only this time, you are pulling the magic from your heart to your hands and holding it there. Push your inner magic out while you create that channel."

Aaron opened his hands in front of him and closed his eyes. He struggled to find his magic, but then there it was. A small light in his heart. He grabbed hold of it and began to push it through his chest, down his arms, and into his hand. He felt the magic throughout his body, but this time it felt much less foreign. It felt comfortable. When it finally reached his hands, he felt the warmth on his palms. He couldn't help but peek and saw a soft white light glowing in each of his hands. Much dimmer than any of his companions, but it was there.

Annathalinda placed her hands above his and whispered, "You're going to have to keep pushing. I'll take it slow."

Aaron felt a tug on his soul. He quickly closed his eyes to concentrate on pushing the magic forward. It almost felt painful. He felt a tightening in his chest. Annathalinda eventually released him. He lost track of time, but he knew it was less time than when he was pulling magic from Annathalinda. He was drained.

"Very good," Annathalinda said quietly. Aaron thought he was the only one who heard it.

"Well?" Klew asked as Annathalinda returned to her seat.

"There seems to be a connection between you two. I felt something in each of your magic that I do not feel in others. I do not know what it means, but it's probably linked to whatever is going on."

"Why do you say that?" Catherine asked.

"Magic is not typically altered in someone unless they are being called for something greater."

Aaron was unsure whether he was tired or if he had really seen a flicker of recognition on her face, but it had only lasted a moment, if it was real.

"Anything else?"

Klew turned to Aaron, but didn't say a thing.

"Keelhola," Aaron said softly.

"You want to pick up where your mother left off?" Emma finally spoke.

Aaron nodded.

"Well, I suppose you came to the right place then."

"What do you mean?"

"The three of you were on your way here when you were a boy," Annathalinda said gently.

All were silent for a while.

Aaron internalized her statement. He was where he was supposed to have gone all those years ago. He's where he was meant to be. He felt someone take his hand, looked down at it, and followed the arm up. It was Catherine. He smiled a half smile at her, appreciating the support. He finally turned back to Annathalinda and asked, "What were you going to tell them?"

"I suppose we have come full circle," the legendary elf said.

"What do you mean?" Aaron felt Catherine squeeze his hand in anticipation.

"I had a vision about Keelhola several years ago, after your parents had passed away, though. I saw it glistening on a table, in the dark, and then a shadow touched picked it up."

"Shadow touched?!" several exclaimed at the same time.

Clay, John, and Klew turned to Catherine.

"I've seen a shadow touched," the young elf stated softly.

Annathalinda looked at Catherine. "I believe the shadow touched are rising again. And they have Keelhola."

"How?!"

Aaron's heart sank. The shadow touched returning was bad news enough, but if they actually had Keelhola, the power they possessed could tip the scales in their favor. Aaron's mind began to echo Catherine's question: How?

"I pray that my vision was a future that we can stop, but I fear for the worst. This is where you two come in."

"Us?" Catherine and Aaron asked in unison.

Annathalinda nodded. "A year ago, I had a dream of a silhouette protecting another and then them leaving Dovan with Klew."

Aaron remembered what Klew had said about Annathalinda sending him on a journey to help them.

"Then," she continued, "last night. I had a dream of those two silhouettes standing before Dovan's castle with an army behind them. A unified army. One that has not been seen in hundreds of years. You two were leading the army."

The weight of her vision fell on Aaron's shoulders. Leading an army? The likes that had not been seen in centuries. He thought of the dream he had where Nissela was informing him dracone were coming to support them. Then he grew confused. "Why would the army be in Dovan?"

"You haven't heard?"

Aaron shook his head, and everyone but Emma leaned in.

"Bellmora has declared war on Zentora."

"Why would King Hargon do that?" Aaron knew tensions were high between the humans and elves in the region, but he hadn't expected war.

"I don't think it was his choice," Annathalinda said calmly.

The half-elf became more confused. "Then how did Bellmora declare war? The king is the one who declares war."

"I had a vision of shadows over the castle. As if an outside power was in control. The person in charge in Dovan is not who we think it is."

"Do you know who is in control?" Clay asked.

Annathalinda continued to look at Catherine and Aaron. "I think it's the shadow touched."

◈•◈

Catherine appreciated that Aaron hadn't stopped holding her hand since they left the meeting with

Annathalinda. Klew guided them all to an inside garden that had a wide variety of exotic plants.

"She's promised us support from the Northern Lands," Klew pointed out as they discussed strategy.

"If you stop by the Isle Lands, I can get support from there. We must announce your return first, though!" Emmyana exclaimed.

Catherine saw a slight flinch on Aaron's face. She was certain she was the only one to see it. Aaron was still struggling to accept everything.

"I suppose we should," Aaron replied.

The elven queen looked quite pleased with herself.

"I will take leave to go to my father," John stated. "I will discuss this matter with him. I will also bring Annathalinda's letter with me to muster more support."

Catherine watched as a blue butterfly landed on a nearby purple flower. It felt calm there, but she knew it wouldn't last. She thought of her dreams. Running through battlefields in Dovan. They were going to happen. The butterfly flew away.

"Would that be enough, though?" Catherine asked softly, still looking to where the butterfly flew away.

"What do you mean?" Klew asked.

"The likes that haven't been seen for hundreds of years. The shadow touched have been in hiding for hundreds of years, with plenty of time to plan, and they might have Keelhola. Would the four kingdoms be enough?"

Catherine felt Aaron squeeze her hand, and she turned to make eye contact with him.

"I'll send a message to Nissela," her beloved said as he looked into her eyes.

"Who's Nissela?" Emmyana inquired.

"The Dragon Lady. I know Saro and Valex cannot afford to sacrifice anyone, but I'm sure Nissela knows a dragon or two that could help."

Catherine saw a pause on his face. He thought something that he wasn't speaking.

"The dwarves will want more than just speculation," Clay stated.

"How do we get that?" Aaron asked as he turned away from Catherine, still holding her hand.

"We need to get proof that the shadow touched are back."

Everyone was silent for a moment. Catherine looked up through the glass ceiling and watched as snow fell, and silently said thanks for the warmth of the building.

"Do you think they would send a representative to assist us and send word back?" Catherine thought out loud.

"That's an idea. We can see if Annathalinda can send them a message," Clay responded.

Catherine was struggling to understand the situation they were in, and yet she seemed to come up with solutions easily. It was like there was a disconnect between her mind and reality. Almost like she didn't know who she was. It had only been half a year, and her entire world had been turned upside down. How was she destined for greatness? For most of her life, she was a poor, lost orphan. She had no idea where she came from and had to rely on the generosity of others for most of her life. Now she was being told that, somehow, she was to save the plane from great evil.

They continued to strategize and make plans. Catherine didn't feel present until Klew encouraged everyone to take a break while he and Clay went to talk to Annathalinda about what they had discussed. John decided to go with them to plan out how he would approach his father and mother. Catherine, Aaron, and Emmyana remained in the garden. They found some benches to sit on.

"I know this is a lot," Emmyana admitted. "But so many will be overjoyed to hear you are alive."

Catherine watched as Aaron looked down at the ground and back up at his cousin.

"I am just feeling overwhelmed right now," he replied.

Catherine squeezed his hand, hoping he knew that she was saying she felt the same way. He squeezed back.

"I know. But please, come to the Isle Lands, and we will gather an army for you. Your people deserve to know you're alive."

"My people?"

Emma nodded.

"How are they my people? I've been gone since I was a child. I barely remember the place."

"Your parents were loved," she said softly. "The people still hold a vigil for them on the anniversary of their ship leaving the harbor. They will be elated to have you return. Even if only for a short while."

Aaron looked at Catherine. "Do we even have the time for that?"

"Again, with the visit to the Isle Lands and the people seeing you are alive, we can stir support easily. You can succeed at two missions at once."

"I think we should go," Catherine told her beloved, knowing it wasn't exactly what he wanted to hear, but it was the truth. "You've seen where I'm from. I'd like to see where you're from. And wouldn't it be nice to go home?"

The half-elf closed his eyes and sighed. Catherine could tell he knew she was right.

Once he opened his brown eyes again, he stated, "Okay. We'll go to the Isle Lands. But only for as long as it takes to rally supporters."

Emmyana's face lit up with excitement. "Everyone is going to be so happy to have you home!" She then asked Aaron questions about his life. Many of the questions reminded Catherine of what her parents had asked her once she found them.

Finally, Catherine heard Aaron ask a question she knew had been on his heart for some time. "What were my parents like?"

"Oh, Aaron!" Emmyana exclaimed. "They were the most wonderful people. Your mother was a fierce leader with a kind heart. She always put the people first. Your father, well, he was always a lively spirit. Your mother swore he could be serious, but I never saw it! But you," Emmyana reached out and touched Aaron's cheek, "You were their world. I had never seen them happier than the day you were born. Your mother would rule from her throne with you on her lap! She wanted to raise you as a true leader."

"A leader for what? She had to know that with a human father, I would die before her."

Emma smiled sadly. "She had always planned to give you Jahola."

Aaron looked down at his ring. Catherine could see the weight of realizing his mother's plan on his expression.

༒

Annathalinda arranged for them to stay in guest quarters in the palace, so after midday, they retrieved their items from the inn and returned. Catherine took a moment for herself as she prepared her room.

The 5th Day of the 6th Moon of the 35th Year of King Hargon

I'm unsure of where to start. Today has been a whirlwind. Aaron's a prince of the Isle Lands. His cousin is here. Who is also Clay's betrothed. The shadow touched are back and they probably have Keelhola. It's likely they've taken over Dovan. Oh yes, and apparently Aaron and I are the key to stopping them. How could we lead an army? Aaron at least has some experience from his time in Thyla. But that was still a much smaller scale. I'm starting to wonder if my dreams will be coming true. Dovan in war. Aaron in armor. Aaron almost dying. This all feels so impossible.

CHAPTER 13

❦

Annathalinda and Emma had joined them for their evening meal. More planning was discussed, and Aaron was growing weary of all the discussions. It far exceeded all the discussions he had had with Valex and was more about diplomacy than strategy. They all continued to sit around the table, talking for quite some time after they finished eating. Finally, once the discussions had quieted, Emma and Annathalinda left to work on preparations for their trip to the Isle Lands.

Catherine eventually stood and said, "I'm going to spend some time in the garden before retreating to bed. Have a good night."

Klew, Clay, and John all nodded and softly said their good nights.

"May I join you?" Aaron inquired, hoping the answer was yes.

His beloved smiled at him. "Of course."

They walked, hand-in-hand, through the glass halls, not saying a word. Once they reached the garden, they saw small, magical, globes of light floating throughout, lighting the area.

They walked together, silently, for a few moments, then Catherine looked coyly over her shoulder at Aaron and asked, "So, *my prince,* shall I bow to you when you enter the room?"

Aaron wanted to be mad, but Catherine began to mischievously giggle, and he couldn't help but smile, pull her close, and kiss her cheek. "I just might make you!" he retorted.

"No really!" Catherine pulled back, a giant smile on her face. She thought she was funny. "I don't know how I'm supposed to behave when courting royalty!"

"I guess we should ask Clay." Aaron found himself smiling for the first time in a while. It felt good.

"A queen?!"

"My cousin!"

They both burst out laughing. Aaron pulled Catherine close and enjoyed the feeling of her against him. Once they caught their breaths, they found a cozy bench to sit on and looked around. His cousin. He found his cousin. Who happened to be courting Clay.

"What are you thinking about?" Catherine inquired.

"What am I *not* thinking about?"

"Fair."

They were quiet once again.

"I'm glad you found family."

Aaron looked over and saw Catherine looking at him with a soft smile. He smiled back. "Me too."

"You do like to take things to the extreme though. Royalty?"

Aaron rolled his eyes. "You're not going to let this go, are you?"

"How could I? Yesterday you were just an orphaned farm boy and today you're a prince! You're going to hear about this for the rest of your life." She looked at him matter-of-factly.

He chuckled softly. "Oh boy, what would Thomas and Tammy say?" His heart sank. He hadn't thought about them in a while. Life had been going by so fast.

"What's wrong?" jubilance left Catherine's tone.

"I wonder how Thomas and Tammy are." Everything they had been discussing flooded back on him. "Dovan."

"Hm?"

Aaron looked at Catherine, panic in his eyes. "Dovan is under shadow touched control. Thomas and Tammy are not safe."

Catherine's eyes widened. "Write to them. Tell them to leave. Annathalinda will be sending out letters tomorrow."

"We can't risk it getting intercepted."

Her shoulders slumped. "What are we going to do?"

"They'll be the first ones we visit when we get there."

The young elf wrapped her arms around Aaron. He leaned in. He loved being her protection and hiding her from the world in his arms, but, in that moment, it felt good to know she supported him the same way. He kissed the top of her head.

"Do you think we were destined to be together?" Catherine asked, slightly muffled by her face squishing against his chest.

"What do you mean?" Aaron pulled back half to look at her and half to understand her better.

"Annathalinda said we're destined for greatness and are the ones chosen to fight this battle. Do you think we were also destined to be together?"

"I have no idea." He brushed back some hair that dangled in front of her eye. "But I want to thank destiny if we were."

A huge smile came across Catherine's face, and she leaned in and kissed him. That is how he would get through, he thought. With Catherine by his side.

"I love you," he said softly.

"I love you, too," she replied.

෨෧

Catherine appreciated the wall-length curtains in the room as the sun peeked through the openings. She sat up in bed, yawned, and stretched. They were to travel out, once again, that day. It felt very monotonous. Not having somewhere to call home. Only staying in one place for a night or two at the most. The ship had felt most like home since they left Dovan. Now they were headed back to Dovan, eventually. She wondered if it would be different. Things had already been degrading when they were last there. She wondered how much worse it had gotten.

She pulled the covers off and got out of bed. She slipped her nightgown off and began to dress. As she laced up the front of her green dress, she noted how dirty it had gotten. She'd only been able to wash it occasionally. She probably needed to replace it, but when and how would she do it?

She brushed her hair, placing pins in it to catch part of it behind her head, and then pulled on her boots. She wandered out of her room and down the hall. John exited a room not too far away and joined her on her journey to the dining hall. Klew, Clay, Emmyana, and Annathalinda were already there. She took her seat, and a servant brought her a steaming cup of tea. She thanked them and took a sip. A few moments later, Aaron joined.

"This is our last moment together for a while," Annathalinda said as they all ate. "I know we've discussed this ad nauseum, but I want to make sure we're all on the same page before we part ways. John, you will take the letter I wrote to Avendale."

John nodded.

"I will send letters to the dwarves in Walfort, the kingdoms boarding us to the south, and Elencka. Aaron, I will send your letter to Saro and Valex. Emmyana, Clay, Klew, Catherine, and Aaron will go to the Isle Lands, and then make your way to Dovan. I will then meet you in Dovan."

She made it sound so simple.

When there was nothing but agreements, Annathalinda smiled and said, "Then let us just enjoy each other's company before heading out on our missions."

Catherine could feel the air get lighter after that statement and began to inquire about the history of the palace and the seeming impracticality of it being made of glass. She learned that it was the glass that made the structure so warm; and that very few armies ventured that far north so there was little worry of attack. Klew also informed her that there was only one moon out of the year when snow might not fall.

Their conversations were light and easy. Catherine welcomed the change of pace. But, eventually, the meal ended, and they were to continue with their tasks. Catherine went to her room and packed her bag with the few supplies she had. Emmyana had all the supplies they would need, so for once they didn't need to stop by the market on their way out. They all gathered at the main entrance hall. Annathalinda and John bid them farewell, and they headed back to the coast.

Emmayana did not have as large an entourage as human royalty might, but she was not traveling alone. She rode a horse, not a carriage, but they did have a wagon with them with supplies. The snow on their travels back to the docks was light and barely hindered their travels. Catherine was starting to enjoy watching Clay with Emmyana. They reminded her of herself and Aaron. Catherine also appreciated having other female traveling companions.

Once they reached the town, they immediately went to the docks but veered off to where the ship with the conch shell flagged ship was. Emmyana had sent word ahead, and the ship was ready for them to board.

"The benefits of having your own ship," Klew smiled, "You don't have to wait for others' schedules."

Catherine marveled at the teak wood. Emmayana's ship was far more elegant than the last ship they were on, which was beautiful in its own right. The figurehead on the bow of the ship was a mermaid holding a shell, with her tail extending around the port side and cresting off the stern. The lanterns around the edges of the ship were in the shape of spiral shells and segmented into squares of pink glass.

One of Emma's ladies showed Catherine to her room. She had a whole room to herself on the ship. It was small, but private.

"And you can place your clothes here," the lady informed as she placed a hand on a small dresser in the corner.

"Oh, I..." Catherine grew uncomfortable, "I only have this dress."

"Oh." The elf did not seem bothered, but Catherine felt embarrassed anyway. "Then I suppose there isn't much use for this, but you can still admire it." She smiled, trying to lighten the mood.

Catherine appreciated it. "It is beautiful."

They both chuckled softly, then the lady excused herself. Catherine placed her bag by the small writing table and looked out the port side window. They hadn't launched yet, but preparations were underway. She made her way back up to the deck.

She saw Aaron talking with Klew and decided to join them.

"I don't think you have to worry about it," Klew said, paying no attention to Catherine's approach.

"Worry about what?" she asked.

The two turned to her and smiled.

"Aaron here doesn't want to rule a kingdom!" Klew chuckled.

"The phrase Emma used was 'heir to the throne.' I'm not ready for that," Aaron explained.

"Was Emma crowned queen?" Catherine inquired.

Klew nodded. "Yes. That's why I don't think Aaron has anything to worry about. Now until lover boy over there finally seals the deal, you're next in line though." Klew waved a finger in the direction of Clay, who was talking with Emmayana.

"He'd better hurry up then," Aaron laughed.

Catherine could tell it was an honest laugh, with a bit of worry behind it. She hadn't thought of the fact that this meant he could possibly be responsible for a kingdom. But that wouldn't be fair, as he's had no training. Granted, he always was a natural leader. She just walked over and placed her arm around Aaron, and he wrapped his arm around her. The three stood at the railing watching as the crew untied lines, lifted anchors, and opened the sails.

The ship took off.

౷

It had been about a quarter moon into their travels. Aaron started to train spell casting with Klew. Catherine was growing to like traveling by water. It was calming.

She was sitting at a table on the deck, enjoying the view of the waves on the horizon, when Emmyana approached her.

"Hello," the queen said sweetly.

"Hello," Catherine smiled back.

"May I join you?"

Catherine nodded and motioned to an empty chair. Emmyana sat down and looked out over the sea.

"I want to thank you for being there for Aaron all these years."

The two women looked at each other.

"Of course."

They both looked back out over the water and were silent for some time.

Emmyana finally broke the silence once again, "Please do not get offended by this."

Catherine looked at her, but Emmyana's gaze remained fixed on the distance.

"I was informed you only have the one dress."

Catherine found herself blushing with embarrassment.

Emma looked at her. "There is no judgement. I understand you left in a hurry and came from humble beginnings. The reason I'm telling you this is that I would like to offer you tailoring services. If you would like, we could make you some dresses."

Catherine froze. "Really?" She had never thought about getting more clothing. It seemed so simple now.

"Of course." The elven queen smiled at her. "I have a limited selection of fabrics on board, but we could make you one dress here and more once we land."

She didn't know what to say or how to feel. All she managed to get out was a, "Thank you."

"Just let me know when you're ready." Emmyana then stood and walked away.

Catherine didn't get the courage to bring up the offer to Emmyana until a couple days later, but when she did Emmyana had the grandest smile and escorted Catherine to her room. One of her ladies was summoned and they pulled out some fabric.

"Here is what we have that is enough to make you a dress," Lady Ahal said. "Pick one."

There were four bolts of fabric. One was a simple cream color; one was a silky salmon pink; one was a velvety, deep green; and one was a fine blue that reminded Catherine of the water. She gently ran her hand over each of the bolts; all of them were pleasing to the touch. Her hand stopped on the blue. It was beautiful.

"This one."

"Beautiful choice," Lady Ahal said with a smile.

Catherine then stood as still as she could while getting measured. Lady Ahal also pulled out a few sketches of some simple dresses she had done. Catherine was drawn to one.

"That will look stunning on you. Once I've finished this dress, I will take your current one and mend it the best I can."

"Oh, you don't..." Catherine started.

Lady Ahal lifted a hand. "I insist."

Catherine felt sheepish. "Thank you."

Lady Ahal gathered her supplies and left.

Catherine looked at Emmyana. "Thank you."

"Of course!" the queen smiled at her. "Anything for those close to Aaron. Come," she offered her arm, "let's join the others."

The brown-haired elf accepted Emmyana's arm and they left the room.

∂°∽

Aaron closed his eyes, focused on the warmth inside himself, and drew it from his chest, through his arms, and to his palms.

"Good job!" Klew exclaimed.

The half-elf opened his eyes and saw the small ball of fire in his palm. He had done it. He cast a spell. He lost his concentration with his shock of success and lost the spell. The fire dissipated without smoke.

"Again," Klew instructed.

Aaron sighed and closed his eyes.

"Excuse me," one of Emma's ladies said timidly as she approached.

Aaron opened his eyes again and looked over.

"You will want to see this." She then led them to another part of the deck near the center. "Watch." She indicated the steps.

The prince of the Isle Lands had no idea what he was waiting for but trusted her. It was a few moments, but soon, Catherine emerged from below. Her hair was half up in a braid with a shell clip holding the end together. She wore a dress he had never seen before. It was a light blue, almost a turquoise of the ocean. The skirt of it was flowy. The main bodice was sleeveless, but had thin fabric attached further down, revealing Catherine's shoulders.

The bodice featured darker teal embroidery on each side, extending from the waist to the neckline. They reminded Aaron of waves.

She looked stunning. There was a glow about her. She smiled at her beloved; he couldn't help but smile back.

She approached Aaron and Klew. "What do you think?" Her cheeks were slightly rosy.

Aaron pulled her close and kissed her. "Beautiful." He looked over her shoulder and saw Emma, glowing with pride, and mouthed *Thank you.*

"Do you think it's too much?" Catherine looked down at the skirt of her dress and lifted fabric to either side, widening the dress.

"It is beautiful," he lifted her face up by her chin, "just like you."

They looked into each other's eyes for a moment. Catherine had a sweet, little smile on her face.

"How did your lessons go?"

Aaron pulled away from his beloved, opened his right palm in front of himself, and closed his eyes. He felt a warmth in his heart and pulled it through the canals of his body and pushed it out his hand.

"Good job!"

The half-elf opened his eyes to see the ball of fire in his hand. It was warm. He tried to remain concentrated on it with his eyes open, but it didn't last long. He still had a lot of work to do.

CHAPTER 14

❦

They would make land soon after dusk. The sun was setting, and the shore was starting to come into view. Catherine placed her hand on Aaron's shoulder as he anxiously stared out over the water and the ever-growing coast.

"Are you alright?" she asked softly.

Aaron heard her, but his thoughts raced too fast to respond. He was about to go home. But was it really home? He had only spent a few years there. What would the people think? Did they really care about a long-gone prince who was supposedly dead? Was that really all they needed to rally an army? He had done so well to ignore most of his worries during the journey, but they were all flooding back to him. He was no prince. He was a farmer's adopted child.

He felt Catherine wrap her arms around his waist and lean in. He wrapped one arm around her and pulled her in, still silently staring at the approaching shore.

Just as he began to make out the shapes of a large castle, darkness shrouded it, and he could no longer see it. A bright light shone from the top of the castle, though.

Emma walked to their side. "We'll eat when we get in. I will introduce you to the court tomorrow."

Introduction to the court.

"Do they know he's here?" Catherine asked.

"Some do. But I've instructed them not to bother us tonight." The elven queen smiled at them. "I wanted to give you at least one night at home before a flurry of activity."

Aaron wasn't sure if one night would be enough, but it was all he had. They didn't have time to linger around.

As the wharf came into view, lights throughout the city could be seen. The tall castle also came back into view. Aaron could just make out the tan stones. He was hoping they would look familiar, but they didn't.

The dock wasn't as busy as the others, but Aaron assumed that was because it was night. They were also pulling into a slightly separated area. Emma left them, but Aaron wasn't paying enough attention to know why. It all felt like a dream. Things felt familiar, but he didn't remember any of it.

After some time, they began to disembark. Aaron kept his arm looped through Catherine's as they walked down the plank. Her presence was a comfort. As they walked the wooden path, he felt as though people were staring, but every time he looked around, no one was. They were led by a group of elves with lanterns up a wooden staircase that scaled a rocky cliff up to the castle. When they reached the top of the stairs, Aaron paused. Before them was a small fountain. It felt familiar. He wondered if there were fish in it. He had the urge to run his hand through the basin of water but resisted and followed the crowd past it. They entered a large door and went through the halls. Aaron was disoriented, but the pastel-colored glass chandeliers and oceanic decorations felt right. Finally, they arrived in a room with a large rectangular table surrounded by chairs. There were enough places for the entire party, with plates, wine already poured, and some bread.

Emma simply extended her hand towards the table as she took a seat. Clay sat next to her. Aaron sat across from her with Catherine on his left side. Klew sat on Aaron's right. One of Emma's ladies did not sit down and left the room through a small door to the side. In moments, she returned and took a seat. Aaron looked around; something didn't seem right.

"I changed the tapestries," Emma said simply.

Aaron looked at her in surprise.

His cousin smiled at him. "The ones that were there when you were here last needed mending, and I quite like these here, so we just never put the old ones back up."

Catherine placed her hand gently on Aaron's leg. He placed his hand on top of hers.

Soon, an entourage of servants entered with cooked fish. Aaron softly thanked the elf placing his dish down in front of him. He picked up his utensil and took a bite. A burst of flavor hit his mouth. He was used to bland fish, but it had so much flavor.

"This is delicious," he couldn't help but say.

"It used to be your favorite," Emma replied. Aaron couldn't tell if she was hiding a smile or forcing one.

Once everyone had their fill, Clay asked, "What is the plan for tomorrow?"

Planning. Again.

"We'll break fast at dawn. Then I will have Aaron measured for clothes," Emma said with her head turned towards Clay, but her eyes darting to Aaron occasionally.

Aaron looked down. He supposed his clothes had seen better days as well.

"Then, midmorning, we have a meeting with the court where I will present Aaron to them."

"Who is in the court?" Aaron wasn't sure if the answer would actually help him, but he felt it was appropriate to ask.

"Ailwen is my advisor for trade, Elnaril oversees all the docks in the lands, Ellisar is my military advisor; he already knows of your presence and mission, Merethyl advises on resources, and Chamylla oversees our libraries."

Aaron sighed. "Did I know any of them?"

Emma gave a sympathetic smile. "They all were part of your parents' court, but Ailwen was a dear friend of your father's. I sent word to him as well."

There was a moment of silence while Aaron processed that there was someone he might have known and didn't remember.

"What will we do after meeting with the court?" The prince felt he ought to at least prepare for the plans.

"That is not planned. I do not know how long the meeting will be, and they will help guide us in the next steps."

The lack of a plan suddenly made Aaron realize how much he had become accustomed to having plans. He had no idea how to mentally prepare for the lack of a plan. He looked over at his beloved and she gave him an encouraging smile. He squeezed her hand.

Slowly their dishes were removed from the table. Emma motioned for one of her ladies to come over. "Please show Clay, Klew, and Catherine to their rooms." She turned to Aaron. "If I may, I'd like to show you something."

He nodded, kissed Catherine goodnight, and watched as they left. He turned his attention back to Emma.

She stood. "Come with me." She exited through the opposite side of the room than they entered through.

Aaron followed.

"I had given up hope on finding you years ago. I assumed your body had drifted off to sea. But every day, since I received word of the attack, I tried to fill your parents' shoes. It isn't an easy task." She paused and looked over her should at Aaron. "Klew informed me you were worried about taking the throne."

Aaron blushed slightly and nodded sheepishly.

"I will gladly continue to lead our people," she turned her body towards him, "unless you want to."

"Oh, no! I have no idea how to run a kingdom!"

Emma smiled. "Then fear not. I'll let you just focus on the war ahead."

He slumped his shoulders slightly. That did not sound much better.

His cousin continued to guide him down the hallways. "There is something I want to show you. I have spent many days staring at it. I hope it can bring you as much comfort as it has me."

They turned into a much larger hallway, with elegant pillars lining the walls. Aaron's heart sank. It felt familiar. He started seeing paintings of rulers of the past. Faces that seemed familiar, but he had no memory of. There was a set of grand double doors at the end of the hallway, with golden handles and oceanic scenery carved in it. That is where Emma stopped, and she turned to her right and looked at the painting on the wall. Aaron followed her gaze.

It took all his strength not to fall to his knees and tears streamed from his eyes. There before him was a painting of a family. A beautiful elven woman with long blond hair and sea-blue eyes wore an elegant blue dress decorated with shells. She wore a gold circlet that mimicked coral. She had a small smirk on her face. A human man was by her side. He had short brown hair and piercing brown eyes. He wore a cream shirt decorated with shells. On his head was a simple gold circlet. He had a serious face. Both rested a hand on a young child who stood between them. The child was probably around three with short blond hair and soft brown eyes. A mischievous grin that bunched up baby cheeks. He wore a simple gold circlet on his head.

Aaron reached out and touched the image of his mother's hand. He no longer saw the painting in front of him. He saw her looking at him, the sun just off to the side, hair blowing in the wind, as she reached down to him. He then felt her embrace him. Someone wrapped their arms around him from the other side and he turned. There was his father. They squeezed his tiny body between theirs and gave him many kisses.

"Aunt Sylance and Uncle Aghust were wonderful people." Emma's voice brought Aaron back to the present. "And you," she paused for a moment, "you brought them so much joy. You brought me so much joy."

The half-elf tried to regain his composure and wiped tears from his eyes. He had thought so much was his imagination. That their faces were not real, but there they were. A painting that matched what he remembered. It was all real. His parents were killed in a pirate attack. He was from the Isle Lands. He was a prince. His chest tightened again, and he coughed a gasp for air as he tried to stifle more tears.

Emma placed a hand on his shoulder, then it traced across his back, and she pulled him in for a hug. "I had given up hope," she whispered. "I thought I had lost all of you. But here you are."

They stood there in an embrace for a while. Somehow every thought was going through Aaron's head at the same time as no thoughts.

Eventually, Emma loosened her arms and backed away slightly from Aaron. "I should show you to your room."

The undoubtable prince of the Isle Lands took one last longing look at his parents. Inside of him screamed, *"I love you and I miss you,"* but he didn't make a sound. He then turned and followed Emma back the way they came.

They went up a stairway a couple of floors and down a few halls. Things began to grow more familiar to Aaron. Finally, they entered a room. It was a fairly large bedroom. Aaron found he knew exactly where to look for everything. The dresser was where it used to be. The armoire was where it used to be. The bed brought back small flashes of memory. He remembered it being so much bigger.

"This was my room," he said softly.

Emma nodded. "No one has stayed in it since you went on that voyage."

They were both silent for a moment, while Aaron looked around, taking in the familiarity.

"I should let you get some sleep. Tomorrow will be a busy day."

They bid each other a good night. Aaron lay down in his bed. He wasn't sure he could sleep. He was correct.

Soon after finally drifting off, he was woken up by a soft knock on his door. He drowsily climbed out of his bed, walked across the room, and opened the door.

An older, female elf stood there. She gasped slightly and said, "It really is you."

"Pardon?" Aaron was so tired he didn't fully remember everything.

"Prince Aaron," she said with a large smile.

All the memories came back. It wasn't a dream.

"Uh, yes," he failed at determining what to say.

"I just...I thought you were dead. But here you are!"

Aaron shifted awkwardly.

"Oh, I'm sorry! You have enough on your plate. Welcome home."

He nodded his thanks.

"I'm here to get you up for morning meal. Dawn is approaching."

"Thank you," he said simply.

"If you wish to wash up, the next room over has a drawn bath. Do you remember how to get to the dining hall?"

Aaron shook his head.

"Not to worry. I'll be back soon to show you."

"Thank you."

As she left, he closed his door and went and got ready. He enjoyed the warm water that was drawn for him, it seemed to ease his muscles for the time being. She kept her promise and was soon back to guide him to where he would meet the others.

As Aaron sat to eat, he felt eyes on him. This time when he glanced around, there were elves standing on the periphery looking at him and whispering. He tried to ignore it but realized he needed to get used to it. To everyone here, it was like the dead had come to life.

"Do I need to know anything in advance of the meeting today?" Aaron asked, trying to distract himself from how uncomfortable he felt.

Emma shook her head as she finished a bite. "They were all very strong supporters of your parents. There is no reason any of them would not be ecstatic that you have been found. Merethyl and Chamylla may not be the keenest on the mission, but I feel they can be convinced."

Aaron felt that there were more questions to be asked and discussions to be had, but he was just too nervous to think of them. So, he ate in silence.

Once the meal was over, Emma escorted Aaron back to his room. It had been transformed. There were tables of cloth, a couple of mannequins, a few standing mirrors, and a closed wooden box.

"I'll be back later," Emma said as she left the room.

The elf with a measuring rope draped over their neck instructed Aaron to stand in a specific spot. They began moving his arms, adjusting his posture, and measuring almost every imaginable dimension. They dictated measurements to the other elf, who was writing things down. Soon he was standing there awkwardly as the second elf pulled out a partially made shirt and placed it on a mannequin. Immediately, the first elf began to sew and cut at the shirt while the other elf began making markings on some of the other fabric. Aaron watched them work, remembering Tammy teaching him to sew and mend clothes.

His mind drifted and he began to wonder how she was doing. Were they safe? Was the war on their doorstep? He missed them.

"Put this on," one of the elves instructed, pulling Aaron's thoughts back to his room.

Aaron pulled his shirt off and put on the light blue shirt. The elves instantly began moving his arms around, pinning different areas, using chalk to mark others, and tugging in various places. The process repeated itself a few times, with at least one shirt being from scratch, Aaron was not quite sure which one. They also followed the process for pants and had him try on a few sets of boots.

As the commotion was quieting down some and they were making final touches to the clothes, there was a knock at the door.

One of the elves absentmindedly said, "Come in."

Aaron looked over to see an older elf enter. He had long white hair, with a small braid on the left side. He had deep blue eyes and wore a deep green shirt and brown pants. A stark contrast to the pale colors of the Isle Lands. They made eye contact.

"I..." he started, then bowed down.

"Oh, you don't..." Aaron suddenly grew uncomfortable.

The elf rose to his feet. "I never thought I'd see you again. You are the perfect blend of your parents. Your father's eyes and chin. Your mother's smile."

"Thank you?"

"Sorry, where are my manners? You probably don't remember me."

Aaron shook his head.

"I'm Ailwen. I oversee the trade arrangements through the Isle Lands. Your father," he paused for a moment, "was a dear friend of mine."

Aaron saw pain flash in Ailwen's eyes. "I'm sorry," he said softly.

Ailwen shook his head. "Not your fault." He smiled genuinely. "I'm glad you survived. Queen Emmyana told me what happened. The kingdom will be overjoyed with your return."

The half-elf was surprised with how comfortable he felt around Ailwen. "Were my parents really loved that much?"

"Immensely so. Your mother expanded the kingdom's influence five-fold during her reign. And your father, well he probably helped with a good chunk of that." He snickered softly.

"How so?"

Ailwen gave a large smile that Aaron could tell was full of memories. "Your father was an ambassador for trade from Bellmora. I had met him many times before finally arranging a meeting with Queen Sylance. Ah, that fool. It was love at first sight. Once they were married, Aghust worked closely with me to establish dozens of trade routes."

Aaron furrowed his brow. "I didn't know there was direct trade between Bellmora and the Isle Lands."

Ailwen shook his head. "When Aghust married your mother, King Hargon took that as abandonment of his post and cut ties with the Isle Lands. Practically banishing Aghust from Bellmora. But don't feel sad," he reassured, "your father wouldn't have changed a thing. He loved your mother more than almost anything in the world. That is, until you came along."

The half-elf pondered a bit. His father was nobility from Bellmora. He wasn't given much time to think, as the tailors handed him clothes to put on. He soon stood in front of a mirror with clean, brown, knee-high boots, tan pants, and a light blue shirt. The collar of the shirt had shells decorating it.

Emma entered the room as the elves marveled over their work. "Now you look like a prince of the Isle Lands!"

"Not quite." Ailwen walked over to the table and placed a hand on the wooden box. "May I?"

The queen touched her chest with her right hand and nodded.

The older elf opened the box. Inside was a simple gold circlet. "This was your father's." He lifted it carefully with both hands and approached Aaron.

Aaron looked back at the mirror as Ailwen placed the circlet on his head. It was slightly too big, so it low.

"*Now* he looks like a prince."

Aaron stared at his reflection and agreed. He looked like a prince. But he didn't feel like a prince.

༃

Catherine sat on a wicker chair, on a balcony overlooking the sea. The misty breeze felt good. She wondered how Aaron was doing. It hadn't even been a day, but it felt like eternity away from him. She knew he was going through a lot, and she wasn't able to be there for him.

Hopefully all would go as smoothly as Emmyana indicated it should. Catherine worried about whether the people of the Isle Lands actually didn't want to join the fight. What if they didn't believe them? She even had doubts. Legends said all of Annathalinda's visions had come true, but those were legends. Reality did not always mirror stories. What if Annathalinda was misinterpreting them? What if they did come true, just in a different way?

"Catherine?" Clay said as he approached.

She turned to look at him.

"Midday meal is almost ready."

She nodded slightly and looked back out at the water. The waves gently caressed the tan, sandy beach.

Clay crouched down so he was eye level with Catherine. "What's on your mind?"

She sighed deeply. "Aaron must be going through so much."

"He's strong. And stubborn. He'll get through it."

Catherine turned her gaze to her lap. "What if all of this is for naught? What if this mission is a failure?"

He placed a hand on her shoulder. "Trust Emma. She is a great leader. She's inspires people almost as much as Queen Sylance had. Aaron's parents were greatly loved here. I can guarantee there will be celebrations across the kingdom with this news. And many will gladly go to war for their family."

That felt extreme to Catherine. She would never have imagined people going to war due to a love of their leaders.

Then again, her experience was with King Hargon. He was not a favorite of the people.

"Yes, but that does mean we have to lead an army." Catherine didn't really like either option.

Clay patted her shoulder. "We'll be here to help."

She looked at her friend. "Have you fought in a war before?"

"There was a minor war between the wizards of Oricla and the dwarves of the Balion Mountains. We assisted the wizards in that. Queen Sylance chose me to lead a battalion. So, I know a thing or two."

Catherine sighed with relief. Maybe they could do this after all.

"Now, enough worrying. Let us go eat." Clay stood up and offered his hand to Catherine.

She took it, stood, and then followed him through the halls. She once again marveled at the pastel colors and elegance of the palace. With the sun shining in, she could see the stained glass better. There were depictions of the ocean, sea creatures, elves of the past, and her favorite: Water Birds. She had no idea how they knew what they looked like, it must have taken years of watching, but the large blue birds were illustrated as having long beaks, a few extra-long feathers on their tails, wings, and head that made it look like sprays of water, and their feathers were different shades of blue that made it look like they shimmered. She paused momentarily at the window but soon continued to make sure she didn't lose track of Clay.

They entered the dining hall, Klew was already there, and there were rolls and wine on the table. Catherine took her seat. The three took part in small talk for a few moments, then a commotion started, and several elves flooded into the outer edges of the room, whispering to each other.

The main doors opened, and a couple of elven guards stepped through. "Presenting Queen Emmyana and Prince Aaron." They stepped to the side and Emma and Aaron entered.

Emma was wearing a salmon-colored, chiffon dress with tight, three-quarters sleeves; it was tight until her waist then flowed loosely out all the way to the floor. She wore a shell necklace and a gold circlet that mimicked coral. Aaron was two paces behind her wearing a brand-new set of clothes: a light blue shirt decorated with shells, tan pants, and brown boots. He had a simple gold circlet on his head. He looked like royalty.

Aaron made eye contact with Catherine. To everyone else, he looked poised and calm, but Catherine saw how uncomfortable he was. The crowd of elves that had gathered began to cheer. Aaron did not do a good job of hiding his shock when that happened. Emmyana and Aaron then joined them at the table; this time Aaron sat next to Emma and across from Catherine. Catherine did not like it but understood there were now customs that needed to be maintained.

Emma made a motion with her hand and the crowd dispersed. Soon they were virtually alone in the room again. Aaron sighed heavily.

The queen smiled. "You did great."

"I don't think I'll ever get used to this," said Aaron.

"You will. And I'll help teach you things you need to know. At the Isle Lands, you will not be judged. We all know your history and that you were not raised here, under our traditions. But there will be a time when you have to interact with people from other kingdoms, possibly representing the Isle Lands. I will help prepare you for that."

Catherine saw a flicker of panic on Aaron's face. She hadn't thought of that either. Official representatives. It made sense with what they needed to do and the fact that Aaron was a prince. But those thoughts hadn't crossed her mind and, apparently, they hadn't crossed Aaron's either.

A few elves brought out food and they all began to eat.

"The court will be meeting us in the throne room after our meal," Emmyana informed.

Aaron dropped his façade and let his emotions show; he was stressed and worried.

"You'll be fine," Emmyana reassured. "We will tell them all we know about what happened. They will just be overjoyed to see you alive."

"And then we bombard them with the mission," Aaron said cynically.

The queen sighed. "They are used to having to move at a fast pace. Even during peace times, decisions must be made quickly. New situations arise all the time and they must think on their feet. It's part of being a royal court. It's their job to be bombarded by new information at a quick pace."

"I understand your concerns," Catherine chimed in, "I have them too, but Emmyana has a point. That's what the court is for."

Aaron nodded in agreement, then adjusted the circlet as it tilted slightly on his head.

"We'll make you one that's the appropriate size," Emma reassured with a slight smirk on her face.

Catherine watched as Aaron's vision grew distant. She could tell his mind was heavy. She didn't blame him at all though.

Soon, their meal was over, and Emmyana and Aaron were once again being whisked away. Catherine managed to sneak a hug from her beloved. She said a small prayer that all would go well.

∾∾

Aaron paused at the painting of his parents. He silently asked them to give him strength. Guards stood outside the large double doors at the end of the hallway. They opened them and Emma guided Aaron into a grand throne room. There was a running rug that led from the doors to the throne. It was a light blue and gold stylistic depiction of water and ships. The kingdom's flag hung on the back wall: light blue background with a pink conch shell outlined in gold with gold rays extending towards the edges. There was a large wooden throne on a slightly raised platform and a smaller similarly styled chair next to it. Emma guided Aaron to the smaller chair. They sat down.

"I don't think I can do this," Aaron said softly. It felt odd sitting on a throne.

"You were born for this," Emma said reassuringly. "I'll do most of the talking."

Soon, a tall male elf entered. He had black hair pulled back in a bun. He wore leather armor. He bowed. "I am Ellisar," he stated with a strong voice. "Queen Emmyana informed me of your return. It is my pleasure to serve you."

Serve him? Aaron was taken aback by the wording chosen.

Emma nodded at Ellisar and he stepped to the side. A female elf entered. She had blond hair tied in a single braid behind her head. She wore a light blue robe with golden edges. She approached and bowed, eyeing Aaron suspiciously.

"This is Chamylla," Emma informed. "She oversees our libraries."

Ailwen then entered. He bowed before Catherine and Aaron with a smile on his face.

A male and female elf entered the room together, discussing something softly. They ceased their conversation once they were about halfway through the room then bowed before Emma and Aaron. The female elf had long white hair, the male elf had long blond hair. They both wore elegant, but simple clothes typical of the Isle Lands.

"Merethyl manages our resources," Emma stated as the female elf stood. "And Elnaril manages the docks throughout the kingdom."

The male elf nodded an additional greeting.

The guards closed the double doors.

Emma stood. "Thank you for joining me today. I'm sure most of you are wondering who this is," she motioned to Aaron, who had remained seated.

All but Ailwen and Ellisar nodded.

"I would like to present to you Prince Aaron."

Chamylla gasped. Elnaril's and Merethyl's mouths opened. Ailwen beamed with joy. Ellisar stood stoically.

"When Queen Sylance and King Aghust's ship was attacked, he survived. Now, the details of what happened immediately after are unclear, but he ended up in Dovan and was raised there by a farmer and his wife. Through fate, we have been reunited. And so, I have brought him back to his homelands." Emma paused for reactions.

Aaron looked out at the court. Soon shocked faces turned to joy.

"My Prince!" Chamylla said with an additional bow. "Welcome home!"

"It will be a pleasure to serve you," Merethyl stated and bowed.

Ailwen had a huge smile on his face. "It brings my heart joy to have you back home." He bowed as well.

"Where you lead, we will follow," Ellisar stated.

Aaron felt comforted by that statement knowing Ellisar knew about the pending war.

Elnaril was silent for a moment, then spoke. "Many had given up hope and believed you were dead. I'll admit that I was one of them. Your presence doesn't feel real, but here you are. Your parents' legacy will live on through you." He then bowed as well.

Aaron couldn't believe he what he was about to do, but he stood and said, "Thank you all for your warm welcome." He glanced over and saw Emma smiling and him, patiently waiting for him to continue speaking. "I know my parents had a great impact on the Isle Lands and I'm sure Queen Emmyana has had, and will continue to have, just as much of an impact. I do not have the best memory of the events that led to my separation from the Isle Lands, but can recount what I do know." Before he could continue, he saw heads nodding. "During our sea journey, we were attacked by pirates. Captain Alik to be precise; who I later killed, but that's a different discussion. Everyone was murdered, except for me. I do not know why they spared me, but they did. I only have glimmers of memory being a slave on their ship. This is where my recollection fails again. I do not remember how I got from their ship to Dovan, but, somehow, I ended up in Dovan, where I was found injured and placed in an orphanage. Several years later, I was adopted by a farmer and his wife. They were kind and loving parents, who I care for dearly." Aaron paused as he thought about Thomas and Tammy again. "Over the last few years, unrest has been brewing in Dovan and Bellmora as a whole. Due to some unfortunate circumstances," he felt it was best not to go into details, "I had to flee Dovan with a companion and friend of mine, Catherine. She is of elven heritage and also found herself abandoned in Dovan as a child. We were led by Klew of the Northern Lands who was sent on a mission by Annathalinda. After a few hiccups in our travels, we made it to Annathalinda in the Northern Lands, where," Aaron extended a hand towards Emma, "we found each other. I honestly have minimal memories of before my time in Dovan, so I didn't even know I was a prince. But here I am. Trying my best."

The court began nodding their approvals.

"We should schedule a celebration!" Ailwen exclaimed. "For all the kingdom!"

Aaron wasn't sure how he felt about that idea.

"Wonderful idea!" Emma agreed.

A small discussion then began to break out, but the prince stayed out of it.

As the commotion began to settle down, Ellisar said, "Enough of the joyous news." Everyone fell silent. "My queen, will you discuss the letter you sent me?"

Emma nodded. "While visiting Annathalinda, she revealed some visions she had received. She believes the shadow touched are uprising."

The room gasped.

"That is quite the vision," Merethyl stated skeptically.

"She believes they are starting in Bellmora."

Merethyl scoffed. "You know King Hargon has always had a disdain for elves. How does any of this prove shadow touched involvement?"

Aaron spoke before Emma could. "I've seen it firsthand. Over the last few years, things have changed. Yes, there was always tension between Bellmora and Zentora, but things were getting worse. Odd things were happening throughout the kingdom. Rumors of strange visitors. Then," Aaron paused for a moment, "trials at night."

The court murmured slightly.

"Trials at night?" Chamylla questioned. "What do you mean?"

"Prisoners would be taken out of their cells in the middle of the night to go on trial." He thought about the disdain of the guards the night Klew rescued him. Something had always felt off.

"I thought trials were public in Bellmora?"

"They were, but something changed."

"We have to take what they are saying seriously," Ellisar interjected. "If they are right and we do not heed their warning, this could be catastrophic. Do we not remember the last time the shadow touched rose?"

"We're a small kingdom, we can't just jump into every war," Merethyl replied.

"This isn't just any war. Do you not remember what happened?"

"Yes, we all know what happened." Merethyl waved her hand in dismissal.

"Entire kingdoms fell! We cannot ignore these signs." Ellisar became exaggerated in his motions.

"What signs? So, King Hargon goes crazy and Annathalinda has a vision. What even was her vision?" Merethyl turned back to Emma and Aaron.

Calmly, Emma said, "That a shadow touched picked up Keelhola."

All were silent.

"But we don't know if that was recent or far in the future," Merethyl tried to argue.

Aaron spoke up again. "Catherine has seen a shadow touched."

"Catherine?"

"My companion. And the other individual Klew was sent to find."

"Sent to find?"

"Klew's mission in Dovan was to find Catherine and I. Annathalinda had other visions that we would lead any army into Dovan." Aaron's tone was calmer than he expected out of himself.

"I think we need to speak to this Catherine."

❧∞❦

Catherine sat at a fountain outside, running her fingers through the water, as fish nibbled at them. She was anxious. She wondered how the meeting was going.

"Lady Catherine?" a guard addressed her as he approached.

She looked over without a word.

"They request your presence."

Her? She stood and followed. They walked through the magnificent halls. Eventually, he led her through a hall lined with portraits of past rulers. They paused at large double doors that were flanked by a pair of guards. She looked to the left and saw a painting of Emmyana. She looked to her right and saw a portrait of a family of three: an elven queen, a human king, and what appeared to be a young human boy with blond hair and brown eyes. Aaron's family. Before she could ponder much longer, the guards opened the doors, and she was let in.

Emmyana sat on the throne with Aaron by her side. Five elves stood before them. They all looked at her as she approached. Emmyana stood and motioned for her to join them on the slightly raised platform. Catherine obliged.

A female elf with white hair spoke first, "Prince Aaron claims you've seen a shadow touched."

Catherine nodded.

"When?"

"Well," Catherine was uncomfortable with the sudden jolt into questions without knowing the context, "while I was traveling with Klew a few moons ago, we were attacked by Ehathians and I saw a shadow touched hiding in the bushes nearby. They saw me and ran."

"Ehathians? So, you were in Thyla?"

"No. We were still on the road there. A few days out if I'm remembering correctly."

"Ehathians were somewhere besides Thyla?" the male elf with black hair interjected.

Catherine shifted uneasily. "Yes."

"There are also Grand Fiends on the plane again," Aaron added.

None of the court could hide their shock.

"Something is brewing, and we need to meet it head on." Aaron subtly clenched his fist.

The female elf with her blond hair braided behind her head shook her head and asked, "How do we know these rumors are true?"

Aaron made eye contact with her. "I've killed one."

Silence fell over the court.

"I think that seals it," the black-haired elf claimed. "We have no choice but to support this mission."

The other two male elves nodded. The two female elves looked at each other, furrowed their brows, then turned to Emmyana.

The female elf with white hair said, "I support this."

"As do I," the other said.

The tension in Catherine's shoulders that she didn't know she was carrying loosened. She looked over and saw Emmyana and Aaron also relax.

"We will need to discuss the details with our constituents."

"I will discuss this with my generals," the black-haired elf said.

"Thank you," Emma said gently.

CHAPTER 15

❧

Aaron and Catherine lay next to each other on the sand, staring at the clouds above.

"Is this all actually happening?" Aaron questioned.

"Either that or we're hallucinating the same thing," Catherine responded.

They turned their heads to look at each other.

"Tomorrow is the big day."

"Don't remind me." Aaron groaned and looked back at the sky.

Catherine propped herself onto her elbow and rolled on her side, facing Aaron. "I think it could be fun."

"You're not the one they're parading around."

"It's a welcome home celebration. Besides, Ailwen said your circlet should be finished later today."

"Well at least there's that," Aaron said sarcastically.

Catherine sighed. "Aaron."

He turned his head to look at her again.

"These people love you, even though they've never met you. They thought you had died as a child. You are all they have left of your parents."

Aaron's expression turned harsh. "I don't have my parents, either."

"That's not what I meant."

He turned his gaze back to the sky, brow still furrowed.

"I'm sorry. Aaron. Please look at me."

He looked back over at her.

"Dovan is our home."

Aaron's expression relaxed.

"If we are to save it, we have to do this. You have to do this."

He sighed. "You're right."

Catherine leaned forward and kissed Aaron, then she laid her head on his chest and wrapped an arm around him. He wrapped his arms around her. They remained in the embrace quietly for several moments.

Eventually, Aaron sighed and said, "I suppose we should go for our final fittings."

Catherine smiled to herself. She knew he hated all this new wardrobe fussing, but she secretly enjoyed it. They stood, shook off sand, and made their way back to the palace. Aaron gave her a quick kiss as they parted ways.

She paused when she entered the room. The dress was on a mannequin, and it was gorgeous.

The seamstress smiled as she walked in. "Come, it is ready." She helped Catherine get into the dress.

Catherine looked in the mirror at the dress. The primary dress was a light teal, much like the sea. The collar sat just off her shoulders and was bordered by a deep teal, embroidered with golden shells. The sleeves were tight on her upper arms and then opened up at her elbow and had identical dark teal borders. The bodice was corseted and so hugged her curves beautifully, then opened to an A-line at her waist. Around her waist was a dark teal sash, also embroidered with golden shells, that had a long piece of cloth hanging down her front center almost touching the floor. She stood in amazement at the loveliness of the dress. The seamstress fussed with a few slightly imperfect spots, but Catherine felt like the elf was being nitpicky.

There was a soft knock on the door.

"Come in," Catherine called out.

Emmyana walked in. "Oh my! You're radiant!" she gushed.

The young elf blushed. "Thank you."

The queen smiled. "I think Aaron will be too distracted to properly socialize."

They laughed slightly. Catherine had to admit to herself, she didn't think Emmyana was joking. And she agreed. She had never felt this beautiful before.

"I brought you a gift." Emmyana revealed a box and opened it. Inside was a beautiful golden necklace. The chain was thin and dainty, with evenly spaced, small, golden pearls. The pendant was half a shimmering clam shell with a white, opalescent pearl mounted inside its cavity. She carefully lifted it out of the box and placed it around Catherine's neck. "Thank you."

Catherine was taken back by Emma's words. "For what?"

"Loving Aaron. Being there for him all these years."

"I...of course." She wasn't sure how to respond.

"I know there is a very long road ahead of both of you. This celebration may be all about Aaron, but the mission is about both of you. I know he would not be who he is without you."

"And I wouldn't be who I am without him."

Emmyana nodded.

Catherine looked back at her reflection and touched the necklace with her right hand. "Thank you."

"It's the least I could do. Besides, it's only proper that a princess of the Isle Lands has a shell necklace."

Aaron's beloved began to protest.

Emmyana raised her hand, silencing Catherine. "I know you're not a princess yet. But you will be. I've seen you two together enough. It reminds me of Clay and I."

"How did you meet Clay?"

The queen smiled sweetly. "About fifty years ago, Ellisar and Chamylla were fighting over a new apprentice. He showed great skill in battle with a strategic mind, but also illustrated a deep understanding of the importance of magic and passing on knowledge. They brought him before Queen Sylance. I was in court that day with her and there he was. Clay. I think my aunt knew I was intrigued by him, because she placed me in charge of overseeing the debates. It became clear that he would be a vital asset in foreign library dealings. Having the strategic mind, he could work through the bureaucracy of other kingdoms and customs, while holding the sacredness of knowledge together. Sylance then put me in charge of coordinating his assignments. I even traveled with him some. After the royal family went missing, Clay was there to comfort me. He supported me every step of the way as I navigated being queen. Finally, twenty years ago, he proposed."

"So, Aaron's mother was a matchmaker as well?"

Emmyana laughed. "Yes. She was."

"When will you wed?"

"We were planning this summer, but with everything going on, we may postpone."

"Oh, please don't! Life has to go on, even when the world is falling apart. You need to hold onto what makes you happy and brings you joy."

Aaron's cousin smiled. "Thank you. We still need to discuss it, but I will keep this in mind."

࿇࿇

Catherine peeked out the door, over the balcony, and at the large crowd below. The palace courtyard was packed. There were nobles lining the room. Her lady-in-waiting adjusted Catherine's braids that were decorated with shells. Soon, Klew and Clay entered.

"Nervous?" Clay asked as they approached Catherine.

"A little bit," she confessed.

"Don't worry, no one will be paying attention to you."

"I'm nervous for Aaron."

"Ah," Klew replied, "that we can't help with."

Soon, Emmyana, Aaron, and the court entered. Emma wore an elegant dress. Its underskirt and sleeves were the same dark teal as Catherine's hems. The top layer was the light teal. The skirt opened at the front revealing the underskirt. The sleeves were tight until just past her elbows then draped open with the light teal on the inside. The bodice was tight fitting, with the skirt poofing out slightly at her waist. There were pearls decorating the skirt in lines with the largest pearls near her waist and the smallest pearls at about the same length as her hands. She wore a pearl necklace with a silver starfish pendant and a gold circlet that mimicked coral. Her hair was loose. She looked like a queen. On her right side was Aaron. He wore a long, stiffer tunic that was the same light teal and had darker teal lines running at an angle. The hems were thick with silver embroidery. The buttons on the front were silver and engraved with starfish. His belt was simple, but elegant, and his two daggers hung by his sides in finely crafted sheaths. He also wore a simple gold circlet. He looked like a king.

The court also wore regal clothes, and followed behind as Emmyana and Aaron walked, side-by-side, down the center of the room to the balcony. The nobles gathered in the room all whispered and gawked. The royal party stopped right before passing through the doorway. The court proceeded Emmyana and Aaron and lined up on either side of the doors, facing the crowd. Emmyana took Aaron's hand, squeezed it, then let go and stepped out on the balcony. Aaron stayed behind.

To everyone else, Aaron looked poised and confident. To Catherine: she saw the fear in his eyes, the uncomfortable way his fingers twitched when Emmyana released his hand. She knew there was nothing she could do at this point, just stay back and watch.

Emmyana addressed the people, "I am sure many of you have heard the rumors by now. Part of our history is being rewritten. When Queen Sylance and King Aghust's ship was attacked, all were slaughtered, but one. Prince Aaron survived." She paused for an uproar of cheers. "Through the blessing of Etienne, we have been reunited." She turned and extended her arm behind her.

Aaron took a deep breath, then stepped out next to her. Catherine didn't know it was possible, but the crowd cheered louder. They really did love Aaron's family.

Once the crowd quieted some, Emmyana continued, "Annathalinda has sent him on a mission, so he will not remain on the Isle Lands for much longer. But tonight is a night to celebrate. Our prince has returned!"

�����

Aaron stood next to Emma, greeting person after person. Every time he glanced at Catherine, who was standing off to the side, she appeared to be having a lovely time laughing and smiling. He was starting to get sick of, "I'm so glad you're alive."

They finally had a moment to breathe.

"I don't know how much longer I can take this," Aaron admitted to Emma.

"Take a moment, you've been doing fantastic. Go get something to eat and drink. I'll handle the crowds." She hugged her cousin and turned to the group of citizens starting to approach.

Aaron slipped behind her and made his way to Catherine.

"My prince!" she exclaimed. "I'm so glad you're alive!"

He glared at her.

Catherine giggled. "Sorry. I really am impressed you've survived this long. Emma is letting you loose?"

"For now. I desperately need something in my stomach."

"Right this way!"

Catherine took his hand and guided him through the crowd. They were stopped several times as people realized who Aaron was but eventually made their way to a table with some finger foods and glasses of elven wine. The prince did his best to gracefully, but hurriedly, eat some food. He was so hungry he didn't really notice the taste.

Once he was satisfied, he picked up a glass of wine and took a sip. For the first time, he looked out over the crowd and saw the joy and celebration people were having. It had been a very long time since he had seen such a happy gathering. He saw a large group of elves had started dancing to the music and began to listen. It was lively and upbeat. It put a smile on his face. He looked over and saw the same smile on Catherine's face.

He began to remember the last time he was at a celebration. It was the harvest festival a few years ago, there had been too much work in Dovan the last couple of years for people to enjoy themselves. He had danced the night away with Catherine.

Aaron reached out his hand to Catherine. She looked at him questioningly. He cocked his head towards the dancing. Her face lit up. Arm-in-arm, he escorted her across the floor to where the dancing was taking place. Soon, all Aaron was aware of was the music and Catherine. They circled around each other, growing closer and farther apart according to the steps. Neither of them knew how many songs they danced to, but finally they needed a rest. They laughed and held each other close as they finished their last dance.

Suddenly, Aaron was brought back to reality. A new wave of people wanted to introduce themselves to him and once again tell him how glad they were that he was alive. However, this time many asked who Catherine was and began to inquire about their relationship. Seeing Catherine's unease, Aaron dismissed those questions.

Soon, Clay approached, "Let the two breathe."

The people began to disperse.

"I want to show you something," he said softly. He then led them through the crowd and out an archway to an empty courtyard. "When I get overwhelmed at these royal events, this is where I come. Somehow only a few people have ever found it."

It was not the most attractive part of the palace. Not to say it was unattractive, just simple and no view of the beach.

"Thank you," Aaron said. "I don't know how Emma does this."

"This was the life she was born into."

"Technically, so was I."

"But you were not raised in it. You will adjust and become more comfortable the more you are exposed. But it will not become second nature as it is for her. Take your time, but I do recommend making your way back to her at some point tonight."

"I will."

Clay then went back to the celebration.

"I hate this," Aaron admitted to Catherine.

They both laughed at the simplicity and frankness of his statement.

"I can tell," Catherine replied.

"You know, I had dreamed about being royalty at one point. Not sure it's exactly what I thought it would be."

"That's just because you're the center of attention. If you were a fly on the wall, you'd be enjoying this."

Aaron shrugged. "I can't believe we have a meeting with the court tomorrow. Everything feels so rushed."

"Well, the shadow touched have already infiltrated Dovan and if Annathalinda's vision was current, they have Keelhola. So…"

"I know." He sighed. "Life has just been a whirlwind since I got arrested."

"I'd say it will calm down soon, but we both know that's not true."

Aaron looked up at the sky. The stars twinkled and the moon was almost gone.

"I suppose I should get back to greeting the people." Aaron resigned himself.

Catherine surprised him by pulling him close and giving him a passionate kiss. "I love you," she whispered.

"I love you, too."

☙❧

Aaron and Catherine walked into the large meeting room, where Emma already sat at the head of the table. There were seats on either side of her. Aaron took the one on the right and Catherine took the one on the left.

"We will need to be completely open with them," Emma instructed. "No secrets."

"Do they know about Jahola?" Aaron asked quietly.

The queen shook her head. "But they will now."

Slowly the courtiers made their way into the room and sat down. To Aaron's surprise, Klew and Clay joined them.

Once everyone was in attendance, Emma spoke, "We do not have much time before Aaron and Catherine need to set sail. We need to finalize our plan. Johnter and Johana have agreed to support the war. They are sending troops to Zentora to start assisting on those fronts. Annathalinda reached out to the dwarves, I have not received their response yet. Aaron," she turned to her cousin, "word may be sent directly to you."

He nodded.

Emma turned back to the court. "If the dwarves want proof, Aaron and Catherine will have to meet with a representative and prove that there are shadow touched in Bellmora. I do not think Catherine's single time witness will be enough. They could argue that it was a rouge shadow touched."

"They should be easily convinced to join if there is proof," Ellisar added.

"How do we get proof?" Catherine asked.

"You could infiltrate the castle," Elnaril suggested.

"That's too dangerous without support," Klew pointed out. "Their numbers are probably growing by the day. And sneaking in a dwarf will be very difficult."

Merethyl spoke up, "They have to get there somehow. There is no opening to the underground near Dovan."

The court pondered her words for a moment.

"If you find evidence of them in Bellmora, that should be enough."

"That could work," Emma replied deep in thought. "So, once you've teamed up with the representative, you will scour Bellmora to find evidence."

"Then what?" Aaron asked.

"Then the dwarves will agree to fight alongside us and send troops. All allies will declare war and we will take them down."

"What about the kingdom of Hinecle? They are right on the border?"

"We will have to start the war before we alert every kingdom in the realm. We will have letters drafted. We don't want the shadow touched to know we are aware of their presence until the war has started."

"How long will we have to wait for the armies to come once we declare war?" Aaron thought about all the traveling they had done.

"We will declare war on Bellmora in support of Zentora," Elnaril announced.

"Are we sure the people support that?" Chamylla objected.

"Zentora is an ally. They would support us. We should support them," Emma stated.

"We have been at peace for almost a century, do you really think the kingdom will agree to this?"

"Peace isn't forever."

Aaron twisted his ring.

"We have no allegiance to Bellmora," Ailwen said coldly, "We do Zentora. Besides, just because the people don't know about the shadow touched doesn't mean we shouldn't prepare for it."

The court continued to debate how much information should be shared and when they should get involved. Aaron said a silent prayer, asking for guidance, as he continued to twist his ring.

Aaron interrupted the debate, "Would the people follow the Bearer of Jahola?"

The room grew silent.

He repeated his question, "Would the people follow the Bearer of Jahola?"

"I'm sure almost anyone would gladly sacrifice themselves for the Bearer of Jahola," Ellisar stated. "But Jahola has been missing for decades."

Aaron, Catherine, and Emma looked at each other.

"What have you not told us?" Chamylla questioned.

The prince slipped off his ring and held his palm open, flat with Jahola sitting on it.

Chamylla stepped forward and looked at the ring. Her eyes widened. "Jahola, the Protector."

"Queen Sylance was the bearer before. She passed it on to Aaron before losing her life," Emma informed.

"Queen Sylance?!" Elnaril exclaimed.

Emma nodded.

"All these years and we never knew?!"

"She was sworn to secrecy. Only Annathalinda, King Aghust, and myself knew."

"She was on a mission to find Keelhola," Aaron informed. "Now it's at risk of being in the wrong hands."

The room was silent for a while.

"We will follow you on this mission," Ailwen declared.

∾∞∿

"As the bearer of Jahola, I support the war on Bellmora in an effort to reclaim Keelhola." Aaron announced from the balcony.

There was an uproar, it wasn't cheering, but it wasn't anger. Aaron hoped it was a good sign.

"They leave at dawn tomorrow," Emma told the people. "We will rally troops and send them to Zentora's aid as soon as we can."

Ellisar and Emma made more proclamations as Aaron stood next to them, poised, but anxious. Eventually, they all retreated into the palace. Catherine, Klew, and Clay were all waiting for them. Catherine wrapped her arms around Aaron as soon as the doors were closed.

"That went well," Emma stated.

"Agreed," Ellisar acknowledged. "I expect we'll get volunteers by morning."

"Time for you to get a good night's rest," Emma turned to Aaron. "You have a long journey ahead of you."

"I'll miss you," Aaron stated.

Emma nodded, "And I you."

CHAPTER 16

⚜

*C*atherine found herself running through the streets of Dovan. She held onto her box, knowing Aaron's life depended on it. Once she reached the infirmary area, an elven nurse wrapped an arm around Catherine's shoulder as she took the box with one hand and guided Catherine to Aaron's side. They had stripped him of his armor, and his teeth were clenched around a rag as another medic stitched a wound in his side. Catherine took Aaron's hand, and his eyes opened for a brief moment. In that moment, Catherine saw his face relax and relief fill his eyes. That moment was harshly ripped away from them as he winced once more in pain.

Catherine woke with a start. She felt the ship rocking back and forth beneath her. She was still on a ship. It was just a dream.

The 18th Day of the 7th Moon of the 35th Year of King Hargon
We are headed to war. With Dovan. I'm having that dream almost every night. I fear it will come true now. It all makes sense. A battle in Dovan, Aaron fighting in it. I don't

know if he survives my dream though. I am so worried. I can't let Aaron know though, he has so much resting on his shoulders. I'm doing everything I can to assure him I'm by his side. But since he wears the crown and bears Jahola, he is the one everyone is turning to.

What do I have to do with all of this? What do I have to contribute to the effort?

Catherine sighed, closed her journal, got dressed, and headed to the deck. Aaron was already up; he had been getting up early recently. She knew he was anxious.

"Good morning," she approached her beloved.

Aaron was leaning against the rail, looking out over the horizon. "Good morning." He didn't look at her.

She placed her hand on his shoulder. His gaze shifted to her hand, he reached up and placed his hand on top of hers, and then he sighed.

They were one day from shore; soon the mission would be in full swing. The two remained silent for some time, but eventually it was abruptly ended by a horn being blown. They both straightened. Elves began running around.

"What's going on?" Aaron asked one as they passed by.

"Another ship has been spotted," they replied.

"Pirates?"

Catherine's heart stopped.

"Bellmoran," the elf answered.

"They don't know we've declared war yet, do they?" Catherine asked desperately.

"No, but that doesn't mean they won't declare war on us." The elf then turned and continued to prepare for battle.

"Go below deck," Aaron instructed.

"No." Catherine wanted to remain by his side.

"If they attack, it won't be safe."

"Nothing we do from here on out is safe."

Catherine could see the resignation in Aaron's eyes. He took her by the shoulders, looked her in the eyes, and said, "Then stay hidden." He then left to retrieve his bow and arrows.

Once Aaron returned, he approached the captain. "Do you need assistance?"

The captain shook his head. "You need to remain inconspicuous. The last thing we need is King Hargon learning about you before our army joins. Any interaction we have with this ship, you are just a passenger."

Catherine thought she saw relief on Aaron's face. They then stationed themselves so that they could see and hear everything that happened but were not easily noticeable.

Everyone waited with bated breath as their ship approached the other.

"Turn port side!" the captain called out. "They're cutting us off!"

Catherine watched as Aaron drew an arrow and nocked it on his bow. The ship heaved to the side, barely managing not to ram the other ship. The captain made his way to the side closest to the Bellmoran ship, where the other captain stood.

Aaron and Catherine followed at a distance, making sure they simply looked like other elves coming to guard the captain.

"What is this about?" their captain called out.

"These waters are closed," the Bellmoran captain replied.

"What do you mean they're closed?"

"No one gets in and no one gets out, without our approval."

"These are not your waters. Your waters are leagues away."

The human laughed a deep laugh. "They are ours now."

Catherine knew that wasn't good.

"We are simply passing through," the elven captain lied.

"Not without our permission," the opposing captain retorted.

"May we have your permission."

He snarled. "No. These waters are closed to all but Bellmoran ships."

Aaron tried to discreetly push forward and whispered something to one of the elves up front. The elf then walked up to the captain and whispered into their ear.

The captain nodded. "I suppose we should turn around then."

The Bellmoran captain cocked his head. "Something doesn't seem right. Mind if we search your ship?"

"I do mind! We have been nothing but cooperative."

"Something seems fishy." The human captain then began to look around. His eyes swiveled back and forth. He eventually stopped and stared at Aaron. "You."

Aaron straightened up.

"What are you doing on that ship?"

"Pardon?"

"You're human, are you not?"

Aaron shook his head. "Half-elf."

The human snarled again. Then one of his crew members whispered something in his ear. His eyes widened for a moment. "Well, well, well. It seems we have ourselves a little problem here." He continued to look at Aaron.

"What might that be?" the elven captain inquired, trying to draw attention back to himself.

"It appears you have a fugitive on board."

Catherine's heart stopped. They were still looking for Aaron?

"Pardon?"

"Oh, you don't know?" He made a motion with his hand and his crew began unsheathing their swords.

"If you attack my ship, you will be declaring war on the Isle Lands!"

The crew readied their weapons. The Bellmoran paused for a moment, raising his hand. He then suddenly dropped it, and soldiers rushed the elven ship. Some swung over on ropes, others laid down planks and ran across. The elves released their arrows and rushed to block. Catherine began to back away but paused when she saw Aaron push forward.

"Stop!" the prince called.

Both captains motioned for their people to halt, and the fighting paused.

"They didn't know."

The Bellmoran captain raised his eyebrows.

Aaron placed his bow and quiver on the ground. "I surrender, just do not attack the ship."

Catherine's heart sank. What was Aaron doing? She started to try moving towards him but felt a hand on her shoulder stopping her.

Aaron raised his hands in surrender. "Do you agree to not attack the ship and let it pass through?"

"Aye," the human captain replied and then motioned to a crew member.

Aaron glanced behind himself at the captain and Catherine, then turned and walked across a plank. Someone immediately grabbed him, yanking his hands behind his back, and guided him away.

"I don't trust him," an elf behind Catherine muttered.

It took everything in her to not break down crying. What was Aaron doing? What could he possibly have been thinking?

The elves began readying their weapons again. It appeared none of them trusted the Bellmorans. As soon as Aaron was out of view, the Bellmorans attacked.

"Steer her out of here!" the captain shouted to the helmsman.

She instantly started turning the wheel.

"We can't just leave Aaron!" Catherine yelled.

The captain turned to her. "They are a military ship. We are a passenger ship. They will destroy us. If we want any chance of making a difference in this war, we run."

Catherine's heart sank yet again. She knew he was right, but she didn't want him to be. She watched as the Bellmorans desperately tried to get back to their ship as the two ships sailed further apart and planks began to fall into the sea. The elves pursued the humans, swinging their swords and firing their arrows. Several humans fell overboard.

Catherine stood where she was, watching as their ship maneuvered away and the Bellmoran ship slowly shrank into the distance. Once she couldn't see it any longer, she sat on a step, paralyzed with anxiety. Someone sat down next to her, but she barely noticed. She thought an arm wrapped around her, but her mind was so numb that she struggled to acknowledge much of anything. Aaron had just handed himself over to the enemy. To the shadow touched. What was he thinking? Her whole world just, once again, flipped upside down. They had a plan. That was not the plan. She finally gave in and began to cry.

∂∽

A soldier shoved Aaron into a cage, slammed the door, and locked it. Aaron looked around. There were two other cells, but they were empty. He really hoped what he was doing was going to work. He sat silently. Eventually the captain came down.

"Your friends got a way," he spat.

"Good."

"King Hargon will hear of this. He'll be pleased to have you again though."

"All this over tax evasion?"

The captain spat. "Full of lies, you are. But I wouldn't expect much else out of someone who associates with elves." He then turned and left, leaving Aaron alone.

"What did King Hargon claim I did?" Aaron mumbled to himself. He sighed, then lay down on the dirty mat. He would have preferred the forest floor.

❧

"What was Aaron thinking?!" Catherine snapped, tears welled up in her eyes, but her veins ran hot.

"He was trying to save us," Klew reassured.

"By doing the dumbest thing possible!" she snapped.

"Catherine, you need to level your head." His voice remained calm.

"How can I be levelheaded when Aaron goes and does something like this!"

"The people need a leader."

Catherine froze. "What?"

"Aaron's out of the picture. Annathalinda chose the two of you for a reason. You're the one remaining."

Leader? She didn't know the slightest thing about leading anyone. Everything was falling apart. Why did Aaron have to be so stupid?

"Catherine."

She looked into Klew's eyes.

"We can't stop just because Aaron has made a rash decision. The fate of the plane is resting on the outcome."

The fate of the plane.

Catherine sighed. She didn't like anything that was happening, but Klew had a point. Something had to be done and apparently everyone was expecting it to be her. She took several deep, slow breaths, and stood up. They walked out of the room and to the captain's quarters.

"Come in," the captain called out after they knocked.

Klew and Catherine entered. Clay was sitting at a table with the captain and two others.

"Any update?" Klew asked as the two joined them at the table.

"I've sent word to Queen Emmyana," the captain responded. "We also are going to sail north a little further and then over to Zentora. Bellmora can't have enough ships to guide every path."

"Why did they call Aaron a fugitive?" Clay asked.

Catherine and Klew glanced at each other. "Well...." Klew said sheepishly.

"Aaron was wrongfully arrested and then we broke him out and started on this journey," Catherine answered simply.

"It's been half a year; they are still looking for him?" Clay questioned.

"Apparently," replied Klew with a shrug.

"Hm. Something seems off."

Catherine and Klew nodded.

"Instead of reaching the coast tomorrow, we'll reach it in three days," the captain changed the topic. "We're going to need some morale boosters though."

She realized she was going to need to be strong if any of their plans were going to work. She sighed once again, focusing on feeling her lungs fill with air. "What do we need to do next?"

৯৹৹ঌ

The captain was right. There were no ships guarding the alternate, longer path. In a few days, they landed on Zentora's coast. A caravan was waiting for them. Without any time to rest, Catherine, Klew, Clay, and their accompaniment were rushed out of the town and towards the center of the battles. They traveled for about half a moon, with little incidents. They reached the camp at night. Each was provided with a tent and allowed to rest for the night.

In the morning, Catherine gathered Emmyana's declaration and met Klew and Clay at the king's tent. It was a circular tent, about four times the size of a standard tent. Two guards stood outside of it.

"We bring word from the Isle Lands," Catherine said, trying to sound as official as she could.

The elves nodded and opened the flaps. The three entered. Five elves sat at a table. Four of them were wearing leather armor, but the fifth was wearing an emerald-green tunic with gold embroidery and wore a silver crown that resembled tree branches.

Catherine, Klew, and Clay bowed.

"Rise," the king stated.

"My name is Catherine. This is Clay from the Isle Lands and Klew from the Northern Lands." Catherine felt horribly uncomfortable. "We bring word from the Isle Lands."

The elven king stood. "Proceed."

Catherine handed him the scroll.

The king opened it and read the letter, his brow furrowed, and then he turned to his companions. "You are dismissed."

Confusion came across their faces, but they did as they were told and exited the tent. The king motioned to the guards, and they left the tent as well.

"There is a lot to unpack in this letter." The king placed it on the table and sat down. He motioned for the three to join him at the table, which they did. "My deepest thanks for your allyship and assistance in this war. But I am curious as to why I am to work closely with a prince who isn't even here."

"Aaron was taken prisoner," Catherine said, calmer than she expected.

"Prisoner?"

"On our journey here, we were waylaid by a Bellmoran ship. Prince Aaron surrendered himself in an attempt to allow us to pass. They still attacked, but we did make it away safely."

The king rubbed his chin. "And this message from Annathalinda?"

Catherine softly sighed, Aaron was going to handle all of this. "We believe that King Hargon is being controlled by shadow touched."

The elf froze.

"Prince Aaron and I have spent many years in Dovan and can attest to odd occurrences that had been happening over the last few years."

"Dovan? But you're elves?"

"That is an unrelated discussion," Catherine dismissed. "Annathalinda has been having disturbing visions of battles in Dovan and shadow touched possibly getting a hold of Keelhola."

"What!?" He stood suddenly.

"We have no proof, Prince Aaron and I were going to go on a mission to find some, but now that he is captured, I'm not entirely sure what we will do."

The king sat back down. "You're requesting my assistance, I'm assuming?"

Catherine nodded.

"A prince who got himself captured before even arriving at war is requesting assistance from a kingdom that is at war and requiring assistance themselves?"

She shifted uneasily. "The Isle Lands are providing support as well."

"Then have them support you."

"This is not just about your war with Bellmora," Clay spoke, "This is possibly a war that will affect all of the plane."

"You have no proof. I have my people to think about."

Catherine was starting to get frustrated. "Aaron is the Bearer of Jahola."

There was silence for a while.

"*The* Jahola?" the king questioned.

Catherine thought the question was ridiculous. "Is there more than one?"

"Jahola? The Protector? The ring the Ainjeal gifted us that bestows every possible protection to its wearer?" He leaned forward slightly.

"Yes. The one and only."

The king was silent once again. "We must plan. Do we need a rescue mission for Prince Aaron?"

"I don't even know." Catherine was feeling the weight of Aaron's absence.

"We will send spies into Dovan to find word of him. But until we know that, we need to find how to get proof."

"Have you noticed anything that might indicate shadow touched?" Clay asked.

The king thought for a moment. "I have heard rumors of disruption in Bellmora, outside of Dovan. It is unclear as to what happened, but I can have people investigate it. Folwin!"

One of the guards entered and bowed briefly.

"Please summon Aeragoth and Thiel. It's urgent."

Folwin bowed and left the tent.

The king turned back to Catherine, Klew, and Clay. "Those are my top two generals."

Soon, two elves entered the tent.

"You summoned?" one asked as they both bowed.

"The Isle Lands have offered reinforcements. They will be here soon. However, their prince was taken captive by King Hargon on their voyage here and Annathalinda suspects shadow touched influence."

The two generals gasped.

"But the shadow touched have been gone for centuries," one protested.

"I suppose it's been long enough then. We must find this prince and rescue him. We must also find evidence of shadow touched in Bellmora. This is not to be spread around. You both are being sworn to secrecy."

The two generals nodded in understanding.

"These three individuals were sent by Queen Emmyana and Annathalinda to investigate the shadow touched. They bring support for the war, but these three individuals will be more valuable than an army if Annathalinda is correct. I know we agreed to hold line and not push into Bellmora, but I think that needs to change."

"Agreed," they said in unison.

"Now, Catherine, was it?"

She nodded.

"I want you to work with Aeragoth to plan the mission to save the prince. Thiel will head the investigation of shadow touched in Bellmora. Time is of the essence."

∾•⟋

Aaron was starving. They only gave him stale bread and dirty water once a day. He was doubting his decision. He just hoped it had given the ship enough time to get away. He lost count of days but thought it had been about half a moon since they transferred him from the ship to an enclosed, locked wagon with only one small, barred window. Hopefully they were taking him to Dovan and the palace. Why were they even still looking for him? At least so much so that someone on a ship recognized him.

One night, Aaron was jostled awake as one of the guards unlocked the door. He was a portly man with stubble on his face. Before Aaron was fully awake, the guard clasped cuffs around Aaron's wrists and pulled him to his feet. Aaron stumbled as the guard pushed him out of the wagon and onto the ground. It was raining. A half-moon peeked through some clouds and was quickly covered again. Aaron looked around. They were in a city. He looked at the towering palace before him. They were in Dovan. His plan worked.

The guard shoved him forward and he was led in a back gate, downstairs, and to the jail cell. The hallways were darker than he remembered; only every other torch was lit. The cells looked different. They were a black metal instead of the steel that he remembered. Every cell he passed by had someone in it. Many were asleep, but a few gathered at their doors to see who the new inmate was. Finally, he was thrown into a cell. The handcuffs were still on. He noticed the cell to his right was empty and somehow this bed was dirtier than the previous ones. Unsure of what else to do, he laid back down and tried to get some sleep. The cuffs were uncomfortable, though. He looked down and began to adjust them. Something didn't seem right. Aaron began to look closer. It was too dark. He went back to the front of the cage and tried to get the cuffs in as much light as possible.

"You're not getting those off," the inmate across the way stated.

"Hm?"

"No keyhole."

Aaron looked closer. He was right. There was nowhere to place a key. "Are yours this way?"

The man laughed and lifted his wrists up. There were no cuffs. "Not sure what you did, but if you have those cuffs, you won't last long."

Aaron slowly lowered his wrists. "What do you mean?"

"Everyone who comes in with those cuffs gets dragged out of their cell one night and never comes back. Other than her," he motions to the empty cell next to Aaron's. "They keep bringing that poor creature back."

"How long do I have?"

The man shrugged. "Usually only a couple nights."

Aaron didn't like the turn the situation was taking. "Thanks. I think."

The man smiled an awkward smile and snidely said, "Don't want you caught off guard."

The prince sat back down on the mat and leaned his back against the wall. Maybe he could remove the cuffs with magic. He'd never done anything of the sort, but it was worth a try. He closed his eyes and concentrated. He felt the light in his heart and began to pull it through his body. The moment it reached his wrists, searing pain shot through both arms and it felt like his heart got stabbed. He let out a small cry of pain and doubled over. He eventually steadied his breathing. The cuffs were blocking his magic. He wasn't sure he made the best decision.

CHAPTER 17

I don't even know if they took him to Dovan," Aeragoth stated. "There are prisons throughout the land."

"That is probably the best place to start though," Klew mentioned.

Aeragoth nodded. "We should have our spies investigate if there are any new elven prisoners in Dovan."

"Well, he's only half-elf and has rounded ears..." Catherine informed.

"Hm...that makes things more difficult. The guards have been arresting people left and right. They even had to build an additional prison outside the city gates." The elf thought for a moment. "I think we need to just start with figuring out where the prince was taken. I will alert our spies to start investigating. This may take some time, so I suggest you all divert your attention to looking for proof of shadow touched influence."

Catherine sighed. She wanted to find Aaron, but, if there was no way for her to help, there was nothing she could do.

Aaron was stirred from his restless sleep by the sounds of armored guards walking down the hall. There were no windows, so he had no idea what time of day it was. Two guards dragged a young woman down the hallway and threw her into the cage next to Aaron. She had blond hair neatly braided into a circle around her head, her eyes were a deep green, her outfit was a fiery red cropped top that revealed her stomach and a matching skirt, and she wore cuffs like Aaron's, but they weren't attached to each other. Aaron drew closer and noticed her ears were pointed. She was an elf.

The elf pulled herself up onto her mat and crossed her arms around her midsection. She sighed and looked around, pausing when she saw Aaron. Her expression dropped. "They caught you?"

She knew him? Aaron made his way over to the right side of his cage. "You know me?"

The elf got up and walked over to Aaron. He noted she was barefoot. They now stood right next to each other with just the bars between them.

"We've never met," she said softly, "But they have been looking for you for quite some time."

"Why? Yes, I escaped, but I was arrested for not paying taxes."

She shook her head. "I don't know, but that was an excuse. I've heard them talking about you."

They talked about him? "What have they said?"

"They've said you're the key."

"Key to what?"

She glanced around without moving her head. "Taking over the plane."

Aaron's heart dropped. He looked into her deep green eyes for several moments. They were kind, but hard. "Shadow touched?" he asked in a hushed whisper.

She nodded.

༺⚬༻

A moon. It would take the dwarven representative a full moon to get to them. But at least he was coming. Catherine placed the letter down on a table. She supposed it gave her time to get proof, so the moment the representative arrived they could send word back and gain more allies. As she left her tent, she heard a horn blow and there was a commotion off to one edge of the camp. She decided to investigate.

"John!" she called out as she ran to her friend.

He smiled and embraced her. "I brought allies." John motioned to dozens of wizards behind him.

"Thank you."

"Where are the others?"

"Aaron was captured, well he turned himself over..."

"What?"

Catherine held back tears. "I don't know. Things seem to be falling apart again."

John placed his hands on her shoulders and looked in her eyes. "Aaron is strong. You are strong. Have faith."

Catherine hugged John again. Eventually, she led him to where Clay and Klew were.

"Welcome!" Clay clasped arms with John.

"You arrived just in time. If you would like, you can join us as we sneak into Bellmora and look for proof of shadow touched influence," Klew informed.

"It would be my pleasure. What is the plan?"

"Well, we've spoken to some soldiers that have snuck further in and they mentioned some disturbance to the east of Dovan, but it is unclear as to what was happening. We're thinking of investigating it."

"Do we know Aaron's whereabouts?"

Klew shook his head. "There is another team investigating that."

Catherine wished she was part of the team looking for Aaron, but knowing she was now the lead of the shadow touched search, she needed to be part of that mission.

"When do we head out?" John asked.

"Soon. We were packing when you arrived."

"Well, I'm still packed, so let's go!" the wizard laughed. Catherine appreciated his enthusiasm. The four of them gathered their supplies and met with Thiel at the edge of camp.

"Due to the sensitivity of this mission, I will be going with you," Thiel stated.

They headed out.

⤛⤜

"Where do they take you every night?" Aaron asked his elven companion, Bree.

"You don't want to know," she mumbled and huddled into a ball near their shared bars.

Aaron sat down on the floor next to her. "I can't come up with a plan to escape, if I don't know what's going on."

"You think I haven't tried to escape?" She scowled

"No, but you didn't have an ally before."

She was quiet. "They take me to Noth."

"Who's Noth?" He wrapped his hand around one of the bars between them.

"A dark wizard, with insatiable lust." She pulled her bent knees closer to her chest.

Aaron was quiet for a moment. "How long has this been going on?"

Bree shrugged. "As long as I've been here. A few moons?"

He felt a pit in his stomach. She had been tortured for so long. Aaron reached his hands through the bars and took one of her hands. "I'll get you out of here. He won't ever touch you again."

She looked up at him, the hardness in her eyes was gone, just pain remained.

"Tell me everything you know."

Bree then began to tell him how every night they would take her to Noth's room, she found if she did what he asked without resisting and served him wine, his lips would be loosened and he would talk about the goings on, which is how she learned about the shadow touched and Aaron. There were times he brought her to dinner, like a trophy, and she saw a shadow touched out of the corner of her eye and a wanted poster for Aaron.

"Do you think you could get information out of him?" Aaron inquired. "Serve him a little extra wine one night and get him talking?"

"I might," she perked up.

"We don't want to be too obvious. Start small, then work your way up."

"What do we want to learn?"

Aaron thought for a moment, they had to prioritize things. "How is the war going? If you can manage to get any plans they have, that would be great. Also, if you can get information on any possible allies for us."

Bree nodded. "I'll do my best."

Aaron quickly shifted away as a couple guards came through. They spat at any inmate that was close to the door of their cage but paid little more heed as they passed by.

Aaron watched them carefully. Once they were out of earshot, he turned to the prisoner on the other side. "Why are there so many prisoners here?"

He looked over and gave a toothy smile. "We're part of the Fiends."

"The what?"

The prisoner sat up, shocked. "You've never heard of us?"

Aaron shook his head.

"Where have you been?"

"Not in Bellmora."

"Lucky you." He leaned against his back wall.

"I suppose." Aaron looked down at his cuffs. "So, who are the Fiends?"

"We're people who love Bellmora too much to let it be destroyed by this disgrace of a king."

"You're rebelling?" Aaron was suddenly intrigued.

"Yes."

"All of you are part of the Fiends?" He looked around, taking in the large number of prisoners.

"Most of us."

"What did you do?"

"A little bit of this, a little bit of that."

"Thanks   for   the   clarification," Aaron   stated sarcastically.

"Hey," he straightened up, "we don't judge what each other does. We allow fellow Fiends to protest in the way they see fit."

The half-elf knew he needed to tap into the group somehow. "What do you know about me?"

"Huh?"

Aaron approached the man's cell and got into as much light as possible. "I've been told I'm wanted. What do they say about me?"

The man squinted and tilted his head, then his eyes widened. "You're the one the king has been obsessing over!"

"What has he said about me?"

"That you stole something of value from the palace and were trading secrets to the elves. What did you steal?"

"I stole nothing. During the first moon I was arrested for not paying taxes despite King Hargon changing the taxes that were due after they were due and then escaped. I stole nothing."

"Then why is the king after you?"

Aaron twisted his ring with his thumb. "What did he say I stole?"

"A ring."

He knows. King Hargon knows Aaron has Jahola. But how?

"Why does he want you?"

Aaron looked the Fiend in the eyes. "I'm here to take him down."

⁊∘⸜

Catherine pulled Chestnut to a stop. Ruins lay before them. The monastery's inner garden was burned. The pillars that held up the inner rim walkway were knocked over, causing the covering to collapse. The stained-glass windows were smashed. The statues were destroyed.

"What happened here?" she asked.

"I don't know," Thiel answered softly. "Keep an eye out."

They slowly began to ride closer. Once they reached the outer edge, they dismounted and began to investigate the ruins further. They spread out but made sure everyone was in at least one person's eyesight.

As Catherine investigated the garden, she found a single plant that was hiding under ashes, still alive. She gently cleared the covering from it, allowing sunlight to reach its leaves. It was small but gave her a bit of hope. She froze when she heard a rustle from off to the side. Slowly, she turned around and a tall, muscular man stood behind her. He wore flowy, white pants with a red sash and no shirt. The pants were rather dirty. He had long brown hair tied behind his head and hazel eyes.

"What are you doing here?" he asked in a gruff voice.

"We're...uh...we're just trying to find out what happened." Catherine was trying to figure out how to get the others' attention without making it obvious.

"The monastery was destroyed. Isn't that obvious."

"Uh...well yes...we were wondering...uh...what destroyed it."

His eyes narrowed. "You're an elf."

Catherine's muscles began to tense up.

"Why would an elf care what happened to this monastery?"

"We just...um...We suspect King Hargon has aligned himself with less than savory allies." She held her breath.

His face and body relaxed. She released her breath and relaxed as well.

"Yammi." He extended his hand.

"Uh…Catherine." She shook it.

"Gather your friends." He then turned and began walking towards their horses.

"Um…Thiel! Clay!" She called out to her two closest allies.

Thiel drew his sword when he saw Yammi.

"No! No!" Catherine shouted. "I think he's a friend."

Thiel and Clay gathered Klew and John. The party met the stranger by their horses.

"Who are you?" Thiel asked.

"Yammi. This monastery was my home." He looked over the rubble. "I now have none.

Catherine suddenly felt sorry for him.

"What happened?" Clay inquired.

"You wouldn't believe me," Yammi answered.

"Try us."

"Shadow touched."

They were all silent.

"They came in the night and burned the place down. I'm the only one who survived. No one knows I survived. King Hargon blames the attack on Zentora."

Catherine felt moved. "We believe you."

Yammi looked at her in shock. "You believe me?"

She nodded. "We're looking for proof of shadow touched influence. I think you're that proof. Come back to the Zentora camp with us. We have representatives from across the plane coming and they want proof of shadow touched presence before they will join the war."

"I can't." He looked back at the fallen monastery.

"We need you. The plane needs you!"

He shook his head.

"Please."

"King Hargon would have my head."

"We'll protect you," Thiel stated.

Yammi looked at Thiel, then back at Catherine. "Alright. I'll go."

Catherine's heart jumped for joy. They had their proof. A first-hand witness. She then stopped and looked at the monastery. "How many monks lived here?"

"About one hundred at any given time."

"How many shadow touched were there?"

"I do not know, but they outnumbered us and came when we were least prepared."

That was a lot of shadow touched. They really did have the numbers to fight a war. All of the excitement she had had with finding proof was replaced with fear. Fear that maybe the shadow touched were too powerful. Fear that maybe they were too late to stop them. Fear that the war was not going to be easy.

∂∘⊰

It was the middle of the night, when two guards dressed in black armor, unceremoniously grabbed Aaron, abruptly waking him up, and dragged him out of the cell. Half asleep, Aaron managed to get his feet underneath him and on the ground. He stumbled along as they roughly guided him through the halls. As his alertness increased, he started to notice the decorations on the wall change. They clearly had left the prison area, but still only half of the torches were lit. Aaron felt a darkness over the palace as they walked through. All of the guards they passed were wearing black armor, not the gray metal or brown leather they used to. Finally, they reached a set of large double doors. There were engravings of rearing horses on each of them. The guards standing outside the room opened the doors for them. They entered the throne room.

Aaron had expected to see the Bellmoran crest hanging on the wall, but instead there were two black banners with identical red symbols on each. The symbol looked like a "T" with drips flowing down from the horizontal line. King Hargon sat on the throne. Color was mostly drained from his face; his hair was white and thinning. He wore dark red robes. An old wizard stood to his left, wearing black robes with red embroidery. On King Hargon's right were two people, dressed all in black, with hooded cloaks casting shadows over their faces.

The guards threw Aaron to the floor in front of King Hargon.

"How dare you steal from me!" the king bellowed.

Aaron stood up.

"Give it to me now!"

"I have nothing of yours," the elven prince retorted.

The leader of Bellmora rose to his feet. "How dare you lie to my face!"

"I am not lying. I have stolen nothing."

One of the cloaked figures stepped forward and walked towards Aaron, saying, "Your lies will not be accepted here. Give us what is ours." They were female.

"I have nothing of yours."

She grabbed Aaron's wrists. Instinctively, Aaron pulled away. She said something in a language that he did not understand but felt like he had heard before. Suddenly, a sharp pain radiated up from his wrists and into his heart. He cried out in pain and dropped to one knee.

"Alaina!" King Hargon said harshly.

"I'm just getting him to cooperate," she hissed. "I won't kill him." She pulled his arms away from his chest and whispered where only Aaron could hear, "Yet." She then looked at his hands, spat on the ground, and said, "It's not here."

Aaron thanked Etienne that he had the foresight to give Jahola to Bree. "I told you. I have nothing of yours."

Alaina swung her arm and struck Aaron across the face. "You will not speak unless spoken to." She then grabbed his face and pulled it in close to hers. "Where is it?"

Aaron saw a glint of her face from the light of a torch. Her skin shimmered like metal and she had purple eyes. He felt his heart stop. He had never seen a shadow touched before.

When he didn't answer, she threw him to the ground. "You will tell us where it is!"

"I told you; I have nothing of yours."

"Lies!" Alaina lifted her arm again, static jumping from finger to finger.

"Alaina!" King Hargon shouted.

She stopped mid-swing and turned to the king. "Remember," she hissed, "this one is mine."

"Not in my throne room."

She turned to the guards that stood nearby. "Bring him downstairs."

The guards grabbed Aaron by his elbows and once again began to drag him. That time he managed to be on his feet the entire time. They led him out of the room, Alaina following behind. He stumbled through the halls towards where the prison was, but when they reached the bottom of the stairs, Alaina took the lead, and they turned a different direction.

"You're going to regret not giving me what I want," Alaina said.

They passed several dark wooden doors, until finally, the shadow touched turned and opened one. She stepped aside and let the guards in with Aaron. Panic set in. There were all sorts of torture devices filling the room.

"Tie him up." She said something in another language and touched Aaron's cuffs. The chain connecting them fell off.

The guards then tied Aaron to a post in the center of the room. He struggled to get free but failed.

"Leave us."

The guards left the room, closing the door behind them.

"I'm done playing games. Tell me where it is." Alaina began examining different tools that were laid out on the table.

"I told you; I stole nothing."

She examined a sharp tool. "I said I'm done playing games." She walked over to Aaron, still holding the sharp tool. "Where is the ring?"

"I don't have it."

Aaron held his breath as she pushed the tool against his side but did not penetrate.

"I see that. Now where is it?"

The half-elf knew there was no hope in continuing to play dumb. "I'm not going to tell you."

She quickly pulled the tool back and then thrust it into his side. He bit his tongue, trying to suppress a cry of pain.

"I wouldn't suggest that course of action. Where is it?"

Aaron chose silence.

"Fine." She twisted the tool.

Tears welled in his eyes and a whimper escaped his throat.

"Hm...tougher than I thought you'd be." She yanked the tool out and went back over to the table.

Aaron breathed heavily, trying to control the pain.

"I told Captain Alik not to let anyone survive." She picked a curved tool up then put it back down.

Aaron questioned if he heard her right. Captain Alik?

"Oh, you didn't know?" There was a cheeriness to her voice. "I hired Captain Alik and his crew. To kill Queen Sylance."

Aaron jerked towards her, but the restraints held him back and the movement caused excruciating pain to shoot up from his side. He released a small cry and stopped moving.

Alaina laughed. Her tone then got gruff. "Then you had to go and live. I know your mother gave you the ring. Where is it?" She walked over to him, without anything in her hands.

"I will *never* tell you," Aaron growled.

"That's too bad."

Blue electricity began to crackle between her fingers as she lifted her hand. She placed her palm on Aaron's chest. He felt pain throughout his body and his heart began to beat fast. Soon he was gasping for air. She pulled her hand back, the electricity gone, but the pain remained.

"Have you changed your mind?"

Aaron spat at her. She struck him across the face with the back of her hand.

"How dare you disrespect me!" She impulsively grabbed a nearby whip and struck Aaron with a crack.

He could no longer hold it back; he gave a cry of pain.

"You will bow to me!" She cracked the whip again.

"I will never bow to your kind."

In a quick motion, she extended her left hand in front of her, towards Aaron, and a dense, dark cloud shot from it and hit Aaron. His insides felt like they were on fire. His mind flirted with unconsciousness.

Alaina muttered a curse word, then shouted, "Guards!"

The two guards entered.

"Take him back to his cell."

The guards untied Aaron and guided him out of the room. Aaron was in too much pain to really control his walking, so he was mostly dragged down the hall. They took him to his cell and threw him in. Aaron just lay there in pain. His vision blurred occasionally, as waves of pain pulsed through his body. He was unsure if it was a short amount of time or a long amount of time, but eventually someone entered his cell and began to bandage his wounds. He hurt too much to do anything in assistance, so he just lay there letting them bandage him. The person then poured something down his throat. He coughed and gagged for a few moments as they left the cell. Once he caught his breath, he realized he felt significantly better. He was still in intense pain, but he was able to pull himself onto his mat. He stared at the ceiling, dwelling on how big of a mistake he had made. He hoped Catherine was in better shape than he was.

Aaron had successfully drifted off to sleep for a short period of time, when he was awoken by Bree crying out, "Oh, Aaron!"

He stirred and looked at her.

"Are you okay?"

He winced as he pulled himself to a seated position. "No," he answered honestly.

"What happened?"

"They wanted answers out of me."

"Did you give them any?"

He shook his head, stood up, faltered slightly, then made his way over to Bree. "Did you learn anything?" he asked softly.

"I did. The war is at a stalemate right now. The king is fairly distracted by a group called the Fiends. He also thinks they have an ally in the palace as they seem to be able to hit vital targets regularly. I didn't dare try to get more out of him."

Aaron winced as he shifted.

"All of that over this?" Bree looked at the ring on her thumb.

"As I said, the less you know, the better off you are."

"We have to get you out of here."

"We have to get all of us out of here." Aaron looked around, then paused as he gazed at his other neighbor. "But I have an idea." He slowly hobbled over to the other side of his cage. "Hey."

The Fiend member looked over. "You're in rough shape."

Aaron bobbed his head in agreement, then motioned for the inmate to come closer.

The human obliged. "Yes?"

"I know you all have an ally on the inside. Can you get their attention to let us out?"

"Do you think I would be in here if I could?"

"Yes. It's not a smart move to have any ally like that risk revealing themselves for a handful of members."

"So, what makes you think it's worth it now? Because it will get you out?" he scoffed.

"I'm one of their targets. I have something that, if they got their hands-on, would-be annihilation for everyone. If you get me out, I can get you allies like you wouldn't have dreamed of."

The Fiend eyed him suspiciously. "Who are you?"

"Prince Aaron, of the Isle Lands. Sent by Annathalinda."

"You're an elf?!"

"Half. Will you help me?"

CHAPTER 18

❧❧

Catherine, Clay, Klew, John, Thiel, and Yammi rode into the camp. Soldiers began to gather and whisper as the group dismounted. Thiel then guided all of them to the general's tent. The elven king was there, discussing matters with the others. Everyone but Yammi bowed. The human glanced around quickly, then bowed himself.

"Rise," the king said.

"We bring a witness," Thiel announced.

The king waved his hand, motioning for the others to depart. "A witness?" He turned his attention to Yammi and looked him up and down.

They all turned to Yammi, who stood there silently.

"Tell him what happened," Catherine whispered to him.

"A moon ago, hundreds of shadow touched came in the night and attacked my monastery. They slaughtered everyone but me. King Hargon blames you. No one would ever believe me."

The king was silent for a moment. "This is more concerning than I had thought. They are comfortable enough to openly attack communities. They have an army."

"The dwarven representative should be here soon," Catherine reminded.

"Yes. We should have them meet with you," he nodded towards Yammi. "Your story should be enough to convince them. I am surprised the shadow touched have not joined the war effort."

"It's only a matter of time," Thiel added.

"At what point do we loop your troops in? I don't think they would appreciate being in the dark until they see a shadow touched on the battlefield," Clay pointed out.

The king nodded. "I want to wait until we have the dwarves' response. Once they join, I will announce both the alliance and the reason why. Do we know when the Isle Land reinforcements will be here?"

Catherine shook her head. "We came here immediately; I have not checked to see if there are any letters."

The king nodded. "Thank you."

"I wish to avenge my fallen brothers," Yammi said simply.

"And how do you propose that?"

"Are you willing to pursue the shadow touched?"

"I am."

"Then I will follow you. I cannot defeat them alone, but with an army we stand a chance." Yammi then bowed once more.

Surprise showed on the king's face. "Your allegiance is accepted. May we be stronger together."

Yammi stood.

"You are all dismissed."

The group turned and left. Thiel quickly parted ways.

"Come," Catherine said to Yammi, "let me show you where you can pitch your tent."

The monk nodded a thanks and followed her through the camp. They got many glances and whispers, but none of the elves seemed to openly object. Once they reached where people had set up their sleeping tents, Yammi thanked Catherine and found a spot to settle in. Catherine then went to seek any updates. There were no messages for her. She then made her way through camp, leaving her allies behind and found where Aeragoth was.

"Hello, Catherine," he greeted.

"Hello."

"Were you successful?"

She nodded. "We found a monastery that had been attacked by an army of shadow touched. Thankfully, there was a survivor. He has agreed to testify about what happened and join the ranks."

"An army?!"

Catherine nodded.

Aeragoth looked down and sighed. "Things are not looking good."

"Any word of Aaron?"

He shook his head. "But I haven't had much word, so there's still hope."

◈◈◈

Aaron tried to hold back tears as the pain surged through his body. He had no idea how much longer he could take it.

Alaina threw the tool to the ground. "Why won't you tell me?!" She turned with a furl of her cloak. "Guards!"

The two same guards came in, untied Aaron, and dragged him to his cell. The world was a blur. He knew he couldn't give in, but he didn't know if he was strong enough. It had been three nights of torture. Three nights of being pushed to his limit. The guards, once again, threw him to the ground. He lay there, finally letting the tears silently fall.

After some time, Aaron wasn't sure how long, someone came into his cage and, once again, patched him up. They did not pour anything down his throat and said, "She wants this one to scar," then left.

The pain made it hard to breathe. He had prayed for the potion he was being denied. There was no sleep for him that night, but he did not move from the floor where the guards had tossed him. Time passed, but he wasn't sure how much.

"This is messed up," the Fiend finally said as Aaron began to come to again.

Aaron tried sitting himself up but quickly gave up.

"They're healing you, just to torture you more. Could you really bring King Hargon down?"

The half-elf was in too much pain to answer but wondered if what the Fiend said was true. Could he take down King Hargon and the shadow touched? Was he actually in over his head? How could he have been so stupid as to just hand himself over? He hoped Catherine was faring better.

He eventually tried to pull himself to a seated position and immediately hung his head between his bent knees. Slowly, he scooted over to Bree. She knelt down next to him.

"My ring," he said softly.

She pulled it off her finger and handed it to him. He slipped it on.

"What does it do?"

Aaron shook his head.

Bree sighed. "I know. The less I know, the safer I am."

The prince prayed that the legends of Jahola having healing powers were true. It made sense with how many near-death experiences he had had throughout his life, but maybe he was just lucky. Over time, the pain subsided slightly. It was nowhere near as effective as a healing spell or potion, but it relieved him enough to think.

"Any news?" he asked Bree.

She shook her head. "He is very frustrated that you have not been killed yet."

"Join the guild," Aaron muttered.

"He doesn't understand Alaina's obsession with you."

The half-elf perked up. "He doesn't know?"

Bree shook her head.

"They're keeping secrets."

Her eyes glimmered. "Should I play that up?"

Aaron nodded. "If they turn against each other, they will be weaker."

Once the day was mostly gone, Aaron slipped Jahola back to Bree. Some of the pain came back, but not all of it. Soon, a guard came for Bree and whisked her away. Aaron then lay down and tried to get some rest before it was his turn.

As expected, a couple of guards came to collect Aaron and took him down the hall to the all-too-familiar room. Alaina stood in the center, waiting for them. The guards tied him up, once again, and left the room.

"Ready to tell me where it is?" she asked.

Aaron spat at her.

"You've healed," she growled. "You have it!"

"Feel free to search, you won't find it!"

Alaina took her hood off. "I want you to see my face when I say this." Her skin was a metallic blue, her eyes a deep purple, and her hair a metallic silver. The colors should have been beautiful, but they just added to Aaron's fear. She got so close to his face that their noses almost touched and looked into his eyes. "I am not going to kill you. But I am going to make you wish I did. I've had enough with you." She stood up. Alaina took a knife and cut Aaron's tattered shirt off, not caring whether the blade slashed his skin or not. She then picked up an iron that had been sitting in a fire.

Aaron closed his eyes and took a deep breath. The hot brand seared his back. The pain was excruciating. Tears streamed from his clenched eyes and a muffled cry of pain escaped his throat as he struggled to keep his mouth shut.

"How?" she threw the brand down in frustration.

Aaron knew he couldn't take it much longer.

Alaina muttered something in a language Aaron didn't understand, then grabbed his face in her hand and forced him to look at her. "Where is it? What did you do with it? Who has it?" Her face relaxed. "Who has it?" she asked herself and then stood up. She placed her hood back on her head, masking her features. "Guards!"

The two guards entered.

"Make sure he doesn't get out. I'll be back." She then left the room.

Aaron gasped as he let emotions out. Once he began to collect his mind again, he had a realization. What did she figure out? Where was she going? Did she figure out Bree had it? Had he failed? He began to feel hopeless. He had tried so hard to not give in. He thought not telling her was enough. He closed his eyes and rested his forehead on the pole in front of him. Eventually, the door opened, but he did not look, accepting his fate.

Aaron was surprised when he heard an unfamiliar, deep voice say, "Alaina sent me to take over."

The half-elf looked over and saw another guard standing there. He wore chainmail armor, had short, slightly curly, light brown hair, and a short beard. The two guards nodded and left the room. The new guard that Aaron had never seen before stood, watching the door for a while. Then suddenly turned to Aaron and rushed over.

"Can you run?" he asked as he untied Aaron.

"What?" Aaron was confused.

"Can you run?"

"I...I don't know."

"Well, you're going to have to. Come on."

Aaron tried to stand and walk without support. He most definitely could not run. The guard caught him as he began to stumble.

"This isn't going to work," the guard mumbled. "Here!" He then grabbed some rope and tied Aaron's hands together. He looped and arm through Aaron's, supporting him, and firmly held the half-elf's shoulder. It hurt, but everything hurt.

The guard guided him through the hallway and up a set of stairs. They were headed out of the palace.

"We have to save Bree," Aaron whispered.

"What?"

"We have to save Bree."

"Who's Bree?"

"She's helping me. She's with Noth. Alaina is going after her now. She has something the shadow touched want."

The guard cursed. "You're in no condition to help anyone."

"We have to. The fate of this war depends on it."

The guard cursed again. "I'm going to get you somewhere safe." He took Aaron out a back corridor and locked him in a caged wagon. "Don't draw attention to yourself."

The moon was waning, but unusually bright. Aaron closed his eyes as he leaned against the wall of the wagon. He was still in immense pain. Who was this guard? Was this the ally Bree and the Fiend were talking about? All was silent but the crickets. He tried to wish away the dizziness that was starting to take over again.

Suddenly, a horn sounded, and guards came running. Aaron had enough control and awareness to duck down so no one could see him. Within moments he heard shouts and the sounds of fighting. Prisoners started pouring out of the palace. He remained hidden. Pure chaos was taking over. Aaron dared not look but heard death cries.

Another horn blew. The cries died down, but the shouting grew louder. It was difficult to understand what anyone was saying as there were so many voices shouting at once. It eventually grew slightly quieter.

Aaron didn't know how much time had passed when the guard who saved him opened the back door and shoved Bree in. The guard closed the door, and it sounded like he locked it. Aaron hoped he really was an ally. The wagon jolted and the sound of horses' hooves clacking against the stone road could be heard. They were moving fast.

"Aaron!" Bree crawled over to him. "What's going on?"

Aaron saw flickers of her face as the moon's light shined through a small, barred opening. "I'm not entirely sure. This guard rescued me. I asked him to save you too."

"He saved all of us!"

"What?"

"He released all of the prisoners! It's a free-for-all back there."

"Where is he taking us?"

"I don't know. He didn't say much because we were in a bit of a hurry. Alaina was fighting with Noth in the room next to where I was when the horns sounded. I'm not sure where they went, but soon after the guard and a few others, including our Fiend friend, showed up to save me."

"He is their ally." Aaron felt a wave of relief for the first time in what felt like forever.

They hit a bump and Aaron's back screamed at him, reminding him how much pain he was in. Bree helped Aaron position himself in as comfortable of a position as he could. They both remained silent for the rest of the ride.

After what was long enough to get them out of Dovan, the wagon slowed down and came to a stop. The door opened.

"We need to abandon the wagon," the guard said and extended a hand towards Bree.

"He can't run," she observed.

"We have horses."

Bree helped Aaron exit the wagon.

The Fiend member from beside Aaron's cage was unhooking the two horses. He looked over and smiled at Aaron. "I told you I'd get you out of here. Now it's time to keep up your end of the bargain."

Aaron nodded.

"You never did share that with me," grunted the guard. "It better be worth exposing myself."

"He said he can end this war."

"Is that so?" The guard's tone sounded like he didn't believe it.

Aaron turned to Bree. "Can I have my ring?"

She nodded and gave it to him. He did not immediately put it on.

"Ring? The ring you stole?!" the guard snapped.

Aaron shook his head. "This was never King Hargon's, but he did want it. Or should I say Alaina wanted it."

"Who's Alaina?" the Fiend asked.

"An ally of King Hargon's," the guard answered.

"A shadow touched," Aaron growled.

Their two male companions froze and looked at him.

"This," Aaron held up the ring, "is Jahola."

"What?!" all three said in unison.

"Get me to the elven army and all of you will have protection."

No one moved. Aaron kept as straight of a face as he could, while desperately trying to remain standing. Finally, his legs began to give out and he leaned against the wagon.

"Oh!" Bree rushed to his side. "I'll join you," she whispered.

"Thank you."

"Help him on the horse," the guard commanded the Fiend.

The three worked together, and Aaron assisted as much as he could, to finally get Aaron on a horse. The Fiend mounted behind him. The guard and Bree shared the other horse. The guard set fire to the wagon and they took off.

They rode as long as they could bear. The sun was high in the sky, and it was about midday when they stopped.

"Aaron!" Bree exclaimed as they dismounted.

Aaron simply turned to look at her. He had no idea how he was still conscious.

"Your back," her voice dropped.

"They branded you?!" the Fiend exclaimed as he came over.

The prince nodded. "What does it look like?"

"It looks like a crescent moon with lightning. What does it mean?"

Aaron shrugged.

Softly, Bree said, "It's a cursed symbol."

Aaron looked up at her. Sympathy flooded her face.

"It's a beacon for the shadow touched. They will hunt down whoever has that symbol."

"Perfect," the guard said sarcastically.

The half-elf's heart sank. A beacon? Things were not going according to plan. It was probably his fault too.

"We need to get rest and keep moving. Do you know where this elven army is?"

Aaron took a deep breath, "A quarter moon east of Dovan, just within the Zentora border."

They were all silent for a few moments as they got comfortable.

"Thank you," Aaron finally said.

The guard looked over.

"Thank you for rescuing us and risking yourself."

The guard sighed. "You're welcome. If everything you have said is true, this war is far more than I had previously thought. The name is Faber, I *was* a palace captain. I haven't approved of King Hargon's decisions for a few years now, and, once the war broke out, I knew I couldn't just stand by."

"That's when he began to help us," the Fiend added. "He would feed us information."

"I knew King Hargon's allies were suspicious, but shadow touched?"

Aaron lay down on the grass.

"How did you know? How did you end up here?"

"Annathalinda had a vision of shadow touched and that myself and someone else were key to everything."

"Because of Jahola," Bree said softly.

"I suppose." He thought of how Annathalinda was worried that the shadow touched had Keelhola.

"Time for rest," Faber restated.

৯৽৻

Catherine, Yammi, Clay, and Klew stood just behind Zentora's king as the dwarven representative entered the tent and sat down.

"Welcome," the king stated warmly.

"I sure hope this isn't a waste of my time," the dwarf grumbled.

"I assure you it is not. This war is turning into more than we had anticipated. Annathalinda spoke of a vision involving shadow touched. And, unfortunately, we have evidence that those visions are true."

The dwarf grunted.

The king motioned to Yammi. The human stepped forward.

"This monk's monastery was attacked by an army of shadow touched, but only he survived."

"Well, isn't that convenient," the dwarf scoffed.

"Excuse me?" Yammi seemed to be getting perturbed.

"Why would a human align himself with shadow touched and then destroy his own kingdom with them?"

"I do not lie."

"I do not believe you."

Clay placed a hand on Yammi's shoulder as he started to lurch forward. The human stopped himself and leaned back slightly.

"Please," Catherine stepped forward, "listen to his account."

The dwarf stood up. "Unless you have some real proof, we will not be meddling in your trivial quarrels." He then turned and left the tent.

"How..." Catherine couldn't find words.

Yammi mumbled something under his breath.

"Apparently we need more," the elven king stated as he turned towards the others.

"But what?! We have a first-hand witness."

The king shook his head. "He needs to see something himself. Something that can't be made up. Something that he can't dismiss."

"Like what?"

"Maybe if he saw one?"

Yammi shook his head. "There had been no rumors of shadow touched before the attack. They are staying hidden."

"Maybe there's something in the palace?" Catherine thought. "Have we gotten word from the spies in Dovan?"

"I have not checked," the king admitted. "Go find Aeragoth. Let me know if you learn anything useful. I will try to think of ways we can convince him."

Catherine immediately left the tent, not caring to check if anyone followed her. She searched through the camp and finally found Aeragoth on the edge speaking to someone.

"Aeragoth!" she called.

He turned, bid farewell to the elf he was talking with, and approached her. "Perfect timing."

"Oh?"

"I just received word from my scouts."

"And!?" Catherine's heart skipped a beat. Did they find Aaron?

"There was a huge disturbance at the palace a quarter moon ago. It appears almost all prisoners were released. Unintentionally."

That sounded like something Aaron would be involved in.

"My scouts were not able to identify anyone involved, but the majority of the prisoners escaped. They are trying to gather more detailed information."

"Please keep me informed." Catherine was becoming excited. Could Aaron be free? Was he headed to them at that moment?

"I will."

Catherine got so distracted by her hope that she started to turn away.

"Did you want something?" Aeragoth inquired.

She quickly turned back around, realizing she had completely forgotten why she went to find him. "Yes! Have they gained any proof of shadow touched?"

He shook his head. "Not even murmurs. Did Yammi's confession not work?"

"No," Catherine admitted disappointedly. "The representative claimed it could all be a lie and that there was no actual proof."

"Hm…" Aeragoth rubbed his chin. "I'll send a message to my scouts to see if they can find something in that regard as well. How long do we have?"

She shrugged. "I do not know, but he doesn't appear to be happy to be here, so I doubt it's long."

The elf nodded. "We'll do our best."

తోం

Aaron was feeling stronger every day.

"Someone's watching us," Faber whispered.

"Halt here," the prince ordered.

The two horses drew to a stop.

"We are allies."

Four elves wielding swords dropped out of the trees. Aaron knew there were more.

"Why should we believe you?" one of the elves asked.

"I was sent by Queen Emmyana of the Isle Lands. The rest of my allies should be at your camp already."

Two of the elves whispered to each other. "Wait here," the first elf said and took off down the path.

It was several moments before they returned, but when they did another elf accompanied them.

"Are you Prince Aaron?" he asked.

Aaron nodded.

He smiled. "Catherine will be so glad to see you." He then turned to the guards, "Let them join us."

The four were led down the path, and soon it opened up to a large military camp. They dismounted their horses and were led to a large tent near the center. The elves guarding the tent opened it up and let them enter.

"This is a waste of time!" the dwarven representative shouted.

"You have to believe us," Catherine pleaded. "The fate of the plane rests on your support!"

The elf guiding the Dovan cohort cleared his throat.

The dwarf, Catherine, Clay, Klew, and the king turned their attention to the new guests.

"Aaron!" Catherine cried as she ran over and threw her arms around him.

He winced, but she didn't seem to notice. He returned the embrace and kissed the top of her head.

She pulled back and hit his shoulder. "Why did you do that?"

Aaron couldn't help but gasp a little bit with the strike.

"Oh my gosh! I'm sorry! What happened?!" She threw her arms back around him.

"They know."

Catherine pulled back. "They know what?"

"I have Jahola."

"Who is this?" the dwarf snapped.

Clay stepped forward. "This is Prince Aaron of the Isle Lands, Bearer of Jahola."

The dwarf grumbled to himself and crossed his arms.

Clay approached Aaron. "Good to have you back. And who might these be?"

"Bree of Kemy," she introduced herself. "I was traveling through when I was captured by shadow touched and taken to Dovan."

"Captain Faber," the human introduced himself. "I was part of the Dovan guard, but do not support King Hargon any longer."

"Nathel," the Fiend introduced himself for the first time. "Rebel."

"They saved me," Aaron added. "I wouldn't be here without them."

"Then we owe you a debt of gratitude," Clay stated.

"If what he says is true, you owe us nothing," Faber replied.

"Annathalinda was right," Aaron said. "There is a shadow touched, Alaina, that is King Hargon's right-hand woman. She was trying to get Jahola and somehow knew I had it."

"That is quite the accusation," the dwarf retorted.

Aaron turned his attention to the dwarf. "It is not an accusation, it is the truth."

"Prove it."

The half-elf lifted his hands, showing the cuffs. "These prevent the wearer from casting spells. I'm sure they're of shadow touched origin."

The dwarf huffed, then approached and examined the cuffs. His eyes widened. "They are."

"They are after Jahola. If they do not have Keelhola, I'm sure they're after it too. But they know I have Jahola. I'm sure they know, or knew, who had Keelhola as well."

The dwarf grumbled in an almost embarrassed fashion. "I will report this to my king. I'm sure he will support these efforts with this new information." He then quickly left the tent.

Catherine closed her eyes and placed a hand on Aaron. He felt a warming sensation where she touched him that spread throughout his body. The remaining pain went away. He pulled her close.

Klew came over and began examining the cuffs on Bree's wrists. "I think I can get these off with a bit of work."

"We'll need an update on everything that's happened," Clay stated, "but I think you all need some rest. Come, let's get you all situated."

Over the next few days, Aaron recounted everything that had happened, glazing over the torture. He did not tell Catherine about the significance behind the branding.

Klew was successful at removing their cuffs and began experimenting on them to learn more. Faber shared what information he could. Nathel prepared what he would tell his fellow Fiends. Aaron agreed they could use the Fiends as allies. The forces from the Isle Lands arrived. Their camp was growing.

❧❀❦

The rain was pouring down. Aaron shifted uncomfortably in his saddle. Their army had pushed a few days into Bellmora, but the opposing forces were getting strong. Catherine rode next to him. Neither knew why, but both felt compelled to join the battle instead of just Aaron. They led the army through the storm. Flickering lights danced before them as the two armies grew closer.

Aaron commanded them to stop as they reached the top of a hill and looked down on their opponents.

"Something's not right," Catherine said, just loud enough for Aaron to hear through the rain.

He shook his head. "I have a bad feeling."

Their enemies marched forward. Aaron tilted his head as he realized almost all of them were hiding their faces and skin. Aaron did not signal for attack as they drew closer.

"Aaron?" Catherine questioned.

Aaron motioned for the army to stay back and kicked his horse forward. Catherine did not obey and signaled Chestnut to follow. One horse strode out in front of the Bellmoran army to meet them.

"Well, if it isn't the prince!" Alaina exclaimed.

"You will not win," Aaron growled.

"You may have escaped that time, but I will see to it you will fall. I see you've brought an ally this time. Don't worry, I'll take her down too."

"Don't you dare lay a hand on her!"

"Now that isn't up to me. I'll give you one last chance, hand it over and I'll walk away."

"You will never get Jahola." He then extended his left hand into the sky and a light soared into the air.

Arrows were loosed from behind him and began to rain down on the Bellmoran army. The cloaked figures all threw off their cloaks. Hundreds of shadow touched poured onto the battlefield. Many of the humans that were intermixed froze in fear. Some turned and began fighting the shadow touched. The shadow touched did not discriminate on who was on what side; if they were attacked, they killed.

The shadow touched were no longer in hiding.

About the Author

Melanie Deer writes primarily epic fantasy that harkens back to the original roots of the epic fantasy genre. Her stories have twists, action, and a strong desire of hope. She has lived in the world of Eylaour for decades and is so glad you are wanting to join her there.

When spending time in our realm, she works at an archaeological repository during the day and enjoys time with her son, loving husband, and (way too many) cats outside of that in the Arizona desert.

www.ingramcontent.com/pod-product-compliance
Lightning Source LLC
Chambersburg PA
CBHW020013120726
47903CB00004B/1261